About the editors:

Alison Campbell is from Aberdeen and presently lives in London. She is co-author of a children's picture book, *Are You Asleep, Rabbit?* (Collins, 1990), and has a short story in *New Writing Scotland*, vol. 5 (Association for Scottish Literary Studies, 1987). She is completing counselling training at Birkbeck College. Her son says he doesn't mind never being rich, so she continues writing.

Caroline Hallett lives and works in North London, where she has helped to set up a counselling service for young people. Writing is a recent interest which persists alongside a job, training and family of three young children. She is gradually adding to a small number of completed stories which she hopes to make into a collection.

Jenny Palmer is a feminist living in Dalston, London. She lectures at Goldsmiths' College in EAP (English for Academic Purposes) and is currently completing a novel and collection of short stories. She has published on Third World issues in *Spare Rib, Everywoman, Tribune* and *Outwrite*, and draws inspiration from Bolivia, her spiritual home.

Marijke Woolsey was born in North London, where she still lives with her husband, and two daughters. She writes mainly short stories, but she has recently completed her third novel, 'The Eye of the Beholder'. Her first novel, *True Love, Dare, Kiss or Promise*, was shortlisted for the Betty Trask Award and for Faber and Faber Introductions. She works part time for the women's co-operative Letterbox Library, a children's book club that specialises in non-sexist, multicultural books. She is a founder member of the Purple Room Women's Writing Group.

Also edited by Alison Campbell, Caroline Hallett, Jenny Palmer and Marijke Woolsey from The Women's Press:

The Plot Against Mary: More Seasonal Stories (1992)

The Man Who Loved Presents

seasonal stories

EDITED BY ALISON CAMPBELL,
CAROLINE HALLETT, JENNY PALMER
AND MARIJKE WOOLSEY

First published by The Women's Press Limited, 1991
A member of the Namara Group
34 Great Sutton Street,
London EC1V 0DX

Reprinted 1992

Mary Ann Hushlak would like to thank Ralph Setian for allowing her to use an extract from his translation of the poem 'The Woman Cleaning Lentils', from the collection *Zahrad: Selected Poems*.

Santa Claus is Coming to Town (Coutts/Gillespie) © EMI – Feist Catalog Inc., USA. EMI United Partnership Ltd, London WC2M 0EA. Used by permission.

British Library Cataloguing in Publication Data

The Man Who Loved Presents – Seasonal Stories.
  I. Campbell, Alison
  823.914[FS]

ISBN 07043 4289 8

Phototypeset by Intype, London

Printed and bound in Great Britain by
BPCC Hazells Ltd.
Member of BPCC Ltd

Contents

To every woman
who has ever wanted
to cancel Christmas

Foreword

Christmas has a particular emotional charge for women, who often bear the major responsibility for making it work well. Since the advent of mass commercialisation of the festive season, its impact has had wide-reaching effects on the lives of most women.

We are four members of a women's writing group, based in North London. We met after Christmas one year, with tales of difficult reunions with families, overspending, absent friends, loneliness and, above all, exhaustion. From this meeting came the idea for this book. We extended our search for stories from women from different backgrounds, culture, race and sexual orientation.

The themes addressed are diverse: birth and death, food and eating disorders, relationships and family, change and renewal. This collection is a tribute to the women, both established and unpublished writers, who submitted such high-quality, powerful stories.

We present a showcase for new writing which we hope will provide entertaining and stimulating reading, and alleviate some of the pressures felt by every woman at this time of year.

Thanks to all the women who have supported our project with contributions, advice and encouragement. Finally, thanks to Hannah Kanter, and to Katherine Bright-Holmes at The Women's Press.

New Year's Eve

Katie Campbell

One way and another it's been a fuck of a year for almost everybody I know. First the storm, which killed half the trees in the park. Then the stockmarket crash which I'm told is no more than a crack compared to what will come, though I don't really care since I haven't got anything to invest anyway. Then the fire in the underground which could have killed any one of us. And as if that's not enough, everybody seems to be deep in personal disasters too. We kept them private at the beginning, but then when Jack got cancer suddenly everyone began to confess their troubles.

It's odd it should have been Jack. He was always on the periphery. As a single man he was a rare commodity, and he knew it. Kept himself to himself: he liked being a bit of a mystery. He was invited everywhere, and he always went alone. Always arrived late and left early. We knew he had girlfriends: their scent hung in his bedroom, their make-up dusted the corners of his bathroom cupboard, he would be sighted walking down Wardour Street or sitting in the new Thai café with some young blonde nobody knew. We would tease him and he'd intimate about this and that but he'd never introduce his women to the group.

He first began looking peaky after a two-week shoot in Trinidad. When he got back we all thought he looked a little lean, but he was a vain old sod – always prided himself on looking young . . . In fact he'd never admit his age so we all assumed he was older than he really was. Anyway, I told him, and I know the others told him too, that he was looking thin, but that just inspired him. The morning after he got back he was down in the gym as usual, then back to the flat for his French language tapes, then his indoor tennis, then he'd hop in the Porsche and be at the office by eight.

I always found it difficult with Jack. In the early days – oh years ago, decades almost – we had a little thing, a fling. It was one of those weekends when Andrew was playing golf. It wasn't what you'd call a success and we never spoke about it, but I suppose it made things a little tense after that between me and Jack. Andrew, of course, never knew about it; nobody did.

Then suddenly, several months ago, just after we heard that Jack had cancer, Andrew walked out. No warning, no reason, just said he needed space. After ten years of marriage he needs space. Space was never a problem in the past but Andrew says he needs space and what Andrew wants Andrew takes. So he packed his case and rented a furnished flat. In Jack's building as it happens.

It was pretty convenient really; he could keep an eye on Jack, pop in on his way back from work and see how he was. Jack must have got pretty bored talking about his chemo and radiation and odds of remission or recovery, so I suppose Andrew must have talked to Jack about us – the marriage, that sort of thing. It didn't occur to me that he would, I mean it's odd for a man to talk about his wife to another man – especially when the other man is the wife's ex-lover – but Andrew didn't know that. They say that men don't talk about those things; it was Emma who told me that Andrew was talking to Jack about our marriage.

Emma was one of Jack's exes from way back. When she heard about his cancer she got in touch again. She got into the habit of ringing him every afternoon after her shrink. Well, Jack would get bored talking about his cancer, and Emma would get bored talking about her neuroses, so they'd talk about Andrew and me. When I heard this, I took to seeing Emma for tea. Since Andrew wasn't communicating, I thought at least Emma could give me an idea what he was thinking through Jack.

Then Chris, who's unemployed – well he's a freelancer but he's always unemployed – when he heard Andrew had gone he asked if he could crash. He couldn't pay the mortgage on his own place so he thought he'd rent it out to some visiting Yanks. I was pretty bored by then and I wanted the company so Chris moved in. He started ringing Jack to see if he knew of any work going – not that Jack spent much time at the office by then – the chemo was much more debilitating than he'd expected, but Jack always had his finger on the pulse; if he didn't know what was going on he certainly knew who would.

Then I thought what the hell, with Chris ringing Jack on a daily basis, why shouldn't I? I mean he was a friend of mine too and Chris and Andrew and Emma didn't have exclusive dibs on him. So I called to see if he wanted me to bring round some soup or something. But he said that Andrew had arranged someone – a woman, I wondered, but I didn't ask – to come in to cook for him. So I rang back later when I knew he had his radiation session, and sure enough she was there.

I said: 'Who's this? I'm a friend of Jack; I'm ringing to see how he is.'

She replied: 'I'm a friend of Jack too; he's at the hospital.'

I recognised the voice, it was Joyce whose husband is an alcoholic. In fact he's a coke addict. Rumour has it that he's stuffed her whole inheritance up his nose, but we all pretend it's a drink problem. Though what difference it makes anyway is beyond me.

Joyce swanned around France on some cordon bleu thing while the rest of us sweated over finals all those years ago. Come to think of it she might have even had a scene with Jack . . . he was always zipping off to Paris for the weekends at that time. That was the last of it for Joyce though. Since then it's been downhill for her: pregnant by the end of final year; the first kid's hyperactive so the psychologist advises she give it a sibling, and then second time round it's those dreadful twins. No wonder she'll use any excuse to get out of that house. Cooking in Jack's silent kitchen must be bliss.

So we chat a bit and I remember that she used to have a partner who did directors' lunches with her. Polly, her name was – we later found out she was another of Jack's exes. Well, I assumed that Polly wasn't working with Joyce because of that, but no, Polly it seems caught herpes some time in the spring. You wouldn't think it was that serious but apparently when it hits it hurts like hell and finally she was taking so much time off Joyce had to let her go. You can see her point; you can hardly concentrate on dotting the quails eggs with caviar when your partner's sticking packs of frozen peas between her legs to numb the pain. I mean how would you explain it if one of the directors ambled in?

I intended to ring Polly to commiserate because I'd had a bout of that sort of thing – it wasn't herpes exactly, and I never told any one at the time – it's often easier not to explain. But as it turned out she'd already been speaking to Jack – well you would if you were one of his exes – and he'd told her about Andrew and me, so she rang me. When we got round to the herpes she explained that the problem was augmented because her husband couldn't understand how she'd picked up the virus. Well, Polly's hardly the type to use a public loo . . . So they're having their dramas too. But he adores the kids so she should be all right. And besides, they've just bought a three-hundred-thousand-pound place in Chiswick; he's not likely to leave and give her half of that.

Anyway, Polly mentioned that their next-door neighbour is someone we all knew at school – Jimmy Goldstein or Bernstein or something like that. I vaguely remember. Well, when he heard about Jack he was full of advice. It seems his new girlfriend is into some strange healing thing. He insisted that Jack see the girl, and Jack was too exhausted to refuse.

It turns out the girl was someone Jack met once on a skiing course. She must have been much younger than him. Polly says she can't be more than twenty-four. Jack always did go for younger women . . . So this girl, well, she tells him she really needs a break; she's just set up her own practice and she hasn't many connections, and if she could cure him of his cancer it would do great things for her reputation. Jack told Emma, at that point he couldn't cope any more. He's pretty conventional – doesn't go for anything not strictly down the line. So he finally got her to leave and he told Emma he didn't want to hear from anyone for a week.

I gave him a quick call to commiserate; I mean I've had my run-ins with Jesus freaks and weirdo healers, so I rang and I rang and all day long all I got was the answer machine. I continued ringing on and off for the next few days but finally even I gave up. I mean you can't keep calling someone if they don't return the calls.

Anyway then I got distracted. First Chris left. When he couldn't get through to Jack on the phone he figured he had to make contacts somewhere else. The next thing you know he's moved in with Jimmy's faith healer. Seems he thought she might be able to realign his energy or change his stars or something. So he went and I'm left alone. I hate being alone.

Then this letter comes from Andrew's lawyer saying he wants a legal separation. Well I must say it came as a bit of a shock. I mean if I'd thought about it I might have guessed. I mean he'd been gone for weeks and no communication. I mean the trial separation was beginning to look like a conviction really. But I really didn't think about it much.

So I rang Emma to see if she'd heard anything about it from Jack. But she wasn't in very good shape because her shrink was in a car crash and would be out of commission for several months at least.

Since I couldn't get much sense from her I rang up Joyce, but the hyperactive kid had just smashed her last Lalique vase over the head of one of the twins so she was coping with hospitals and social workers and all.

So I thought Polly might know something, but it seems that her husband had disappeared several days before with his passport and the contents of their joint account, so she hadn't spoken to Jack and of course her herpes was raging again.

So I still don't know what Andrew is playing at, but I suspect it's serious if he's hired a lawyer. I suspect this is it . . . The end.

So you see, one way and another it's been a real fuck of a year for everyone I know. Especially Jack, who died three days ago and no one even told me.

The de Montfort Essay Cup

Zoë Fairbairns

There's one thing I wish people wouldn't do at
Christmas. By people I mean old lovers who have gone off
and married someone else. This happens to me over and over
again. I don't mean I have all that many lovers, but the ones
I do have invariably leave me after a few months and marry
someone else.

I don't think I am unduly bitter about this. I'm certainly
not surprised. A list of my lovable qualities would be very
short. Or even my likeable qualities. It's a hazard of being a
writer, as opposed to having a more sociable occupation.
You don't develop your likeable qualities. You don't have
to. You don't have to see anyone, apart from publishers, and
they are trained to deal with you.

You don't have to get on with normal people, so you
don't learn how to. You don't develop tolerance for other
people's idiosyncrasies, you just grow idiosyncrasies of your
own. When lovers happen along you may try to keep your
idiosyncrasies under wraps, but after a month or so the wraps
start to slip. Then love turns to hate and before you can turn
round the lovers are off marrying somebody else. This is
both inevitable and understandable. All I wish is that they
wouldn't send me joint Christmas cards.

'To Nicola with love from Carl and Cynthia,' they write.
Or, 'Love from Len and Beth.' What a shabby business. I've
never met Cynthia or Beth. I don't want to. I'll lay odds,
furthermore, that Cynthia and Beth don't want to meet me.
They'll have heard all about my idiosyncrasies. Yet here they
are, sending me love. Or rather, having love sent in their

name, quite possibly without their knowledge. Why should they be conscripted into greeting me, just because it's Christmas? Why should their love be commandeered and their names be scribbled on the card by Carl or Len or whichever moral coward it is who lacks the guts either to send his own love on its own, or alternatively forget me, strike me off the Christmas card list, hate me?

'You know, Nicola, it's quite exhilarating to be hated.'

Who was it who said that to me?

It sounds like the sort of thing a publisher might say. Yes, now I come to think about it, it was a publisher. Not my present publisher, who I don't think hates me, yet, and not the one before him, but the one before that. I don't know why she said it. I can't remember the context, but I do remember that shortly afterwards she cast me out of her company on the grounds that she had dealt with a few difficult authors in her time but I took the biscuit. I was the most impossible author it had ever been her misfortune to work with.

I didn't care. I would have left anyway. Why should I work with people who hate me? And I hated her for her smug assertion that it was exhilarating to be hated.

It's all very well for them to find it exhilarating. They go everywhere in packs. When they're being hated, at least they've got each other. Who have I got?

I have got a friend, as a matter of fact. His name is Colin, but he just laughs and says, 'What do you expect?'

I don't *expect* anything. I expect to be hated. But I don't find it exhilarating and I'm not going to pretend that I do.

Being hated makes me feel despairing and panicky, as if I won't live much longer. I get a small circle of bitterness on my tongue, the sort of taste you get from licking a coin: metal and dirt and covetousness. I don't lick coins so I think it is probably the taste of death, and it comes from being hated.

When I detect hatred coming my way, I become helpless

and wretched. Wherever I am, I want to go home. It doesn't happen at home. I don't allow into my home people who hate me, or even people who like me now but who I fear might hate me one day. One of my main bones of contention with Carl (as in love from Carl and Cynthia) was that I wouldn't let him into my home in case he might grow to hate me, and of course it has turned out that there is no might about it. My one consolation is that there is no trace of him in my home because he has never been there. The same goes for Len, as in love from Len and Beth. It goes without saying that I have torn up their Christmas cards.

My first memory of being hated comes from when I was at school, in the sixth form. Actually, I don't think that can be right. It seems rather late in life for a first memory of anything. I expect I was hated long before I reached the sixth form, but I don't remember, so I expect I have repressed the experience. In all probability I will get cancer one day from my many repressed memories of being hated, but here is the first occasion I do remember.

There was this prize called the de Montfort Essay Cup. It was awarded once a year to the girl in Upper Six who wrote the best essay in her A level mock.

I got a fabulous mark for my A level mock essay, 98 per cent or something like that, the sort of mark teachers give you to let you know that the only reason they're not giving you 100 per cent is that nobody gets 100 per cent.

I didn't see why not. If a piece of work is worth 100 per cent, why not give it what it is worth? I would have loved to get 100 per cent, but nobody ever did, particularly in a mock where they kept the marks down artificially to stop you getting cocky. I wouldn't have got cocky, but still. In any case, I wasn't going to make an issue of the odd 2 per cent. Nobody ever got essay marks as good as mine. Not even Patsy Holroyd. Not even Clare Davis. I can't remember what they did get. Probably about 70 per cent. Perhaps 75.

It seemed obvious that the de Montfort Essay Cup was in

the bag for me. It was just a matter of waiting for the announcement. But the announcement, when it came, was 'The de Montfort Essay Cup is not being awarded this year because there were no entries of a sufficiently high standard.'

This friend I have, Colin, accuses me of being obsessed with this incident. He's exaggerating, of course. It's his way of being funny. He knows his exaggerations amuse me.

The Christmas before last, he bought a presentation cup from an antique shop and had it engraved 'de Montfort Essay Cup, awarded to Nicola Baxter', together with the name of my school and the year I should have won.

I was surprised he had all that information but he said he had heard the story so many times that he regarded the details as part of general knowledge, like 1066 the Battle of Hastings. He could go on *Mastermind* and answer questions on the great de Montfort Essay Cup scandal. He made a formal presentation and gave me a one-man round of applause, after which he said, 'Perhaps you'll shut up about it now.'

I didn't need to shut up about it. I wasn't even aware that I had mentioned it. Granted it bothered me at the time, but it doesn't bother me now. Not any more. Anyone who is still bothered, twenty-two years later, about the prize they didn't win at school, has bigger problems than the prize they didn't win at school. But I admit to a continuing sense of puzzlement.

If 98 per cent isn't a sufficiently high standard, what is?

I had had my eye on the de Montfort Essay Cup since kindergarten. I liked the fact that while the cup itself remained in the school, on display with your name on it, year in, year out, you yourself got given a little silver replica, with two handles and your name engraved, to keep.

I'm not sure how I knew this. Someone must have said within my hearing, *That child will win the de Montfort Essay Cup one day!* Even at that age, I stood out as a writer. Writing was the one thing that I was better at than anybody else. Better at than Patsy Holroyd. Better than Clare Davis.

I won prizes for it. Non-school prizes, I mean. From the

local Literary Circle, and the BBC. And I was published in *Children as Writers*. That title had a tone of surprise that I didn't care for, but still. I think that's what spoiled my chances of the de Montfort Essay Cup, actually. I didn't realise this at the time but in retrospect I think I can tell that my school was offended by my winning outside honours. They saw it as treachery. *If our honours aren't good enough for her, she can go without.*

They thought I was too clever by half. But why shouldn't I be clever? What were schools for, if not to promote cleverness amongst their pupils? I wasn't as clever as all that, anyway. I was clever at writing, but I wasn't an all-rounder in the way Patsy Holroyd was, and Clare Davis. They were good at science and games and history and a great many other things that merely bored me. Everything bored me, apart from writing, which I adored. Writing was the only thing I wanted to do. The answer to the question 'Where's Nicola?' was always the same: curled up somewhere, writing. Everything else I was required to do was an interruption of writing, and I saw no reason to make a secret of this fact. The teachers accused me of inattention and dumb insolence. They hated my guts.

I'd always assumed that Patsy Holroyd and Clare Davis hated my guts too, and that that was the reason why we haven't been in touch for more than twenty years. This made it all the more surprising the other day when I received a Christmas card from Patsy, whose surname now appeared to be Davenport.

She had spotted one of my books in a library and read it and thought it was tremendous, and she had written c/o the publishers saying congratulations and good show and would I come to her Christmas party? Clare Forrester would be there, née Davis.

I wasn't sure. I don't like parties much. You get a lot of hatred flying around at parties. On the other hand, I do like receiving invitations, and you have to accept invitations now and again if you want to go on receiving them.

Invitations prove that not quite everybody hates you. In theory they prove that. But you do get occasions when people invite you to parties *because* they hate you and then run the whole event as a punishment, with people saying things like 'I could write a novel if I had time,' and 'Why are the only interesting novels being written by Latin Americans?' How was I to know that Patsy Holroyd and Clare Davis weren't putting on their party for this very purpose?

Patsy Davenport, she was now. Clare Forrester. I wish women wouldn't change their names. I'm not a feminist or anything, it's just that it upsets me to think that you could have a hypothetical situation in which two women could correspond with each other for years and years, and if they never saw each other and never discussed their backgrounds – and it could happen that way, if they were business associates, for example – they would never realise that they were old friends.

You could have a woman writer's books being read by all her old schoolmates or university chums or people she was in the Brownies with, and if she had changed her name they would never know that she was the author.

I've never changed my name so people always know when it's me, but how am I supposed to know when it's them?

I wouldn't have known it was Patsy. Not if I had passed her in the street. But she came to her own front door to welcome me, so obviously it was her. She cried, 'Nicola, Happy Christmas, thank you for coming!' and gave me a hug and a kiss, and another woman came rushing out behind her with tinsel in her hair and little squeals of excitement, so I assumed she was Clare.

'I'm Clare, remember me? It's marvellous to see you again!' she said. 'You've done so well! You're such a celebrity!'

'Me, too,' I muttered.

What I meant by that was, *it's marvellous for me too, to see you* but it came out wrong. It sounded as if I were agreeing that I was a celebrity, which is the last thing you should agree on if you don't want people to hate you. It was too late now. I knew that Patsy and Clare would take the first opportunity to duck out to the kitchen on the pretext of fetching mince pies but really in order to fume and giggle and say, 'Did she *really* say that? Can you *believe* it?'

I wished someone would develop a system under which you could proof-read what you say in the way you can proof-read what you write, and correct it before it comes out. A piece of computer software under your tongue or something.

'. . . computer software,' Clare was saying, as Patsy gave me a glass of hot punch.

'Oh really?' I said. 'How long have you been doing that?'

'It's very boring,' said Clare. 'Not nearly as interesting as what you do. I couldn't write a book in a million years. Could you, Patsy?'

'No fear. Nicola was always the one with the flair in that department.'

'Don't do yourself down, Patsy,' said Clare, in the way of grown people discussing their achievements at school, pretending to be joking but really serious. 'Your essays were quite something. Remember when you won that cup?' And she nipped over to the holly-strewn mantelpiece and fetched a small gleaming silver object with handles.

'Oh, *essays*,' said Patsy. 'Anyone can write essays, Nicola writes books.' She examined the cup in a nostalgic sort of way, and passed it to me, not as if she really thought I would be interested, only as if she thought it would be impolite to withhold it, now that it had been brought into the conversation. I read the engraving: 'The de Montfort Essay Cup, awarded to Patsy Holroyd'. It was dated the year I should have won it.

I swayed a bit and put my drink down as my whole life seemed to flash before my eyes. I said, 'Patsy, could I use your phone?'

'Over there,' she said. 'Or there's one upstairs if you want to be private.'

The sort of privacy I needed at that moment isn't generally

available outside a coffin but I managed to control my shaking fingers sufficiently to get through to Colin.

He said 'Are you having a horrible time?'

'Colin, you know the de Montfort Essay Cup?'

'The what?'

'*The de Montfort Essay Cup.*'

'The what essay cup? Speak up. Never heard of it.'

'Colin – '

'Is it like the FA Cup?'

'Colin, *please.*'

He stopped laughing and said, 'What about it?'

'Patsy won it,' I said.

'Eh?' he said.

'It's sitting on her mantelpiece.'

'It could be a fake,' he said, after a while.

'It isn't.'

'I see,' he said. 'Well, this is a very serious matter.'

'I know. I've made a terrible mistake. Could you burn it?'

'Burn what?'

'The one you gave me.'

'What are you talking about, burn it, it cost me a fortune.' He sounded rather outraged.

'Please, Colin.'

'Silver doesn't burn,' he said sulkily.

'Melt it down, then,' I said. 'Smash it to smithereens with a pickaxe. Please do it now, let yourself into my bit of the house – '

'How?'

'The key's under the blue vase, *destroy that cup.*'

'If you want it destroyed,' he retorted, 'destroy it yourself.'

'But what if I die?'

'Do it before you die.'

'I might get killed on the way home.'

This mollified him a little. 'Don't do that.'

'What I mean is, when my affairs are being wound up, someone might find that cup and not realise it's a fake – '

'It is not a fake, Nicola. I gave it to you, the Christmas before last.'

'*Listen to me.* It might fall into the hands of my obituarist or my biographers and they might say something like "even at school, her promise was evident. She won the de Montfort Essay Cup". They might even publish a photograph of it and Patsy will see it and say, "It's not true! I won it, and Nicola had her nose put so far out of joint that she sulked for twenty-two years and repressed the memory and made something up about the prize not being awarded. And then she awarded it to herself!" Think how much people will hate me then – posthumously!'

The prospect was growing more and more real to me as I described it, and striking horror into my heart, but he was completely unsympathetic. I pleaded and pleaded with him but he refused to accept my authorisation to take my key from its hiding place under the blue vase and enter my part of our house to destroy the cup he had given me. If that was the way I felt about his gift, I could destroy it myself. His sole concession was to give me his word that he would explain the true status of my cup to my obituarists, should the occasion arise in the meantime.

The occasion didn't arise, as you will have gathered from the fact that I am alive to write this story. I am writing it in order to explain to future obituarists and other curious persons why I have in my possession a cup engraved 'de Montfort Essay Cup, awarded to Nicola Baxter', dated the year when it was in fact awarded to Patsy Holroyd. I decided not to smash the cup, or melt it down, or burn it. It would be a shame to do that, because it was a gift of love, and gifts of love should be valued, particularly when everybody hates you.

The Death of Men

Linda Anderson

I was eating Christmas pudding when the news broke. The first sign was my brother's alarmed voice in the hallway. He was on the phone.

'You're joking. Naw. You're kidding. But . . . you're joking. Oh Jesus. Yes. I'm sure my mother will go round and see Laura . . .'

'Samuel's gone and died in his sleep,' Jimmy announced, returning to the dining room. My mother's hands flew to her face. 'On Christmas morning,' Jimmy said. 'Imagine.'

I considered for a moment. 'Well, why not? There is no amnesty.' I didn't know what to do next. I resumed eating. Dark bitter-sweet pudding. Dollops of brandy butter.

'They would like to see you, Mum,' Jimmy said sheepishly.

'I'll go with you,' I volunteered. 'But later. Not yet.'

We took hours to get ready. We knew we had to go. We had to comfort the bereaved.

'But you won't have to attend the funeral,' I said.

'Their church is just round the corner. They'll expect me to go.'

'No one will expect it.'

'Should you wear that red scarf?'

'Yes.'

I had been wearing a red scarf every day for months. Except for the occasion of my father's funeral when I swapped it for a black one. Red and black. Anger and death.

We stepped outside. The evening was beautiful, cold and starry. 'Oh, Christmas night!' I exulted for a moment. We linked arms. I wished that Samuel's home were further away, that we could walk and walk.

'I never liked him,' I said. A natty little man, florid complexion, stentorian voice.

'Yes, he always sounded as if he was quarrelling with you,' my mother said. 'He wasn't bad, though.' It was her habit to echo my furies and then let gentleness and justice reclaim her.

We were nearly there. The bungalow of mourning was in sight.

'Will the body still be inside?' I asked. 'Do undertakers work on Christmas Day?'

'He got off lightly,' my mother said with sudden bitterness. 'No suffering. No awareness. Just fell asleep.'

I had a vision of my father in his coffin. A diminutive waxwork with golden skin. A shrunken look-alike.

'We won't stay long,' I assured her.

'Oh Patricia, there you are!' shouted the widow. Laura. My father's cousin. She wept, waving her crumpled handkerchief.

The poky room was overheated and packed with people. Daughters of the deceased, their husbands, their children. Everyone looked huge, giants in a Wendy house. Samuel's daughters gawped at me.

'You've put on weight,' Brenda said eagerly.

'The poor girl's lost her daddy and now we've lost ours!' Sally spoke almost reproachfully as if I had instigated some distressing trend.

The much-married Marlene ignored me. Brenda, Sally, and Marlene. I had not met them for twenty years. A trio of platinum blondes with discreetly ample figures encased in good suits and frilly blouses. They all looked impeccable and yet strangely vulgar, like strict barmaids.

'We're in the same boat, Patricia,' the new widow declared. I registered my mother's imperceptible wince.

No, you're not, I thought. My mother is on a raft. A raft for one.

'Aye. Dear dear . . . To think it was only six weeks ago that we put your Robert in the ground. And now my Samuel will be laid beside him. Aye. Friends in life they were, and now . . .'

I remembered my mother in the bedroom trying to choose the clothes for my father's body. His good dark suit. There was a Masonic pin in the lapel. A dazzling white shirt. I touched each garment. I had rarely touched my father. Now I could take liberties with his clothes.

'A tie?' said Moira. 'What about a tie?'

We stared at the fat tangled maypole of his ties hanging in the wardrobe. My mother removed a wide striped one.

'That's unfashionable,' I protested, snatching out the green silk one instead.

'Shoes,' said Moira. 'Will he need shoes?'

My mother began to weep. Moira was standing behind her. She placed a hand on her right shoulder. And I put my hand on Moira's shoulder as if to transmit more strength. We stood there like that, in a line, like Pharaoh's wives.

Your husband is an also-ran, lady, I thought.

' . . . God moves in mysterious ways,' said Florrie, Laura's sister.

'Yes . . . I just thank God that my Sam didn't suffer. For the Lord knows he didn't deserve to. No, and I couldn't have borne to watch him . . . Such a good soul . . . Oh, not that anyone deserves to suffer, of course!'

'That's right,' I said, making my voice as chilly as possible.

'Isn't she just like her father?' Laura responded. 'They live on, they live on . . .'

'Just like her father.' That sentence had followed me since childhood. A chip off the old towerblock. The old iceberg. I did not want to resemble my father. A joyless and forbidding man. Until cancer stripped away his flesh, and with it all signs of his cruelty and remoteness. It reduced him to a tenderness I had longed for but could not stand. Too much, too late.

The widow launched into an inventory of her husband's final day. He made the breakfast. He polished his shoes. He went to the shops. He peeled the potatoes. He looked after his granddaughter, Amanda Jayne. He drove Laura over to her sister's and fetched her home later. That night he kneeled by his bed and prayed, listing everyone in his family by name. He prayed then for some trawlermen lost off the Antrim coast.

'Did he pray aloud?' I wanted to ask, but managed to stop the impulse. I had a sense of trespass. I hate the way the most private things about the dead become instant public property. But I was intrigued by this new image of Samuel. The jaunty splenetic Samuel transformed into a kind, vulnerable old man in pyjamas. After a day crammed with chores, favours and piety, he drew a neat line under himself and unobtrusively stopped breathing.

Laura's monologue moved on to other recent deaths in the district. The Reaper had been busy. There was Arnold Mulholland who paid all his bills one day, ironed all his shirts, went to bed quietly and never rose again. And then there was Stanley who made his wife a cup of tea before sinking unfussily into his armchair . . . Such orderly demises. I began to hear an implicit criticism of my father, his noisy toilsome death, the wild incontinence of it.

Laura turned to my mother: 'How did you get your Christmas in, Patricia? Did you have a dinner? Of course, none of us can eat a thing. Whole place coming down with turkey and mince pies and we can't manage a bite!'

'You're going to have to eat some of that turkey after all the trouble I've had with it,' Brenda said sullenly.

'Aye, our Brenda has had a hell of a time with her turkey this year,' Laura confided.

'It was a bloody fiasco!' Brenda said.

'She was done,' said Sally. 'Well and truly done.'

'What happened?'

'I went to that butcher, you know the one, McMullen's. Couldn't have a better reputation. Well, I asked him for a fresh turkey. I warned him, "None of your frozen!" It was the last minute on Christmas Eve and I needed a fresh turkey. He gives me a bird. "Madam dear, here's one that's as fresh as your face." But here, when I tried to cook it, it just would not cook. And gallons of water pouring out of it! After hours and hours it was still as pale as a snail drowning in a pond. So it was a frozen bird that he had thawed and passed off as a fresh one.'

A chorus of advice chimed out: 'She should have stuck it in the microwave . . .'

'She should have held it under the hot tap . . .'

'She should have hurled it through the butcher's window . . .'

'I'm going to see that man as soon as his shop opens up again! I'll put him out of business. I'll sue the arse off him!'

'You're just right, Brenda. Imagine doing the like of that to someone on Christmas Eve!'

'Man's inhumanity to man,' I muttered to myself.

A debate ensued on the comparative merits of frozen versus fresh poultry.

'You can always tell frozen. I don't care what anyone says.'

'No, you cannot. If you were blindfolded and had to taste a range of samples . . .'

'Now, don't you contradict me, Sally.'

An exchange of recipes followed. 'I'll tell you something that makes a good meal for a Saturday night . . . Economical, too.'

Samuel probably died of boredom, I decided. I intervened by telling them my turkey anecdote. A true story. My sister Moira prepared and cooked her turkey a couple of weeks before Christmas. It was stuffed, basted, roasted, glazed, cooled, and wrapped in a freezer bag. All sacraments completed, Moira placed the bag on the floor and instructed her husband to put it in the freezer outside in the garage.

On Christmas Eve she retrieved the bag, opened it and found . . . rubbish! Litter – a stiff collage of discarded food, old teabags . . .

'Kenneth!' she shrieked, realising in a flash what had happened. Freezer and pedalbin bags being indistinguishable, he had deposited the turkey in the bin, the rubbish in the freezer. Kenneth was a man living in a perpetual fog. His wife was always unconsciously devising 'Spot the Mistake' contests for him to fail.

The hapless husband bought her a surrogate turkey.

'Ah well, no harm done then,' I had suggested.

'But it just wasn't the same! It just couldn't be the same as my lovely, my *original* turkey that I slaved over. I suppose that in the context of Lockerbie and Armenia, it seems trivial but . . .'

I knew my sister, and could imagine the celebratory dinner at her house. The superior beloved lost bird would be invoked at every penitential mouthful.

I told the story in my best 'comedienne' manner. I waited for laughter. A ring of scowling faces, a tribunal.

'That's not funny,' Brenda chided at last to a chorus of agreement.

'God, what a moron!'

'I'd have made him eat the rubbish.'

'What was he playing at?'

These women took their fowl seriously, I was beginning to understand. My story was not one of womanly over-reaction but of husbandly transgression.

'She punched him in the jaw,' I said, despising myself for making the placatory offering. I had omitted this fact at first, regarding it as shameful.

'Just right!' Brenda was mollified.

I realised suddenly that Moira was just like these sisters. Even in appearance. They were of the same tribe. Bright blonde women, divas of the kitchen, each with a brace of dainty coddled children. Each with a defeated man in tow. Loud women with lulled men.

Oh Dad, why did you inflict these relatives on me? These smug saturnine Protestants? I wished I could resemble them less. I wished I could be utterly different. I became aware of my body, the dense materiality of it, its overstatement. Why couldn't I be a willowy Catholic with a soulful face, a pilgrim to Croagh Patrick with stones lacerating my ascetic feet?

My aunt Florrie came and lowered herself cautiously into the sofa beside me. Her eyes were alarmingly magnified behind thick lenses. I stared at the faint hem of her moustache.

'How are you doing, darlin'?'

'Fine.'

'Miss your father?'

'Yes.'

'God's will, darlin'. Long time, no see.' She laughed. 'Do you remember the time you slammed the door in my face?'

'No.'

'Yes, you do. When I was collecting money to build an Orange arch at the entrance to the housing estate.' She smiled indulgently, sure that I must have long outgrown such youthful waywardness.

'To keep the Catholics in their place?'

'Your father was ashamed of you for turning me away. Mortified he was. He called you a Fenian-lover.'

'You got your revenge. At my wedding,' I reminded her. She looked baffled, no idea what I meant.

My wedding joined my best Catholic friends and my worst Protestant relatives under the same roof. I had to watch with horror while alcohol drew Florrie and her boss-eyed husband out of their usual semi-autistic slumber and into a high-decibel belligerence. She danced a jig around my friends, bellowing insults at the Pope. Sean, Sinead and Michael. My lifelong friends, all disappeared now. Ditto the till-death-do-us-part bridegroom. But I was still linked to this affable gorilla sprawling beside me on the sofa. Blood is thicker than glue.

'No sign of more wedding bells for you?' she asked coyly.

'Is that your Marlene's new husband over there?' I said, indicating a bashful little man perched on the side of an armchair across the room.

'Aye. Numéro trois . . . Husband number three,' she translated helpfully. 'Third time lucky, maybe.'

'Maybe,' I said. First a wifebeater, then an alcoholic, and now a dwarf, I thought charitably.

'Are you courting?' she persisted.

'I have no use for men,' I said, noticing the ambiguity of that. Was I subject or object? I have no use? I am of no use?

'Oh, I can't believe that. You were always a dark horse.'

Dark riderless horse, I rose, and gathering some used cups as pretext, I left the room. I went searching for the kitchen, afraid of the unknown geography of this house. What if a door were ajar and I might glimpse the corpse? We've forgotten him, I realised. Poor Samuel, upstaged by a turkey! The light was on in the kitchen and there was the lamented carcass of the half-raw bird on the table. Bald and yellowish, there was something both doleful and festive about it. I stared at its pitiable dark cavity. They'll have you tomorrow, I told it silently. They'll want to eat a piece of death. Bite back, so to speak.

'You look as if you're communing with that turkey!'

I jumped. It was the jarringly robust voice of one of the mute men who had followed me out.

'Only intelligent form of life round here, I suppose?' he added. He opened the back door, letting in the crisp night air. The sky was navy blue. Without thinking, I stepped outside.

'You can see the stars here,' I said. 'You can't in London.'

'Yeah. The cloudless skies of Northern Ireland . . . You live in London, then?'

'Yes.'

'Are you on drugs?'

'Drugs?'

'Cocaine and stuff.'

'Of course. I've got half of Peru up my nostrils.'

'What? Oh. Don't treat me like a country bumpkin.'

'Don't treat me like a big city debauchee!'

'Sorry . . . I'm ever so slightly . . . drunk.'

'Who are you?'

'Son-in-law of the late great.'

'I know . . . I mean, what's your name?'

'Jack. Jack of Brenda and Jack.'

'I see.'

'Yes, I know you see. I watched you in there, looking at everybody like a she-wolf . . . And who are you? Do you come here often?'

'I'm the daughter of . . .' I stopped. 'I'm Helen Forrest.'

We were silent for a moment.

'It's a bad thing to happen at Christmas,' I said awkwardly. 'Christmas will never be the same again.'

He snorted. 'Oh, that's too much to hope for. It'll be the same all right. Gloom and gluttony. Laura will have to eat for two.'

Silence again. Then he looked at me with sudden concern.

'It must be dreadful for you to have to come round here? You're demoted. Overnight you've gone from chief mourner to mere bystander.'

'Oh well. Samuel was my father's best friend. He helped us when . . .'

'How did he help you?'

'He came round.'

'And?'

'You know. He extended his sympathy.'

'How extensive was it?'

Jack stared at me. There was something needling and coercive about him. He began to whistle through his teeth, a tuneless sibilant sound. Then he tapped his feet. I began to laugh. He was mimicking Samuel, the maddening whistler.

'Yes, yes, that's what he did. While my father was dying and after he was dead, Samuel just sat there and whistled!'

' "And flights of angels sing thee to thy rest!" So Sammy whistled your dad into the hereafter. It was his all-purpose response.'

I felt a sudden pity. 'Poor bastard. Whistling in the dark. Just six weeks later . . .'

'Yes. Togetherness has its drawbacks, eh?'

We giggled.

'Is the body here?' I asked, ashamed of something avid in my voice.

'Sure. Tomorrow's Boxing Day, isn't it?'

'That's a terrible joke.'

'Don't smile, then.'

'You didn't like him much, did you, Jack?'

'No. Although I'm already getting confused. I hate the way the dead change, don't you? Suddenly Sammy is this very good-natured guy. A tireless helper of mankind. By tomorrow morning he'll be a saint.'

'Oh yes! I couldn't believe what my sister said to the mourners at my father's funeral. He was the handsomest man we ever saw, the kindest man we ever met. No one could surpass him in generosity. He was even developing a belated sense of humour. I thought we were burying the wrong man!'

Jack smiled at me. I could see the wet gleam of his teeth in the dark. 'You're a bit of a fervent disliker yourself.'

I noticed the dark stubble on his jaw. I had a momentary impulse to stroke it.

'There must have been something you liked about your father?'

'He went out a lot. I liked that. I used to pray he would never come back.'

'Was he violent?'

'He made me afraid. He sank my spirit. There was something poisonous about him. A rage held back by a terrible blankness. I used to hate the way he would do all kinds of pointless stupid things with this solemn look on his face. Like he had this Swiss army knife that he was proud of and he used to sit whittling sticks with it, gathering up little shavings and chips of wood . . .'

'The rage? What was the rage about?'

I shrugged. It was too big to describe. 'One day he was staring out of the window and he looked so full of wrath.

There were two dogs outside greeting and wagging their tails at each other. He said: "See dogs. First thing a dog does when it meets another dog is . . . it sniffs its behind." And he was scandalised. I guess that's what it was all about. He hated animals to be animals and he hated human beings to be animals too. He policed his body and his feelings all his life.'

'Poor man,' Jack said.

'I stole his knife.'

'Like some old schoolmarm confiscating a toy?'

'I needed it.'

'What for?'

'I used to cut myself.' I looked at him quickly. 'People think you have to be mad to do something like that.'

Jack said nothing but he seemed unflinching.

'I used to do it in the bathroom while I listened to him prowling about downstairs. I was calm when I did it, almost meditative. I made very neat incisions, in the thighs and arms mostly. It made me feel better. It was like drawing boundaries to keep him out. Does that make any sense?'

'Oh yes. Blood-lines. The bloody old blood-lines.'

'I had my rituals. I cleaned up afterwards. Lots of TCP and bandages.'

'When did you stop?' Jack's voice was near and very gentle.

'When I met a man.'

'Of course.'

I thought he was going to kiss me. That was the expected outcome, after all. Strangers in the night, impulsive confessions. The meeting of bruised minds, the mating of bitter lips . . .

'You don't have to cut him out of yourself,' Jack said. 'Just cut him down to size.'

'Like the cancer?' I spoke so venomously that he turned away. In that moment I started to guess something I could only fathom later. I hated the cancer for its vengeful revelation of my father's frailty. I was in love with his bogus

power. He was the hollow colossus in my featureless landscape. I did not want him toppled.

'Want a smoke?' Jack offered a pack of cigarettes.

'No, I don't.'

'Oh, I'm sorry. I forgot. I'll wait.'

'His lungs were rotten. In the end. He had to keep the
oxygen mask on almost all the time. The seals were dying
all through the autumn. Every night on the news they would
report how many seals died on the north coast, how many
on the east coast. It was as if they were circling us. My father
and the seals gasping to death . . . His whole life was a long
slow suffocation. He took his own life.'

I felt Jack's hand soft on my hair. 'Take *your* life. Take
your life and use it.'

'Helen!' My mother came into the kitchen. 'There you are!
Do you think we could go now?'

The retrieval of coats, the gauntlet of goodbyes, the con-
dolence routine again. Sorry sorry sorry for your trouble
trouble trouble. At last we were outside. Our feet rang on
the pavement. I began to do a sort of backwards laugh: 'Ah
ah ah ah!'

'God, that was dreadful,' my mother said.

'And where do you stand, Missus, on the controversial
question of frozen versus fresh?' I asked.

'It hasn't hit them yet,' she said.

'No.'

'I don't know what to do.' I knew she was talking about
her whole future.

'Neither do I.'

Take your life and use it.

She started to laugh. 'We could always do the turkey trot!'
Suddenly we skipped and ran like girls getting out of a bad
school.

It's My Party . . .

Bernadette Halpin

Except it wasn't, my party, that is. I was in no good shape that winter for having a party, and not in much better shape for going to one. The nights were drawing in fast, and if I could have drawn a blind down across the days too and sat out the dark till the clocks leapt an hour again, I would have. But there were two compelling reasons for not refusing this invitation: the party was at the house of my best friend, Clare, plus the weather and TV trailers had been warning me all week that it was approaching New Year. The one overwhelming reason for not going near Clare's house that night was that my ex-lover of more than four years would be there. Almost five years. We might have chalked up the Big Five had I not thrown one of my DM loafers at her head the morning she told me she was in love with another woman. I guess there must have been something in my eyes that told her the other shoe, and more, might follow if she didn't quit my flat fast. I hadn't seen her since.

Two months later I was past the howling at all hours and on public transport phase, and into that besieged mood of terror that I would see her – and the unattractive stranger I used to call a friend – at every venue where dykes gathered in numbers.

'You *have* to come to my party, you can't be alone on New Year's Eve,' Clare had insisted earlier in the week, while I was still holding out for a rigorous evening of solitude and booze.

'Why not?' I'd answered belligerently.

That was the kind of wilful indulgent mood I was in, and

that was Clare's cue to say, 'Because I'd miss you, everyone would. New Year wouldn't be the same without you.'

Tears stang my eyes in anticipation.

'Because that would be stupid,' Clare had replied. 'What are you going to do on your own? You'll only feel shitty.'

I had planned not to be feeling too much at all come midnight. I had already booked the bottle of Hogmanay whisky that would keep me company till kilts and haggis and the chimes of Big Ben happily signalled the end of a god-awful year. By that time I would have reached the familiar state of stupor that had been home to me for most of the past two months.

'*Be* there,' Clare had warned, 'or I'll come over myself and drag you out. Show her you don't give a fuck – show her you can have a good time without her.'

Jesus! Show her I could roll a cigarette with only two fingers might be just as likely . . . But Clare had faithfully tuned to my weakness: a challenge, a dare – the seductive pull of doing something outrageous or nigh impossible. I smiled at the end of the telephone and said I would come to the damn party, forgetting, as it was necessary I did, that the end of these 'dares' had too often been humiliation.

'Great! There'll be loads of nice woman there. Y'know, I think Angie fancies you.'

'She does not fancy me!' I protested. But in the same moment a vagrant memory returned, of Angie brushing past me in the hallway of another party – rather closely, I'd thought at the time, given how skinny we both were – and raising huge lingering eyes to mine. Clare talked on about how nice Angie was, while my own eyes narrowed at the other end of the phone in the effort of imagining kissing her. She had a nice mouth, that was true. But as imagination strove to press my lips into hers, another mouth intervened, a mouth turned hard despite the passionate night before, saying 'I'm in love with Linda'. The shoe I was about to pull onto my foot flying despairingly through the air. *Damn.* How long before I could forget *her* taste and smell and ges-

tures, before I wouldn't care? But still how willingly I
accepted the wisdom of my best friend that another woman
(any woman, it might be, but as unalike her as possible)
could erase all of that overnight.

'So get dolled up,' Clare was finishing, 'and I'll expect you
not later than ten.'

I spent the next four days getting dolled up. That is, I
scrutinised my entire wardrobe – hot weather and cold – but
found nothing that might transform me from the hateful
reject I felt myself to be, to an object of desire. I went out
armed with plastic to the local smart casuals shop and
endured the torture of tugging new jeans on to a body I was
despising. Booze and indolent misery had done little either
for my shape or skin.

'That pair's really *you*,' the mellow black guy in the shop
purred, while I glared unhappily in the mirror at my transformed lower self. What was it about denim that it could
flatten out my bum to nothing, make something baggy and
obscene of my pubic area? I leaned my weight heavily, first
to one side then the other, to watch how the fabric creased.
Show a little, but not too much. I chose finally a pair of
chinos that gave nothing away. Leaving the shop much later
with a shirt too that I hadn't wanted – 'With those pants,
y'gotta have the shirt . . .' – I clung to the hope that the
woman who wore them might seem as fresh and unused as
they were.

I had my hair done too. Or rather, I asked a friend with
steady hands to run a razor up the back of my neck and trim
the hanging basket that had grown into my eyes.

'Fab!' she exclaimed, standing back and studying me, then
plunging forward again with scissors to butcher another curl.
'A little mousse, a little make-up, and you'll be fit.'

Mousse? Make-up? When had these alien words from
another female world entered the lesbian vocabulary? Two
nights before the party I experimented with unfamiliar aids
I had only ever seen before at close quarters in my sister's
bedroom. The mousse clotted and fought my fingers' strug-

gle to shape it to something untamed but immovable. The make-up made me look a little like Dusty a little too late. I abandoned them both and stayed faithful to the natural look.

The night of the party I pulled on stiff pants and shirt and gazed in the mirror at a face naturally ashen and apprehensive. I thought of the endless bottle all for me. I thought of the reassuring kilts swinging with abandon at midnight. I thought of Clare's voice on the phone demanding 'Where the fuck are you?' and left.

'Hey, you look great!' Clare greeted me at the door. 'New shirt, eh? *And* new chinos. And your hair . . .' Her voice trailed off, eyes resting on the fringe that had somehow fallen onto my forehead during the walk over. 'Could use a little mousse, maybe – there's some in the bathroom.'

'Mmmm. I thought I'd leave the mousse out tonight.' I looked up at Clare through a bead curtain of hair.

'Sure,' she answered. 'Anyway, mousse leaves a stain on the pillow-case, I find. Come on up, Angie's here.'

If these two remarks had a connection, I chose not to make it, brushing curls aside and letting my eyes question her.

'No, she's not arrived yet.'

Upstairs in the kitchen only a dozen or so close friends of the house had arrived, mostly lovers, and ex-lovers with new lovers, of the other women who lived there. I raised a smile and said 'Hi' to the whole room, heads turning from conversation to greet me.

'Hi, Annie, good to see you.' Surprised to see me more like, I thought as I dumped my six-pack on the already cluttered worktop and searched for the heavy booze. Only a quarter bottle of Haig registered from the array of supermarket wines and cans lassooed with plastic. I turned my back on the crowd to disguise how eagerly I vandalised the Haig. My least favourite whisky, but it went down like saccharin, softening the edges of the flinty unhappiness that had begun to shape at the sight of so many women who must all know

I was in a state. I pulled on the whisky, and felt it course hotly through the knots in my gut.

'Hello, Annie, how've you been? I haven't seen you for a while.'

I looked up to find the lingering eyes I remembered from a hallway looking into mine. Angie. And now a different detector was telling me for sure she was going to find another reason to brush against me that night.

'No, er . . . I've not been well. I think it might be this bug that's going around. I haven't seen you since, mmm . . . Leah's party. That was a good night, wasn't it?'

I could hear myself, running on like a bore at a bus-stop, but Angie didn't flinch or seem otherwise to notice.

'Yes, it was,' she answered, with a certain light in her eyes. 'I had a really good time. But I think this one will be better – I hear everyone's coming.'

Oh gooood! I thought grimly, picturing a room of 'every-ones' made up only of my ex and her new passion, replicated over and over, appearing everywhere I turned. I wondered if I could simply put a fat straw in the whisky and draw serenely on it in some quiet place. The downstairs outdoor toilet, for instance, that nobody would be using much on this cold night. Perhaps the booze and the cold would leave me as numb as I wanted to be. Perhaps I could go home now . . . Clare's eyes caught mine from across the room as though reading my thoughts.

'I mean, how can you live with a woman who never changes her cat litter?' Angie was asking me earnestly as Clare slipped an arm conspiratorially through mine. I had barely heard a word of what Angie had been telling me of the civil wars in her collective household.

'Sure, that's bad news all right,' I replied, as Clare drew me away, and we drifted arm in arm from the already claus-trophobic kitchen.

'Sharing intimacies over the cat litter already?' she smiled, turning towards what was customarily her bedroom. 'Let's go and sit down in the dance room – we can have a chat there.'

It was too early yet for the dance room to be living up to its name, but it had been stripped bare, in readiness, of Clare's insomniac futon, her chic pastel duvet, the jungle of house-plants that had given it, many nights, a subterranean inti-macy. A sound system was running idly through a party tape, a succession of raves and smoochies flowing over us as we settled ourselves on the floor. I felt a little safer with the cool hard wall against my back.

'So: how are you doing?' Clare asked, giving me that friend-to-friend look more practised, I'd noticed, since she'd been doing therapy. Sometimes it made me feel like the cushion – like at that very moment, hardly able to meet her eyes.

'Oh, okay, I'm fine, really . . .' I gave her a wan smile, but couldn't disguise how my body flinched each time the bell downstairs sounded another arrival.

'You're doing really well!' she insisted, clasping my hand intently. 'I know how hard this is for you. But you've got to face it, face them, some time.'

Yes, but not tonight, a child inside me wailed. Not now, not here. Perhaps in a year or so when I could stare hard at her photographs and not remember her night-time profile. Maybe in a decade, when I wouldn't envy every other woman who could spend time with her, mention her name indifferently.

'You won't get *too* pissed tonight, will you?' Clare pleaded, as I pulled the Haig furtively from my pocket and killed stone dead the little orange juice in my glass. Light thrown from a street-lamp outside glinted on the warm-coloured bottle.

'Why not? It makes it better . . . well, easier, anyhow. Don't worry, I won't make a scene.'

I rarely made scenes. I could stand upright against a wall and pour booze into me like a rising thermometer and not register a heatwave inside, not shift an inch. Not unless they took the wall away.

Clare gripped my hand once more then left me, to mingle with the crowd that was by now spilling over from the kitchen into the large bare room. The DJ had arrived, casting the party tape aside with some contempt, running her finger-tips across grooves with a surgeon's precision. Headphones muffling her ears, hips twitching to the beat, she moved in a different orbit from the women who still stood or sat, indifferent to the music. Maxi Priest reached silkily into my left ear, and I began to feel better. The whisky had raised me to that happy plateau where nothing mattered and no one could reach me. Euphoria swept me to my feet and towards the kitchen again. Perhaps I was about ready to dance, per-haps about ready for Angie and the promise of waking to the New Year under a different duvet.

The kitchen was a smog of tobacco smoke and gossip going down. I leaned on the bodies jamming the open door, searching out for Angie, then pressed between thighs and shoulders to find what the new arrivals had added to the bar. A glance at embossed labels told me that an hour before midnight the serious and expansive drinkers had arrived. As I tipped another bottle into my drained glass, a tiny aside murmured that juice would do just as well to keep me on this level plain, that another drink might only tip me down-wards onto that rockier and descending path. But I ignored the warning as I habitually did, and poured the large one that would ease me into the New Year. Time enough tomorrow to deal with the fags and booze.

'Hello, Annie, I haven't seen you in ages.' A low-toned voice sounded close at my shoulder and the euphoria died. I knew the voice; the woman it belonged to was one of those I'd hoped to avoid that night . . .

'Hello . . .'

I could never say the woman's name with any conviction, unable to suppress my memory of her 'real' name. Then I felt guilty. Why shouldn't women change their names, names they'd had no choice about at birth? Hadn't I wanted to change my own a score of times? But every time I practised approaching Clare and saying, 'I want you to call me Medea from now on', I couldn't do it. But this woman seemed able to carry it off, to have buried Rosemary Saunders as though she'd never known her, never lived her comfortable life for more than thirty years. She was a *serious* writer – depicting the lives of working-class women with a tedious sentimentality that was devoured by the feminist press as 'authentic' and true.

'How's your writing going?' she asked then, with the gravity of someone enquiring after an incurable disease. 'What are you working on these days?'

I was working on my own authentic story of working-class life, but it was like giving blood and I doubted any publisher would touch it. *Her* writing had a dogged we-survived-despite-it-all quality that somehow I couldn't reach. I hated telling her too much. In her eyes was something predatory that made me suspect she'd like to take notes and sew my history too into the pastiche of other women's lives that she sold as her own.

'My novel,' I bluffed, 'but I'm having problems . . . with the storyline – can't seem to get past the chapter I'm writing.'

I wanted to escape, but pulled out my Rizlas instead and practised a one-handed roll in case I might need it later. Sympathetic eyes shone close to mine, sensing a kindred soul.

'I know *exactly* what you mean, Annie,' she said fervently, 'I found it so *painful*, writing some parts of my last novel – especially the scenes between Norma and her mother.' Her lips trembled to convey to me without words how Norma's life had exhumed her own. Or rather, her own life as she wished it might have been, but without Norma's despair, could Norma have stepped from the pages and spoken for herself. All her heroines had these unpretentious pretend names. I sucked hard on the roll-up I'd pinched too tight, and made my exit.

The dance room was heaving by the time I returned; a mass of breasts and arms merging and dividing again in the insubstantial light from the one lamp above the sound-deck. The DJ had drawn almost the whole room into her orbit, swaying crazily but intent as she lined up the next track through her becoming headphones. I took a stand alongside an open window and glanced down at the street outside. It looked chill and empty, like a foreign landscape from a stopped train. Only a clutch of partygoers, arms heavy with bottles, walked quickly, anxious to be withindoors when midnight came. I wanted badly to get off the train, to be an uncertain brushstroke against the grey. I leaned back again and surveyed the pulsing room. Who was with who tonight? What had changed since the same hour and place last year, except the soundtrack? And could I connect up all the women in sight, dot-to-dot fashion, via who had ever been lovers with whom? I'd all but plotted every woman in the room into what might have been a dartboard when Angie appeared beside me.

'Are you all right, Annie? You're squinting in a really weird way.'

'I'm fine,' I answered, distracted suddenly from the woman who appeared to be the bull's-eye.

The music had slowed from frenzy to the moody opening chords of a song that had been background to most women's bars for months. Bodies came together like pooling water, dots merging to make slow-shifting dark amoeba, filling the room.

'Do you want to dance? I love this one.'

'Sure.'

My hands were full of the half-drunk glass, a cigarette smoked low. I tossed the butt through the window and stood the glass close in against the wall. Angie and I wound ourselves between bodies weighty with a desire that seemed at that moment foreign, almost foolish, to me. Join the dots and pray that something lasting, or at least sufficient, is drawn. As we moved I strained to solve the equation of her body and mine – the rhythm behind, that should have held us both together. My feet had hit the rocky descending path; I was very drunk. But if I closed my eyes I found I could almost make sense of where Angie's body was taking me. Familiar territory: this scent rising from her throat, this warmth, her light composed body moving into mine. Angie's arms came up around my shoulders, fingers curling into my new-shaved neck. I let myself go with a desire I hadn't felt in a long while, our bodies turning like a mobile in a bare breeze.

Lazily I opened my eyes, found I was facing the door ajar, and in the lighted space my ex-lover stood.

'I see she's arrived.' Angie spoke tonelessly into my ear as the music faded, leaving us stranded.

'Who?' I asked stupidly.

'Annie, you don't have to cling to me like that. The music's finished, and I'm sure you have other places to be.'

She pulled away and walked out of the room. I headed back to my drink, finding it mercifully intact, I swallowed it whole, wishing it might be some kind of memory potion – amnesia would have been a joyful state right then.

She came over to stand very close to me, so close I could feel my arms around her. She was wearing new trousers too, and had her hair shaped to a different style. Something more had changed, but I couldn't find the one thing that had made her so much a stranger.

'Hello, Annie, you're looking good.'

'Looking good' – what did that mean? Was it a 'I want you back' looking good, or a 'You can't be missing me too badly' looking good?

'So are you,' I replied, not looking at her at all but past her shoulder to see where her new half was.

'Linda's in the car. We're not stopping – there's another party in south London tonight. I just came in to say happy New Year to everyone, to you . . .'

'So happy New Year,' I said, with as little emotion as

possible, eyes fixed anyplace except on hers. The whole room seemed to have become an audience.

'Annie, don't be horrible . . . I'm sorry. I didn't want things to turn out like this – it just happened.'

Oh yeah, I thought with bitter misery, like murder just happens. I felt the wall behind me crumble, a chasm opening into an inferno. The flames were in my throat, the anguish I couldn't swallow at her standing there so indifferently, but eyes pleading. For what? I remembered my promise to Clare not to make a scene. I could have buried my glass in the face so close to mine, but instead I pushed brutally by.

In the kitchen my hands shook violently as I poured the glass full. I needed desperately a quiet place to be and, as I'd suspected, the outdoor toilet was empty. I pulled the heavy wooden door open and closed it after me like a shell. A sallow light painted in the gap at the top of the door, and it was bitterly cold. The hot room, the scores of bodies – the one close body – retreated; a tide of relief flooded through me, leaving in its wake an appalling emptiness. Another party in south London? *Whose* party? We hardly knew anyone in south London. But 'we' wasn't *we* any more; 'we' was Linda and . . . In my mind I saw her car: a tiny toy gliding over a wide bridge across the river – probably they'd hear Big Ben for real from there. On the other side another life, leaving me behind. A faint memory of kilts turned to the plaid upholstery of her car I'd always despised till then, Linda's fingers shaping her thigh as she drove. She might have said I'm going rafting up the Nile, so remote it seemed.

I struggled, with grey shaking fingers, to roll a cigarette. Two *hands* couldn't do it, how bad I felt. The door shook suddenly as someone pounded urgently on it from outside.

'Annie, what are you doing in there?'

'Being a piece of shit.' I reached up to pull the bolt across, and Clare's face was framed between the house and the ragged fringes of the garden. There was a bottle of champagne in her hand to celebrate something, and her face had that cushion look again.

'Can I come in?'

Only Clare could be so polite about sharing space in a toilet.

'Sure – if you can stand the pace. This is where it's all happening.'

Clare took the crumpled bouquet of tobacco from my fingers, settled herself on my knee, and wrapped strong arms around me. I saw their raft, battling a tropical Thames, and began to cry.

'It's okay, baby, she's gone,' Clare murmured into my hair.

We sat silent a long time holding each other, then heard, as though from a planet circling above, the hectic suspended countdown that hailed the New Year. I imagined the kisses, plotting dots again. Clare fired the cork from her bottle through the gap in the toilet door, miraculous as a comet that moment, and passed me my glass teeming now with pretty bubbles.

'Happy New Year, sweetheart,' she whispered, kissing me.

'You too, baby,' I replied, dragging damp strands of hair from my eyes. 'This just might be the year I learn to use mousse.'

Not Another Clucking Christmas!

Fiona Cooper

Christmas. I don't know about you, but mine starts about October; that weekly duty phone call to my dear mother gets an added edge.

When I call my mother I usually get the births, marriages and deaths list, and then a re-run of the Bishop's latest sermon, then it's gardener's weekly: 'I told your father not to put that bonemeal under my standard rose, but he wouldn't listen and now the garden's full of dogs.'

Then we have the galloping gourmet session. For this I pay a phone bill? 'We had our lunch today. Carrots. Peas. Potatoes. And the new baker on the High Street has started doing individual meat pies. So your father can have chicken and mushroom to his heart's content and I can stick to steak and kidney. He's never liked steak and kidney. But he's very good. He doesn't complain.'

And then comes the first cough. It's serious; it's bronchitic; it's accident and emergency all the way from Lincolnshire. I have a choice at this point. I can give her the weekly weather report, and a price check on vegetables up north, but usually I make the fatal mistake of saying 'That's a nasty cough.' Four little words and she goes straight for the throat. My throat.

Her voice suddenly gets tremulous; she starts to sound like Grandma Walton after her stroke: it's the victim number! And of what is she a victim, my dear sweet fragile mother? My cruelty and neglect, that's what. How dare I have my own life at the age of thirty-something? Why am I not At

Home looking after her? After all, I'm not married. I've got no one else to take care of, have I?

My mother makes me feel like Lucrezia Borgia.

But I still say it; I say, 'That's a nasty cough, Mother. Are you taking your vitamins?'

'Vitamins?' The voice is fading now. 'Oh, there are some things vitamins just can't help. If you had a proper balanced diet you wouldn't need vitamins. Vitamins wouldn't help your father and me . . . we're not getting any younger.'

Well, shit, Momma, is that the truth? I must write that down. But that's only the beginning. Here comes stage two in *How to Guilt-trip your Grown-up Daughter.*

'We don't seem to have seen you much this year.'

'Well, you know, I've been really busy. It's not that I don't want to come home.'

Baby Jesus is watching me, girls, and he is not pleased. My nose starts growing. And here comes stage three. The last request.

'Have you got any plans for Christmas?'

Yeah. I'm gonna nuke the shopping centre, Mother. I'm not coming home. I'm gonna liberate a thousand turkeys, Mother. I'm gonna paint pink triangles all over 10 Downing Street. I'm not coming home! I'm gonna rob a bank and run away to Mexico. I'm going to make a bonfire of all the Christmas cards they send me. I'm gonna buy a crate of gin and lock myself in my own living room until it's all over. *I am not . . .*

'Well, I don't know.'

What is it about my mother that makes me go high-pitched? Why can't I just say I don't *like* Christmas? I am a pagan. I hate it! I don't have anything to say to her or the old dad or the aunties or my fascist sister and her jolly husband and their three spoilt kiddies and pedigree dogs. Mother, I'm a pagan!

And that's only October.

By November, she gets to sounding like Joan Crawford in *Whatever Happened to Baby Jane?*

'You wouldn't treat me like this if I wasn't in a wheelchair, Jane.'

My mother says, 'I know your father doesn't say much, but we both miss you.'

I'm feeling just a little bit guilty. But this year I'm not going to do it. I am not going home for Christmas.

December she's fading fast.

'Christmas is the one time families really should get together.'

And it always gets to me! I find myself slush-wrestling with the entire population of Newcastle in Eldon Square, me and my flexible friend.

Try to find something suitable for my sister: the woman who has everything bad taste and thirty thousand a year can buy. She was born wearing junk in a High Street emporium, that one, with a mix-and-match mentality. Mentality? I flatter her! And then it's Christmas Eve and I pack up the car. All the prezzies; a crate of wine: my family thinks one bottle of wine is quite enough for five people. Then there's the stash. The stash that refreshes. My own personal litre of Greek brandy and just the teeniest bit of herbal extract for my poor lungs. And what do you wear? I go for something really safe. One year I wore my scarlet leather flying suit. Auntie Winnie almost had a heart attack. So it's the interview outfit. Subtle. Grey and blue, the colours of peace and harmony.

Driving home for Christmas. A traffic jam. I look around. Almost every other car has a single person sitting staring ahead grimly, like they'd volunteered for euthanasia. Then there's the families: the kids are worse than the back benches at prime minister's question time. Crew-cut Darren's zapping My Little Pony with a transformer stun-gun, little Tracey's dismembering a toxic plastic Turtle and their poor mother is twisted round in her seat-belt talking to her darlings. Great fun if you can lip-read.

'Just sit down you little bastards! And you'd better behave when we get to Grandma's.'

And then there's Daddy. See Daddy, Daddy is driving. Daddy is driving the car. Makes me wish I was normal, really. All that could be mine.

And then I get home, park a block away and try the Christmas Eve joint for size. It feels like *High Noon* walking into the family kitchen. And they're all there.

'Hello, Mother.'

'A shame you couldn't get here sooner, really. I wanted you to wash the curtains and put down a new stair carpet. But you will lead your own life, won't you?'

'Hello, Auntie.'

'What have you done to your hair? It was such a pretty colour when you were a baby.'

'Hello, Sister.'

'Are you putting on weight – again?'

'I've never thought that blue and grey went together. But you've always had to be different, haven't you? Turn round.'

'Now, don't slouch. Hold your tummy in. I always think a corset might help.'

Why is it your family think they have the right to talk to you this way? Maybe I'm too polite. I don't think a lot of my sister's non-crease cerise floral ensemble. My mother's always colour co-ordinated too. Brown on brown. Cream on cream. Beige on beige. And the brother-in-law's beer gut's doing very nicely too. Oh, I forgot. Silly me. He's a Man. Now why couldn't they simply say 'Well, welcome home, Fiona, how nice to see you!'

They said they'd missed me. Nothing to laugh at for 365 long days I suppose.

But they are in a festive mood. Here comes the thimbleful of sherry and a hot mince pie. What a treat! But here's a tip: sherry's the same colour as Greek brandy so, glass in hand, I make a discreet exit to my room. The Real family have taken over all the spare beds and I've got a lilo in the airing cupboard this year. It's very cosy. I lock myself in the bathroom. What am I doing there? Now that's better. Kill the illicit smell with a squirt or two of Paco Rabanne – that hunky perfume my flabby brother-in-law likes so much. I float downstairs.

There's a dead bird on the table and bowls of stuffing. I'd just love to peel those blanched almonds, Mother. Bugger my nail varnish, the one I put on specially. Lovely. And grating chestnuts? Gee what a lot of fun we're having. We're in the living room now. My sister's dogs are the size of sheep and they're grazing on my new DMs. Her children are fast asleep, the little dears. Fast asleep in bed. My bed.

Nine o'clock and I've decided not to argue about what's on the telly. I want *Sticky Moments* and *French and Saunders*. But my family thinks that Channel Four's a communist plot and BBC2's not much better. Besides, we must catch the re-run of *A Tribute to Margaret Thatcher, the Years of Growth*. My sister and brother-in-law are the secretary and treasurer of the local Conservative Party after all. Hurrah for Maggie! What a loss to us all!

And then it's Christmas morning. Now I don't mind being woken up in the morning – you know, a gentle kiss on my sleeping brow, a discreet offer of at *least* coffee. Well, tough shit, bitch, you lucked out! It is Christmas Day and the door bangs open at eight in the morning. Is there an eight o'clock in the morning? I thought it was just an ugly rumour. There's a silhouetted figure standing there! It's wearing a huge hat weighted down by fruit and flowers and a kamikaze pigeon. It starts poking me with an umbrella. It's the mother, God save us, and she chose it herself!

Does she say 'Good morning, child of mine, I hope you slept well and here's some coffee'?

Oh no, girls. My mother says in her best fête-opening voice, 'It's a lovely morning, a bit windy and there's storms on the way! You'll waste the day lying in bed. Too many late nights! You'll catch your death of cold one of these days; I don't know why you won't wear a nightie. I can lend you one. There's nothing like flannelette on a winter's night. If you're quick we can give you a lift to church. You *are* going to church, aren't you? It *is* Christmas!'

Some people never give up. I pretend to be dead. The door bangs.

Eventually the clatter of jolly feet and the patter of tiny ones is over. I race down to the phone – to call the one I love. The first human voice for twenty-four hours. Somebody loves me! The real me! I do exist! Then I have an hour of peace in the bathroom shattered by the return of my nearest and dearest. And they're all singing: 'Good King Wenceslas' and 'God Rest Ye Merry Gentlemen'. There's no rest for me, but then I'm not a gentleman, am I?

And soon it's Christmas dinner and God help me, we have to talk to each other. Now then, have you noticed what you can talk to your parents about? There's the weather. And the garden. And the price of veggies. And the car. But you can bet your sweet bahoolas that they're gonna ask you: 'What have you been doing since we last saw you?'

Well, I've had two lesbian novels published, been to a few drag shows, broken up with my lover, fallen in love, spray-painted an RAF bomber, picketed some X-rated movies, got a caution for Supergluing all the magazines on the top shelf of Smiths, joined the Gay Pride committee, walked on a beach at sunset with my lover and this time it's the Real Thing . . .

'Well, this and that. Not a lot really.'

'And how's the new job?'

Brilliant. I've met the most amazing women writing the most amazing stories.

'I don't know why you're only working with women. Isn't that sex discrimination as you'd call it?'

Well, Mother, I just don't feel right working with Martians. I wish they'd sod off back to their own planet and stop messing up mine.

It's a shame you can't just say 'Pass' really.

'They're all Labour up north anyway,' says my sister. 'You only went there because they got rid of Ken Livingstone and the G.L.C.'

'Snipped any good fences lately?' says the brother-in-law.

'We thought of getting you some thermal underwear for your little camping trips to Greenham Common.'

So witty. There's only one thing to do. I do it.

'Must freshen my mascara,' I say, a true girly to the last, and escape to the bathroom. Oh dear. My knuckles seem to be white and clenched. Whoops. I appear to be clutching the dining room door handle.

A Stone

Mary Ann Hushlak

The Woman Cleaning Lentils

A lentil, a lentil, a lentil, a stone. A lentil, a lentil, a lentil, a
stone.
A green one, a black one, a green one, a black. A stone.
A lentil, a lentil, a stone, a lentil, a lentil, a word.
Suddenly a word. A lentil.
A lentil, a word, a word next to another word. A sentence.
A word, a word, a word, a nonsense speech. Then an old
song.
Then an old dream.
A life, another life, a hard life. A lentil. A life.
An easy life. A hard life. Why easy? Why hard?
Lives next to each other. A life. A word. A lentil.
A green one, a black one, a green one, a black one, pain.
A green song, a green lentil, a black one, a stone.
A lentil, a stone, a stone, a lentil.
ZAHRAD (ZARSH YALDIZCIYAN) (translated from Armenian by
Ralph Setian).

      'You gonna open up your bag, little lady? Big hold-
all, eh? Lots of presents, eh? Wrapped them up all fancy, did
you? What's in this one?'
    'Wheat. Cooked wheat.'
    'You got cooked wheat wrapped in red tinsel paper?'
    'It's a Christmas dish.'
    'How about this one?'

'I think – cabbage rolls, cabbage rolls with either rice or buckwheat.'

'You think cabbage rolls. Jesus Christ. Just what I need after my break. Who're you visiting?'

'My cousin. She's studying in San Francisco.'

'Let's have a little feel of this glitzy green one. Soft.'

'Dumplings. Dumplings with mashed potatoes, and with sauerkraut.'

I was ready to crawl under the long, low metal table.

'Dumplings in glitzy green. Cabbage rolls in shiny blue. Sure. You developed a colour code? What's royal purple?'

'Fassouli. Beans with prunes.'

'Hey, Roberta.'

Roberta, middle-aged, blonde curls, feminine in her tailored custom's officer uniform, at the next table, her plump arm plunged deep into a bag.

'Yeah, Hank.'

'You listening, Roberta?'

'I hear you, Hank.'

'I got a little lady here in a check tracksuit who says she's got . . . how'd you like beans with prunes for your Christmas dinner?'

'Christmas Eve.'

'Roberta?'

'I hear you, Hank.'

'Correction, Roberta. The little lady says it's beans with prunes on Christmas Eve, not Christmas Day. The little lady said I made a mistake.'

Hank's voice carried across the custom's hall. Everybody turned to look.

'It's all cooked,' I said. 'There's no meat in any of it. There's no chance of foot-and-mouth disease. It's all lenten, nothing animal in it.'

'Lady, foot-an-mouth disease ain't our biggest worry right now. You read newspapers? Terrorists. Terrorists hijack planes. Terrorists nurse bombs. People carry drugs . . .'

My God, behind his drawl, he's gauging my reaction.

'. . . ordinary-looking people, except for a little giveaway sign. What's in the separate bag?' he asked, his eyes not shifting an inch from my face.

'Kalach. Braided bread. For the centre of the table.'

'Bread always the size of a pull-along vacuum cleaner?'

'There are three round loaves, one on top of the other. Do you want me to show you? All of it's just food.' I can't explain that Sharon and I haven't seen each other for three years and . . .

'Where you born?'

'Canada.'

'Your parents?'

'Canada.'

I flushed. I felt a clamp round my chest. What if he asks about grandparents? Say they were Canadian citizens if he asks about grandparents. Great-grandparents too. Start talking about all of them buried in the same graveyard in Alberta.

Does he have to lick his teeth as he watches me?

If he picks up on citizens, say Bukovina. Austrian-Hungarian Empire. Stress Austrian. He'll never know Bukovina is in Ukraine. Just don't say Soviet Union.

'Your cousin's parents born in Canada?'

'Yes.'

'What's this? Pretty tough on the teeth.'

'Those are candles.'

'Hey, Roberta.'

'Yeah, Hank.'

'Roberta, the little lady says they eat candles for Christmas. No bundle of baby birthday candles either. Pepperoni-size candles.'

'Three of them go in the bread. The others are for windows. They're put in the window – an invitation for any homeless stranger.'

'You all concerned about the homeless?'

Please God, don't let him pick up the straw. How can I explain I wrapped up straw? Sure it's put under the tablecloth. I can hear him. Memory of the Christ-child in a manger. Sure. Big joke.

'Who's "Missie"?'

'My cousin's cat.'

'What'd you buy the cat?'

'It's a custom to mix a spoonful of every dish for house animals because animals were the first creatures to see Jesus.'

'Unwrap them. All of them. Yip, all your fancy paper and shiny ribbons.'

'I'll miss my plane.'

'Your plane won't go without you until we tell it to go without you. Now you just unwrap every little parcel and line them up in a nice straight row and we'll have a little look at your Christmas dinner . . .'

'Christmas Eve supper.'

'We'll have ourselves a little inspection. Including the candles. Candles are very interesting these days.'

Won't he just be thrilled with church candles? He'll probably confiscate them. He won't ever have seen such plain ivory candles. To think I trekked over to the Ukrainian bookshop in Notting Hill to find genuine Orthodox church candles; so Sharon and I could have a giggle, especially considering what a stash of them Baba had in shoe boxes under her bed.

Why did I think it would be such fun for Sharon and me to have a traditional Christmas Eve supper, like when we were kids? I must have been out of my mind.

'Don't tear the paper,' I murmured to myself. Not so fast. Slip your nail under the tape carefully. What a bastard. When I took such care making tucks and folds with the paper and curled the ribbons and frayed the bows.

I feel faint. How did Baba fast all day long on Christmas Eve and not wolf her food down when I brought it to her? She spent all day long in her warm little house, not changing aircraft going to the United States, that's why. She would have been pleased; two granddaughters spending Christmas together. I'm glad I decided to fast today. In Baba's memory.

How Dad shouted at her about her religious fasting. 'It's unhealthy to drink only water for two weeks,' he railed.

And she shrugged back, 'It hasn't killed me in eighty-one years, and I'm not dead yet.'

I'll miss the plane. There won't be a seat left on the other flights to San Francisco. No seats to San Francisco and none back to Edmonton either. Stuck in a hotel room in Vancouver or taking a bus. I mustn't be so catastrophic.

Let Hank confiscate the food. Great. The last two days with my *Traditional Ukrainian Cookery* wasted. Mother adding instructions while she made the Christmas honey cake wasted. The honey cake, her contribution. Her contribution wasted. Maybe my suggestion that we set out a large plate and small bowl on a tray as if it were for Baba wasn't so silly. Would be as useful and real as when Hank gets his hands on it all. In the bin, down the garbage chute, dumped.

May Hank trip over his neatly tied shoe laces and may the knife-edge crease of his trousers crumple. May his wavy hair erect into spikes.

Christmas Eve. What a place to be on Christmas Eve. If I was in London, I'd be going to St Paul's for eleven-thirty, my once a year collective singsong. If I was still a kid, I'd be taking a sample of this food to Baba; to Baba wearing her best silk headscarf and embroidered blouse and bold flowered skirt.

How she sat, facing the door, on the wooden plank bench next to her long wooden table, waiting for me. The room smelled of floor wax. I must have been eight. I fluffed up three grand feather pillows for her head, and three smaller ones for her feet and helped her settle on her brass poster bed, positioning her cane so she could easily reach it. I handed her the small bowl of *kutya*; she crossed herself, and slowly chewed one spoonful of the cooked wheat, and crossed herself once more. The candle in the snow-coated window flickered. Only candlelight in her middle room, a candle beneath every icon, every icon draped in embroidered cloth.

How I wanted to race back to the big house, our house, where everybody was decorating the tree.

'Grandma, your Christmas Eve supper is getting cold,' but she wasn't about to be deflected. I stood at her bedside and sang. Rising and falling 'Nebo i Zemlya'; rollicking 'Na Rozhestvo', and all six verses of her favourite carol, the rumbling 'Boh Predvechnyi'. I sneaked a look at my right wrist. I was picturing my first wristwatch. I was sure Saint Nicholas had a wristwatch for me.

And I left her alone. I never thought about leaving her alone.

Why did she always want to be alone on Christmas Eve? We always asked her to join us; Sharon's dad and mom always asked her, but she always stayed alone.

Same with Gido; Baba and Gido both choosing to be alone on Christmas Eve. In their separate houses, alone.

Will I forget his tears and that cup? Never. My hand tucked in Dad's, climbing the two steep steps into his converted granary, stomping the snow, fingering the sensuous grey wood panelling.

His back to us, hunched over the square table in the centre. I skipped round in front of him, framing my 'Christ is Born, Grandad.' Catching his tears in a metal cup. I still wince. How Dad cradled my head, covered my eyes, and turned my face away. He took the candle from the window, placed it on the table, set out his father's dinner, and gently pried the metal cup away.

I still can't quite incorporate that it was the same Gido, jolly Gido, a few days later. 'What a clever daughter-in-law I have,' he teased my mother, shaking his head and crooked finger. Cutting holes in every pair of his Christmas-present new thick socks and in every pair of new thermals, and neatly darning the scissor cuts. She knew the darn meant the store wouldn't exchange them. Oh yes, she knew him; she knew he exchanged his presents for Hoffmann's drops. He wasn't a fool; he knew gripe water was alcoholic. She was determined; he was going to be warm through the winter in spite of himself.

How Gido could trigger her sparkling, ringing laugh. I love that lilting laugh of hers. So different from her proud, formal, frosty, quiet internal self. Except when she cleaned wheat.

She talked when she cleaned the wheat. A kernel, a kernel, a kernel, a stone. Like in that Armenian poem. 'A lentil, a lentil, a stone, a lentil, a lentil, a word . . . A life, another life, a hard life. A lentil. A life.'

On the oilcloth table covering, it was a stone, a straw, a stone in a scrap pile on one side, and a rising mound of pure wheat kernels in a porcelain bowl as Mother talked. As in Zahrad's poem: 'A lentil, a word, a word next to another word. A sentence.' Baba was cranky, even as a young woman, not only now she's old and crippled and achy, a kernel, a kernel, a straw, a kernel, and Great-grandmother had warm dimples when she smiled, and she found it easy to smile, but Great-grandfather, a kernel, a stone, a stone, had a foul, angry mouth, a stone, a stone, he beat Great-grandmother, a kernel, a kernel, a kernel, a kernel, a straw, a kernel, they thought Great-grandmother had healing hands.

Zahrad must have cleaned lentils with his mother or grandmother or aunts or neighbour-women. How many days I spent memorising his poem on that beach in Cyprus. 'An easy life. A hard life. Why easy? Why hard? . . . Lives next to each other. A life. A word. A lentil.' Lentils in his world; wheat in mine.

How Mother cleaned only a little wheat each day. Never cleaned it all in one go. For a month before Christmas, every day, she cleaned and every day she talked.

Yes, how much better things are nowadays, she said. Better that people talk about alcoholism and wife beating, and child abuse too; in the newspapers, on television. Everybody kept quiet about everything in those days. Much better now, a kernel, a kernel, I was an easy baby, easy birth too, a kernel, a kernel, a stone, but with . . .

'What're the black bits in this stuff?'

I was startled. I'd forgotten; I'd been mechanically unwrapping the twenty presents, all laid out.

'The black bits.' Hank was rapping the customs counter.

'Poppy seed. Ground poppy seed, honey and walnuts.'

'Ground poppy seed. Ground-up poppy. Poppy. You know what poppy is? Sure you know what poppy is. Very versatile plant, the poppy.'

'There's nothing in anything. It's all normal food.'

'Little lady, you're coming into the United States of America. You gotta be clean coming into the United States of America, you understand. You got your driver's licence, little lady? Good. Good. Alberta, eh? Lot smarter up there with pictures on licences. Helps us. They don't let us have pictures. Civil liberties crap.'

I mustn't react.

'I thought I told you to unwrap everything.'

'I've unwrapped one, two, three, four, five, six, twelve, twenty . . .' The record, oh my God, the Cyrillic script on the record.

'It's a record. I thought you were only interested in food.'

'You gonna unwrap it? Well, what we got here? You see this writing? Sure you see this writing. This writing looks "commie".'

'They're Christmas carols.'

'You read this writing?'

'Vaguely.'

'Vaguely, eh? Now, vaguely's a word I got trouble with. You know, it's kinda like . . . either you have a drink or you don't . . . you don't vaguely, know what I mean? You got your passport with you, little lady? Hey, Roberta, how's a Canadian get a K12 in their passport?'

'I live in England. I arrived British Airways into Boston.'

'What were you doing in Boston?'

'Visiting a friend.'

'Your friend know how to read this writing?'

'No.'

'Where'd you go after Boston?'

'Edmonton.'

'You stop here in Vancouver?'

'No, I'm just changing planes. There's no direct flight from Edmonton to San Francisco.'

'How long you lived in England?'

'Eight years.'

'Lots of "commies" in England, eh?'

'Okay, Hank.' Roberta clapped her hands, clanking her rings.

'Okay,' she said to me, yawning. 'Stuff it all back in your bag and get to your plane.'

'Hank,' and she elbowed his lean stomach, 'my instinct's never been wrong yet.'

Hank pulled a penknife out of his trouser pocket, and drew out a toothpick. 'Little lady, next time you'd do a whole lot better leaving your "normal" presents at home. Have a good Christmas.'

The Christmas News

Maeve Binchy

There was an old story that when Paddy Crosbie was recording *School Around the Corner* on Radio Eireann for the first time, he asked a small boy to tell him a funny incident.

The child took a deep breath and said, 'It was Christmas Eve, and my sister came in the door from England and said, I'm pregnant, and Da said "Beautiful effing beautiful" and we all laughed.'

Dot laughed more ruefully than others because, as she used to say to herself, it was her story exactly.

It had been Christmas Eve when she had announced the same news. Thirty years ago when things were a bit different. Very different. Her father hadn't laughed at all. He didn't even manage a smile during the chilly January wedding. It wasn't as if he'd been an old man, he'd only been forty-five; that wasn't time for an old man's attitudes and hardness of heart. But then those were different times, and the town was small. And most of all he blamed himself; he felt he hadn't been parent enough for Dot, that somehow he had betrayed his promise to Dot's mother who had died long long ago.

It was useless Dot trying to tell him that no amount of mothers would have kept her out of Martin's arms and that she felt nothing but delight to be having his child. Her father had turned his head away, holding up his hands. The situation was bad enough, must she now glory in her ways?

Dot used to look at pictures of her dead mother and wonder would the reaction have been the same? Might her mother have held her and consoled her, congratulated her even?

But it was foolish to be sentimental; 1960 was 1960, the Middle Ages in a small country town. No doubt the calm eyes of this woman in the photo frame would not have been calm at such news. And anyway it had all turned out so well, a beautiful daughter, Dara, born in the springtime, a happy marriage for years and years. Well, twenty years. And that was more than most people had. It was more than her parents had.

It had seemed natural to go and live with her father again. Why should the two of them live in big empty houses with their memories?

Dara had been against it. It would mean an end to freedom, she had warned, her mother would grow old before her time caring for Grandfather. It wasn't what Father would have wanted – Mother entombed with an old man, an old man who had been so disapproving of her. There had been no point in Dot trying to cover up her father's long sense of grievance about the shotgun wedding. It was there in every sigh and head shake.

Dara begged her mother not to go back to her old home. 'He was so cold to you there when you told him about me. Don't go back now just because he's ancient and decrepit and can't manage any more.'

Dot smiled. Her father was a sprightly sixty-five; anything less incapable she had found hard to imagine. And they wouldn't be on top of each other. Dot would move into the basement. She could give her piano lessons there easily; the pupils wouldn't even disturb her father, they could come in by a separate entrance.

'You think too much about him,' Dara had grumbled. 'Mark my words, it won't work out well.'

But it had worked very well, the years living with her father. He had a busy life, filled with committees and friends, and little outings.

Time passed peaceably. Dara moved in and out of their

lives, bringing laughter and friends. But never just one friend. Never the man she was going to marry.

Dot longed to be a grandmother. She wished that her dark handsome daughter would find a man she loved and start a family. Next year Dara would be thirty, but Dot reminded herself that Dara knew only too well what age she was; she would scarcely appreciate her mother reminding her.

So Dot was always bright and interested in stories of new friends, new interests, new and bewildering successes at work. Dara, small dark eyes, Dara the light of her life, was apparently a killer in the money market. She talked of stock exchanges in Tokyo and New York as easily as her mother and father had talked of music examinations for their pupils, as her grandfather talked of the Parish Council.

Dot sighed. They had wanted the best for their only daughter. She and Martin had travelled long hours on buses in the rain to teach in schools; they had taken the tone-deaf children of ambitious parents and forced scales and tunes into them in hours of joyless work. There had never been a car even when they could afford one; always keep a nest egg there, just in case. Dara might want to do a Masters in America; they would need the funds.

And they had never regretted a minute of it. Martin and Dot rejoiced over their daughter, and they forgave Dot's father his head shaking, his sense of lives destroyed, marriage anticipated and lingering shame. That was the way he was; it was his generation they had told each other. The man had been born in 1915, before the Easter Rising, before the founding of the state. How could he be expected to understand what was going on?

Always around Christmas-time Dot felt glad that there had been no serious coolness, no falling out or even a sense of distance between them. She decorated the old house as she had done for as long as she could remember.

It was somehow unchanging. Dot would put on her wellingtons and go out to the walls in the long wet lane behind their garden, and pull great fronds of ivy. She ironed and folded the red ribbon each year so that it was ready to drape in big loose bows around the house. Even when Martin had been alive they used to bring a lot of their Christmas cards here to make the place look more festive.

Dot looked back on it all, the Christmases when Martin had carved the turkey, twenty of them, and the ones that went before and came after; they were all a long continuous line, same red ribbons, same kind of ivy. Just Dara's face changing, growing up, growing older even. Last year she had looked drawn and tired. But she had assured her mother that she was well and happy. Dot knew better than to pry, and was never tempted to offer advice. What could a middle-aged piano teacher offer in the way of counsel to a bright young star of the money market?

Dot's father had brought out a tired, neglected potted palm to be added to the decorations. It was far from lustrous, but he was fond of it.

'I thought we could use this.' He sounded a little different. Still at seventy-five he was his old self, sure in the rightness of everything he believed in, which included leaving plants in the dark.

'It's lovely, I'll put a ribbon around it,' Dot said. Carefully she painted the leaves with colourless nail varnish. It gave them a shine. She sprinkled a dusting of Christmas glitter over it before the polish had dried. It looked quite splendid she thought happily. Maybe this is what she and Martin should have done with their lives, run a flower shop, created sparkling Christmas decorations rather than teach unmusical children to play the piano. She was smiling to herself at the thought, and didn't hear the door open.

It was Dara, back from wherever she had been . . . certainly another country, maybe even another continent.

They sat in the firelight, companions and friends as well as mother and daughter. Dara told of the terrible rush to catch the plane, of the traffic, the crowds, the shops. At the mention of shops she leaped up and opened a parcel. It was a beautiful red silk jacket for her mother.

'I couldn't possibly . . .' Dot was astounded. It was designer fashion, something for a younger woman, not for Dot.

But her daughter's eyes were shining; she said that when she saw it, it reminded her of the scarlet ribbons and all the wonderful Christmases here at home.

Dot blinked the tears of gratitude out of her eyes. She tried on the jacket. She didn't look like someone who would be fifty very soon; she looked terrific. She stared with amazement at her reflection in the mirror.

Behind her she saw Dara's face. It looked different somehow. Perhaps that was just because it was a reflection. Dot turned around but she had been right, there was something different. Dara was going to tell her something.

'I have some very seasonal news,' she said.

Dot's heart missed a beat. 'What are you telling me?' she said. Her face was full of hope.

'What you told Grandfather in this very house a long time ago,' said Dara.

It was 1990; it was another era; the girl stood there proud and sure, happy that her Christmas news was welcome, that this baby would delight as she had done.

Dot folded her daughter in her arms; she stroked the dark hair; she cried with happiness.

'And tell me about him, when will we meet him? When will you get married?'

Dara pulled away. 'Oh Mother, I'm not getting married or anything,' she said.

'No, no.' Dot's voice was soothing. She didn't want to spoil the moment, the wonderful Christmas moment.

'It was never on the cards. I mean that wasn't part of what this is all about.'

'I see,' said Dot, who didn't see.

They sat together in the firelight. She held her daughter's hand as she had done during Christmas-times long ago. She rejoiced that next year there would be another person here, a baby looking up and smiling at the lights and the ribbons.

She wouldn't ask now, about the man who had fathered this child but was apparently never part of anything that this was about. She would hear eventually about why marriage had never been on the cards.

She must get the words and the tone right when she was telling her father about it. She must try to make him see what she couldn't see herself.

'Now my love,' Dot said to her daughter, 'we must be very careful about how we tell your grandfather.'

'Why, Mother?' The clear untroubled young face looked at her. Dara genuinely saw no problems in a second disgrace being visited on this household, a second Christmas revelation to an old man who had already heard too much.

Dara, who understood so much about the world, surely must understand that her grandfather would have to be jollied along, protected, cushioned in some way. Dara *must* understand this. Mustn't she?

'I think we should sort of hint at some marriage plans,' Dot said tentatively.

'Absolutely not.' Dara was firm, not even remotely argumentative but utterly sure of her ground. 'Why fill an old man up with lies and fictions, and then have to unpick them?'

Dot felt herself biting her lower lip as she always had done when she didn't trust herself to speak. She saw Dara watching her, calm, loving, but with the impatience of a mother who is waiting for the toddler to get it right. They had reversed roles. Dara was not the erring daughter who had come home with a tale of a Christmas pregnancy outside wedlock, she was the wise all-knowing adult trying to cope with juvenile confusions.

Almost as if she were watching a play, Dot saw the drama unfold in this house all over again. But the lines were different. The girl of the nineties told her grandfather of the great wish she had to bring a child into the world, how she had planned carefully to look after the baby, to work from home, to job share with another woman. Unbelievingly Dot saw the craggy disapproving head of her father nod with interest and approval. Everything this beloved granddaughter was saying seemed to make sense to him. Where was the coldness of three decades ago? Where were the speeches about shame and disgrace? Had he forgotten the tirades about being cheap, and sluttish servant girl's behaviour? Yes, apparently he had.

Even after Dara had gone to bed and Dot sat watching his face, she could find no sign that he might not have meant his enthusiasm towards Dara's infant.

'Why is it different now?' she asked eventually. The unspoken rule had been broken; they never referred back to the way he had behaved thirty years ago.

'Everything is different.' Her father seemed surprised that she had asked.

'But how? I mean isn't it even worse with no marriage or . . . or anything?' She felt her voice trickle away. She sensed she was betraying her own Dara, trying to whip up resentment against her.

There was a lot of head shaking. He said that he could see no similarities. All those years ago Dot had been ashamed, and tearful; she had been apologetic and known she had done wrong. This was something entirely different. Dara, a mature woman, wanted to bring a child into the world; she had provided for the contingency in advance. There was nothing feckless and ill advised like a rushed marriage to a penniless young man, a tying down of two young people before they were ready. What had Martin or Dot ever got from their lives except a long grinding struggle trying to rear the child they had conceived so irresponsibly.

Dot sat there looking at the fire, as she heard her father justifying his own hard-heartedness of years ago. She thought of the many tears that she had shed, the million efforts to regain his admiration and affection. And all that time he had written off her marriage to Martin as nothing!

In all the years that she had tried to please him, in the foolish contest which she thought she had won because he accepted both her and her daughter, she had not realised that he had merely dismissed her.

The Christmas news had a bitter taste to it. The news that she had so wanted to hear had been strangely delivered. She tried to remember Martin's face, his good sense, his way of turning away the bad side of things and mining until he found the good.

What would he tell her now? That their life hadn't been thrown away; that the continued struggle had not been grinding. That he was overjoyed that their line would go on. Perhaps he would have told her to rejoice that times had changed and that it was easier for a girl today; that a baby planned, and waited for and welcomed, would have an even greater chance of happiness than one which came too early and nearly frightened them both to death.

She looked long into the fireplace trying to see his face among the flames, and take the good of the Christmas news into her heart.

He Delighteth in Mercy

Joanna Rosenthall

The phone ringing on Yomtov? It couldn't be. It must be Auntie Sadie worrying about her. It would have to be something important for her to decide to use the phone. Perhaps she should answer it and tell her she was okay, then it would stop ringing. There would be peace. She could hear herself saying, Sadie. I'm not going, Father died a year ago today, and I'm just not going. She could hear Sadie's sharp intake of breath. Ash? You're not going to shul, it's Rosh Hashonah! It's no good for you to stay at home alone. Come and be with your family.

If she could think of one answer that would stop the conversation right at the beginning . . . Her hand hovered over the receiver, she even touched it, gave the red plastic a little stroke. She wished Auntie Sadie could see her toying with the idea; the old lady would be anxious about her. It seemed very mean. She walked around the room, stopping in front of the bookcase as if she were browsing. Her arm went up to loosen a title that caught her eye. She pulled the top of the spine forward and the book stayed there, in a tipsy balance, poised to fall, yet safely jammed into the overfull shelves. *The Golden Notebooks*. If she committed suicide and they searched the flat looking for clues they would look at that book and wonder why it was like that. Was it the last thing she had read? Was there a message concealed between the pages? She could see Auntie Sadie trying to be head of the family, red in the face, wanting to get rid of the policemen. After they were gone she would allow herself all manner of prayers and curses interspersed with cluckings and 'pfut' sounds to ward off evil spirits, reverting suddenly in times of need to her Polish peasant roots.

Auntie Sadie had been like that when Father died. She had spoken only Yiddish, and kept repeating incantations, unrecognisable to Ash, and yet clear in meaning: something terrible had befallen them all and they had to make sure nothing else as bad would happen. She didn't talk to Ash for days but stroked her hair and offered her the dish of tagels which had been so carefully prepared for the New Year celebrations. The celebrations had had to turn into the Shivah.

There were people coming to the house each day for seven days, to pray, to sit, to talk. It was exactly a year ago. Ash only remembered bits of it. The tagels, gorgeous little knots of biscuit swimming in ginger syrup, and the fact that Auntie Sadie closed all the curtains. She covered the mirrors with a cut-up white sheet. It all had a peculiar, disconcerting feel. Everywhere in the house where she was used to seeing light, reflections and movement, there was only dimness and whitish shadows. Dark white. Still white. It made her think of ghosts. She had not asked why they did it. Auntie Sadie, or her mother, would have said, Jews do. Ash had a feeling that her father was there and if she looked in the mirror she might see him looking back at her. At the end of the seven days, she took down the sheets with relief and the mirrors too. What did she want with a house full of mirrors? She put them in the boot of the car and took them to the Oxfam shop.

Bad thoughts. Dismal, morbid thoughts. She left the room, walking into the hallway. It was an act of defiance against the memories. She pulled her dressing gown around her. It was a thin cotton Indian print, she was cold. A bath would warm her up. She would feel the day had started proper. It was always a mistake to put off getting dressed.

She felt like an egg being coddled in the hot water. She suddenly remembered it was the New Year. It wasn't that she had forgotten, but more that the memory of last year had flooded everything else.

She sat on the closed toilet seat, hot and heavy as if the

water had swelled her up a little, staring at her towel-covered knees.

She must dry her hair and dress. She had been so slow. She was late. Of course she must go to shul. How could she miss it? She had never missed it. She could see herself entering the building at the side, running up the steps and searching the semi-circular sweep of the balcony for where she would sit. It was like the upper circle in an old Victorian theatre, giving everyone a chance to see the service below. Where were Sadie and the girls? She would be at the front, her usual place, in her Shabbos coat with a mink stole and the cream hat that looked like a cowrie shell. Ash giggled silently at the thought that the hat would look less incongruous on a beach, tucked up into the side of a rock, than it did on Sadie's head. It was the thought of seeing her aunt waving madly at her, relieved, delighted that she had taken the advice and come, that finally convinced Ash she would not go. This year had to be different.

She opened her wardrobe solemnly. She would go to synagogue, but a different one. She would walk to that little orthodox shul at the side of the park. It would take at least half an hour to get there, maybe nearer an hour. No one would know her. What would she wear? She picked out the usual Shabbos outfit, a pleated navy skirt and matching jacket. Sombre and smart, an outfit for a woman who doesn't want to be noticed. She always wore that pale blue shirt with it. She dressed quickly, then stood in front of the mirror, critical. Yes, she looked okay, smart. Her father would have been proud that she was carrying on, doing the same things without him. Without anyone.

The phone again! Sadie. God, she would have to answer all these questions at some time. Now. She would do it now. She picked up the receiver, instinctively holding it away from her ear.

'Ash? Hello? We were wondering if you'd like to come around tonight and help us make up a little party?'

Who was this? Who could this be on New Year, ringing and forgetting what day it was?

'Ash . . . Ash?' The voice now sounded uncertain. She asked who it was. It was Rose! How simple things were. It was an invitation from her friends from college. It wasn't a special day for them. She had another life! This was the new life that she had struggled so hard to find. She had almost forgotten its existence. No, I'm sorry, she said, I can't tonight, and the phone went down. She had forgotten to be friendly.

She was standing in front of the bookcase again with that strange sensation of not knowing how she had got there. A little bit of her life had happened without her. She kept the prayer books on the top shelf. She could reach. Just. Festivals? No. Atonement? No. New Year. There it was. The set had been her father's, bound in rough, cheap leather. She opened the book, flicking through the start of the service, she had missed the first hour or so. She calculated where they would be up to by the time she got there. Her father's pencilled scribbles sprang out. How strange that he wrote these words, that they were here and he was not. *Open ark, Close ark, Open ark, Close ark*, he had written repeatedly through the whole book in a wavery but unfaltering scrawl.

She slipped her feet into a pair of broad, flat shoes by the front door. They had elastic pieces at the sides and rounded toes. She wouldn't need a coat – the walk would keep her warm.

She could see herself walking to shul with her father. She had a long thin body and a very strong back. Her aunt had said she was just like her mother had been, but her father said nothing and she knew not to ask. She was dressed in her Shabbos best, that long blue coat with a velvet collar that lasted for years. By the time it was the right size it was already looking shabby.

It was quite a long way to shul. They would start out from the house in silence. She would think for a while, should she link his arm? She would wait until they crossed a main road and then she would thread her hand underneath his bent elbow, making a space between his arm and his body. When they had crossed the road she would leave it there. After a while he would talk. He would tell her, Today, Ashra, it is a High Holy day, a Day of Awe. She would know it from before but he would explain how Rosh Hashonah is the New Year and yet it comes always in the autumn, how it is the only Jewish festival that falls on the first day of the month, and how the Jews of the diaspora had a problem because news of the sighting of the new moon often took time to travel from Jerusalem and so they couldn't be sure of their dates. All they could do, he explained, was to celebrate for two days in a row. For Ash that would mean two days off school, two days of long walks with her father to and from the synagogue. She thought the Jews of the diaspora were good people, they believed in holidays.

Nearing the shul, she would see more and more people walking in family groups. She would feel important. She and her father were going to the synagogue together. People would see them. They would notice how straight and tall she was, how old she looked now. When they reached the building, he would hand her a siddur and give her a thin, scratchy kiss, before they went their separate ways.

She wasn't sure which way to go in. There seemed to be doors on every side of the building. People might have their special seats. They would stare at her. Why had she come to this strange place to pray with people she didn't know? It was Father. She had to come because he had died a year ago, and because she had never missed a High Holy day. Coming here though was different. She felt lonely as she climbed the stone steps to the first floor of the building.

There was only one door at the top. A heavy wooden door. She pushed it, walked through, and held the cold brass handle until the door was fully closed. As it came to rest it made a swishing noise like a small sigh. She was in a section of balcony filled with women and a few girls. She had made no noise but they knew she was there. She was a stranger and she was late. A tall child in the front row was the only one to look round. She had large brown eyes and stared at Ash, fearlessly, and for a long time. The woman next to her didn't stop her. Ash was left with a cold feeling that the child was doing it on behalf of them all.

There was one row at the front that was virtually empty. She walked down to it, feeling pierced by watchful stares. As she sat a small rebellion inside her made it impossible not to turn around and look, take up the challenge. Each woman was buried in prayer, there was only the child to her left who was still there with wide open eyes, looking. Looking at someone from a different community, someone from the outside world.

She had only just taken off her shawl when her prayer book was taken out of her hands. An older woman in the same row, who had moved to be next to her, was showing her the place in the book, her finger moving across the words in time to the chanting. Ash turned and smiled, thanking her silently. She had been welcomed.

It was so different to being at home. These were seriously devout people, there was no gossip, no nudging, only whispered prayer, each woman holding her own private service, singing, chanting, standing, sitting, intent and totally alone.

The disappointment! She tried to look down to where the men were, the ark, the rabbi. All she could see were trails of light coming through the white gauze, the blurred shapes of the men, rocking, praying. She concentrated her eyes, sure that if she tried hard enough, she would decipher a face, a hand or see the scrolls. But she could see only long, white, faceless shapes moving in a ceaseless frenzy, holding for her both mystery and menace.

Her father might be down there somewhere, amongst the shapes. She would never know. They looked like the Ku Klux Klan. They looked like angels in sparkling white robes. They looked like women, brides for the day. She smiled. Men in dresses. She was celebrating New Year with them. No Father, I don't have to do it your way. She could hear him telling her this was a dying community, that Jews have to live their lives to the full. That's why they had survived centuries of hardship and oppression. At that point he would be quoting Deuteronomy at her, God's words: 'I have set before you life and death, the blessing and the curse, therefore choose life and live, you and your children.' He was right in a sense: there were very few children here, very few younger women. There were a lot of Auntie Sadies with cowrie shell hats. She was warming towards them. They had let her be here. But suddenly there was a fierce anger. It was for the women and herself. They had been excluded from the service. She decided there and then, she would never come here again.

She could see her father standing opposite her on the tennis court, big belly and long trousers, incongruous with gym shoes, the ones he wore on Yom Kippur. He hated running, he was doing it for her, trying to make her life normal because she had no mother. She could see him controlling his irritation, bellowing, 'Watch the ball!' and lumbering because he didn't have enough breath to run. She could see him sitting in the car afterwards, returning to normal and saying, 'Later on we'll go through your homework.' She could see him controlling his irritation at her slowness, at first needing every little thing explained, him wanting her just to know. Like he did. She could see him on her thirteenth birthday handing her a dark red box. Inside she could see the ring with a pale blue stone. He was saying, It's a sapphire, and why should it only be the boys who get something special when they're thirteen? She could remember the disappointment that it wasn't drawing things or books.

'Marvellous, O God, are thy works . . . O my God I am overwhelmed with shame when I appear before thee . . . I am lowly and weak.' Ash, why did you leave me? Her father was joining with God, telling her she was useless. She had let him down. She was shameful, he had needed her and she had left. She had broken the bonds that should be there for ever. He had no one else. Of course there was Sadie and the cousins, but it was her he needed. She felt the weight of him.

She could smell his rough woollen overcoat, damp from rain, suffused with his own slightly bitter smell. She had had to get away.

She was shocked by the intrusion of the woman's hands over her own. Her prayer book was being removed, pages were gently turned. The woman smiled. She thought Ash couldn't follow it. Damn them, it was like her father! She could feel laughter rising within her. Wild joyful laughing. He was an old bastard. He wouldn't let me go. He made it so hard. I did go, I left to live, but he punished me.

She could see her father standing at the top of the drive, waving her off. It was not the house she had grown up in. She could see him as a cardboard cut-out, he had been stuck on to this pretty picture. He was so far away from all the Jews, the community he had lived in all his life. She could see him framed by the garden, the English garden, roses round the front door and billows of flowers all through the summer. His face red and lined, pinched by years of restraint. He wouldn't say much, afraid of losing control. He would raise his arm in a funny little wave that looked a bit like a salute. She would feel a yearning to look after him, to love him, to make up. As the car reversed slowly, turning awkwardly at the gate, he would try to follow her, to close up the gap a little before she accelerated. He would stumble, clumsy with age and suppressed tears, his hands clasped behind his back as if there might be comfort in that. She would drive fast on the country lanes, vowing to phone him more often.

On the way home she felt chilled. She walked fast. She should have brought a coat. All the Jews were praying and she was walking through the streets. She had killed him. Damn the man, he was everywhere. He died a year ago today. Perhaps he's telling me. He won't leave me alone. Nothing's changed. He's not here but he is.

She passed a church, hesitated, turned back on her steps and walked up the path. Inside it was cold, dank. She took a few steps and craned her neck forward hesitantly. She felt on very foreign territory. Was anyone here?

The cold air crept around her face, down her neck, its further progress luckily barred by her clothes. The body of the church was hollow and dark. Little shapes moved in front of her eyes until she grew accustomed to the shadows. Then she could see that around the edge of the church there were smaller enclosures, each one a little chapel, separated off by wrought-iron gates, all locked. You were meant to look, not enter. She had the urge to push her head through the bars, just to see if she could fit. She imagined she would have to produce physical contortions in order to hold her ears flat so that she could pull it out again. Father would have been so cross at such a' thing, if she had got her head stuck, and caused a fuss. They would have had to bring a welder, somebody who knew how to cut through iron bars. It was that sort of thing that brought home to her how much he felt like a visitor, an unwanted foreigner. Jews should do their best at whatever they do but not draw too much attention to it. Stay in the background, he had told her.

She walked around, looking into each chapel, staring at all the mothers and babies. Mothers and babies in absurd and wonderful profusion. She peered into the gloom: angels, dogs, cats, men, women, children and creatures who were a strange mixture of all of those emerged from the dark. Before long she felt some excitement rise within her. Her initial reluctance at the age, the dark and the damp had turned into delighted curiosity.

She had nearly completed the whole circle. It had been like walking around the edge of a huge cave, discovering offshoots, lots of smaller caves like little satellites disappearing into the gloom. She stood in front of the last chapel, and peered through the railings which kept it separate, holy. It was a particularly dark enclosure, cold and musty. To her right was a long table covered in an embroidered cloth. Above it was an enormous oil painting. It was of some indefinable religious scene. A lot of old men with their eyes cast upwards, wearing very sorrowful expressions. Surrounding the picture were plaster explosions, rams and other heavenly creatures she couldn't name. It was the centrepiece of this enclosure that was unexpected. A long sofa, with a gilt, carved frame and a plush red seat. It looked as if it were from a palace or a castle. She studied it with surprise. It dawned on her, this wasn't 'only' a church. Each chapel was different, the result of planning and care. Each held a million meanings. Her mind surged forward, the church receded. She was inside, closely examining the upholstery on the sofa, and then trailing her fingertips appreciatively over a cool marble figure lying supine over his own tomb.

'Father? Are you here?'

'In here?' he replied, laughing, friendly, scornful. 'In here? An old Jew boy like me? Not bloody likely. Jesus, no.' He chuckled appreciatively, as if he'd just made a good joke. She felt close to him, excited.

They were walking home from shul. He had just keeled over on the pavement. One minute he was walking along and then he was on the floor. She had already gone on one or two steps before she took it in. His face was white. Quite white. Then the most horrible thing: there was a flood of blood from his mouth. She held his hand until the ambulance came, sitting on the pavement worrying about going in a vehicle on Yomtov. He would be angry. How stupid! He was dead.

She let herself into the flat, it was about four in the afternoon. She felt hungry. She would phone Sadie and tell her she was all right. Perhaps she would go over there this evening for supper. But before she did that there was just one thing. It was a line from the service, it had struck her at the time, but she couldn't remember . . . she had to find it. She rifled through the pages. Yes, it was here. 'He retaineth not his anger forever, because he delighteth in mercy.'

She struck a match and held it to the gasfire. She would

warm up a bit before going to Sadie's. She would sit here
and relax. She had already had a lot of fresh air.

A Christmas Story 1935

Ann Chinn Maud

'She must be sick,' Mama Georgia announced emphatically to 'Aunt' Mabel in English. 'She's usually delirious over Christmas. We have to hear every Christmas carol on the juke box and take her to every store with a Santa in Salt Lake City. Now she says she doesn't even want to go to ZCMI's Toyland.'

Mabel wouldn't understand, of course. Barbara knew that if Mama Georgia didn't know how she felt, 'Aunt' Mabel wouldn't have a clue. Still, Mabel seemed surprised that Barbara would be willing to miss ZCMI's lavish decorations: all eight windows with scenes of the 'Night Before Christmas' and the Santa's fairyland on the fourth floor. She gave her stock advice.

'Take her to Dr Brown. After all she does have a weak throat, but really, she looks all right to me. It's just that she's always so nervous. She's always been high strung and moody.'

Barbara sighed and escaped the conversation through the dining room to the sunroom extension of the parlour in a series of Captain-May-I scissor steps. The voices hummed on behind her, discussing the pros and cons of consulting a doctor, her unpredictable behaviour, her irritating activeness, and other shortcomings. Outside the windows she saw that the snow (*lohksyet*? in Chinese) was beginning to fall. There was even going to be enough to make a snowman, perhaps.

'I'll go outside in a little while, make a snowball, roll it around the front yard and make it bigger and bigger.' She started to imagine the bracing cold of the snow.

The second ball did not take so long, not being so big, and finally only a small one was needed on top. An old broom handle was pushed through the second one for arms, and then features fixed on the head. Barbara always felt that the eyes and mouth should be made of clinkers and the nose with a carrot as she saw it in the comic strips and *Liberty* magazine illustrations around the house. Sometimes she found clinkers left over from the old furnace, but she was never given a carrot. Wasteful! Also, although her snowmen had gloves, they never had a hat. Such departures from tradition always bothered her a little. By now she had forgotten that Mama Georgia and 'Aunt' Mabel were talking about her. She loved snow and making fox and geese tracks to play with the other children. On Edith Avenue, unfortunately, there were hardly enough to play with, but sometimes Mama Georgia was a fox to her goose or 'Aunt' Mabel goose with her, but never never Papa, of course, because he was too busy and important. She watched the snow piling up in the corners of the french windows and the hot, hard fist inside her chest began to loosen its grip.

Humming, Barbara hopped on her left leg into the parlour. She opened the doors of the radio cabinet and switched it on. KSL Utah gave voice with Bing Crosby singing 'Silent Night'.

Sitting snug in Papa's lap, vacation trips with Mama Georgia and 'Aunt' Mabel, the beginning day of school, Christmas, going to Lagoon Amusement park, fun with the cousins on their rare visits, and playing in the snow were the highlights of her life. And now snow and Christmas were fitted together in the carol.

The sisters had stopped talking and now Barbara could hear the rhythmic chopping of the cleaver and make out the smell of Mama Georgia's cooking: rice, *lap chéung* sausage and *cháau yuhk*, but a kind she didn't like, not tomato rice, her favourite beef and tomato stir fry. Oh, well, Mama Georgia always cut up the delicious alternately fatty/meaty pork sausage carefully and divided the pieces equally between each of them. Then Mama Georgia, 'Aunt' Mabel and Papa would slip her an extra piece of their own on the sly. They always did.

The music changed its mood:

> You better watch out; you better not shout,
> Better not cry; I'm telling you why:
> Santa Claus is coming to town.

'*Héifáan lā!*' 'Aunt' Mabel called. That meant 'Let's eat' and that she must set the table, so for variety she hopped into the kitchen on her right foot, mindful of the warning in the song being sung:

> He's making a list; he's checking it twice.
> Going to find out who's naughty or nice.
> Santa Claus is coming to town.

She put out the bowls neatly and the chopsticks beside them. As a way of muffling her ears against Georgia's continuing complaint she silently practised the Chinese words and phrases Georgia had given her to learn that morning during their daily Chinese-lesson-hair dressing session. Each morning Georgia pulled her children's table to the middle of the kitchen, set a kitchen chair on top of it so she could sit high enough, and then proceeded to use the curling iron to produce Shirley Temple ringlets. Barbara's hair was of the thickest coarse Chinese type and so the ringlets never lasted very long, for which her activeness was always blamed.

'*Néih hóu ma?*' Mama Georgia would say.

'*Néih hóu ma?*' Barbara would repeat, and then translate – 'How are you?'

'*Ngóh sing Wong. Ngóh haih Wong Suk-ping.*'

'*Ngóh sing Wong. Ngóh haih Wong Suk-ping.*' My surname is Wong. I am Suk-ping Wong.

Her papa had chosen that she should learn English as a first language so she would have no accent. But with no Chinese children in the neighbourhood and no brothers or sisters to speak with, and the adults speaking Chinese mostly when they didn't want her to understand what they were saying, her Chinese was halting indeed.

'I took the whole afternoon off to take her to all the stores, Uncle Willie. I spent all of last evening helping make up her list.' Mama Georgia served up her grievances to her papa like the portions of his food.

Papa said something in a commanding voice in Chinese, and Barbara caught the word '*Gau*'.

'That's enough' it meant. She remembered about when she had repeated the swearing exclamation she had overheard one cook hurl at another in the restaurant kitchen. That was when she had learned the phrase '*Gau!*'

He sees you when you're sleeping.
He knows when you're awake.
He knows when you've been bad or good;
So be good for goodness sake.

Barbara tried to pay attention to the rest of the song because so many things could go wrong at the dinner table, and with only four days left before Christmas she felt she had to watch her step. She ate her sausage and poured tea into her rice to finish it off. She sat with her left side to the wall as much as possible so they would forget her using her chopsticks with her left hand. Sometimes when no one was looking she dropped a hand on her knee to restrain herself from tapping her foot. She was old enough now to know better than to believe there was really a goblin underneath the table ready to bite her hand, but she did know it was impolite. Then she showed them that she had carefully eaten every grain of rice in her bowl (left rice meant you would get smallpox and have as many scars on your face as the wasted rice grains), and got down from her seat.

> You better watch out; you better not shout,
> Better not cry; I'm telling you why:
> Santa Claus is coming to town.

A very strong impulse to run away from it all came over her. She gave a little jump and said breathlessly, 'Mama. I want to go now. I want Santa Claus at Paris Department Store first and then to go to Kress's for the school presents. I have to give one to Wayanna and Leroy tomorrow. Miss Gerber said 25 cents each.'

Her sudden change caught Georgia's resentment unawares. 'Now she wants to go . . .' she began.

A look from Papa. 'Lui Fong will be here to talk business this afternoon,' he said.

Mama Georgia fell silent and collected dishes like she was upset. Neither Mama Georgia nor 'Aunt' Mabel looked much like Christmas was coming.

Only five days before Christmas and she was so excited that she slept badly. She heard the kettle whistle to make tea and 'Aunt' Mabel hang the electric candle wreaths in the windows. Next she would put all the things on the tree.

Barbara closed her eyes and saw the strings of light that would go on first – so many of them blinking off and on, one after another, sometimes two in tandem, and then that magical moment when they all went off together. Then after an anxious second they all turned on again in a particularly triumphant blaze.

After the lights 'Aunt' Mabel put the ropes of tinsel. Tomorrow she herself would help with hanging ornaments: all kinds of fruit, birds and horns (even violins) with whistles in them, and houses with Santas on the roof, all glittering and delicate. Last of all they would put on the trickle ice and cover the bottom of the tree with the cotton wool that looked like snow. The lights were turned on at dusk every evening, and from Christmas Eve through the morning after Christmas Day they were left on all the time. She heard 'Up on the Housetop' on the radio, and then she must have dozed off because next it was quiet and dark and she heard Mama Georgia and Papa talking in the next room.

'*Ngóh fàanheui Jùnggwok,*' Papa told Mama Georgia.

Mama Georgia's voice startled, concerned, her words tumbling over one another. 'When? How long? Why go now, Uncle Willie, when there may be a war?'

'*Ngóh fàanheui Jùnggwok. Ngóh fàanheui Hèung-góng.* I am going back to China. I am going back to Hong Kong.'

And then some more in Chinese she didn't understand. Finally, in English, 'Right after New Year's Day.'

More Chinese. More argument.

'Don't tell Barbara yet. Don't spoil her Christmas.'

She heard no more, but when she woke up her head hurt and she felt something tight and hard in her chest.

The Paris Department Store had the simplest arrangement of them all. A jolly, white-bearded man, stout and with a large pack on his back, was wandering throughout the store leaning over and listening to children's requests. After each one finished he handed them a piece of candy out of his sack. When he came up to Barbara she said hello in her politest voice.

'Here's a child who'd like to ask me to bring her something,' he said to her. She paused momentarily. The first Santa of the year always daunted her a little. Then, with a clear voice she asked for a Lincoln log set and cowboys and Indian figures to go with it. (This was a fairly safe request because she was sure she had seen 'Aunt' Mabel with a Lincoln log box in her shopping bag last Tuesday. She felt it would not be good luck to ask the first and least important Santa for something and not receive it. It might mean that there would be less chance of her getting what she asked for from the more important Santas later.)

Barbara had quite a long gift list, but she always divided it between the Santas at several stores. There were the three important stores, Paris, Arballs and ZCMI. Then, if Mama

Georgia had time they would visit the Santas at Sears Roe-buck, Montgomery Ward and J C Penneys, but requests made to these Santas had less impact. They never bothered with those at the 5–10–25 Stores or even their own Chinese National Dollar Store. Anything asked for and received from these last two sources would simply be an accident.

'Mention only two gifts, or maybe three if they are small,' both Mama Georgia and 'Aunt' Mabel had said. She wouldn't want Santa to think her greedy, or she might not get anything at all.

At Arballs the affair was more impressive. A corner had been set off for a large throne. Christmas carols were sung by invisible choirs over the canopy and continuous paper snow fell. She climbed the three stairs up to the candy cane throne and dutifully onto the knee of the Santa.

'*Glinda of Oz* and *Ozma of Oz* books, and a live miniature turtle,' she intoned to this Santa.

'Ho ho! ho! I think I might manage that for a good little girl. Well. Here's a little something anyway.'

She received a striped candy cane with a green ribbon and a piece of holly tied to it that looked just like the poles holding up the canopy over his throne. She shook Santa Number Two's hand and scampered back to Mama Georgia.

On the way to ZCMI she noticed none of the store win-dows or decorations on Main Street. The next occasion was important and she was excited as well as worried. At ZCMI, besides the windows, there was a whole floor devoted to Christmas decorations and toy displays, and a 'North Pole Fairyland' had been created at one end where Santa inter-viewed each child. One by one they were ushered through successive Christmas tableaux, each presided over by an increasingly important magic figure – a gnome, an elf, a fairy with a wand – and each one gave a reward for passing through their domain, namely a reindeer seal on the forehead, a red balloon with a green string, and a green and red lollipop wand with sparkles on it. Finally came Santa Claus in his own throne room, surrounded by Christmas trees and flanked by a stout Mrs Santa Claus whose function seemed to be to monitor the entrance and exit of the children. She swept Barbara forward and lifted her on to Santa's lap.

'And have you been a good little girl this year?' he queried.

Barbara made a little nod and then gulped. She hastily reviewed her activities as far as she could remember them. There was a pause while she recollected the poster paint on the living-room carpet. This was the sort of pause with which Mrs Santa seemed well equipped to cope.

'Now, now. *This* little girl obviously couldn't have done anything really bad. I can see it in her eyes. Come on, dearie. Tell Santa what you want.'

Reaching up, she whispered in his ear so quietly that he had to ask her to repeat it. This time it was distorted by her trying not to cry at the same time as she was speaking.

'Please, Santa, I want Papa to stay home with me. Don't let Papa go away.'

Her time was up but still the big red man held her on his lap and patted her back.

'Well,' he said finally, in a non-Santa kind of voice. 'Sometimes it's hard to give people the things they ask for. I'll see what I can do. But it's hard times right now. Anyway, maybe a nice kid like you would like this.'

He looked through the sack at the side of his throne and carefully picked a pink Christmas-paper-wrapped box and gave it to her. She was too near to tears to thank him but he gave her a smile that made her feel he knew how grateful she felt. She waved goodbye, and looking back until Santa could no longer be seen, she went off further down a decorated tunnel.

She thought that Mama Georgia would be cross that she had taken so much time. But when she got out of the rainbow labyrinth with all the scenes from her favourite fairy tales Mama Georgia was talking to a friend. She was another Wong – Auntie May they called her, although Barbara knew that she was sister to one at her home. They talked half in Chinese, half in English, as they all did. Auntie May was talking very fast about the Hong girl actually marrying that Japanese doctor. Even if he was the president of the Japanese–American Citizen's League, what was that to them? Look what was happening in China. It was like going over to the enemy. No one was likely to come to China's aid, not even President Roosevelt.

Barbara went and looked at some more toys. She saw a basket-making set that looked interesting and wished she had put that on her list. She wandered back to Auntie May and Mama Georgia. They were still talking. The three o'clock bell rang and finally Auntie May stopped. Mama Georgia said goodbye and, 'Ngóh fàanheui Gwòng Náam Làuh.' That meant 'I'm going back to Kwong Nom Café', her father's restaurant.

'Ngóh fàanheui siúhohk,' she said to herself. That meant 'I am going back to school.'

'Ngóh fàanheui Hèung-góng,' she remembered Father's voice saying. 'I am going back to Hong Kong.'

Auntie May offered to walk back to Kwong Nom Low Café with the two of them. Mama Georgia needed to go back to work. Barbara skipped beside them holding her candy and little box and tried to forget about last night. Perhaps it was a dream. She was always making mistakes with her Chinese, anyway. Auntie May went on again about the Japanese–American Citizens' League and continued right on into the restaurant because Uncle Quentin, who had taken Georgia's shift for her, was president of the Chinese–American Citizens' league and did not get on with Dr Suyamura.

Uncle Quentin (so named by Mama Georgia because he was Barbara's fifth uncle) was much younger than Papa and even than Mama Georgia and 'Aunt' Mabel. He seemed always to be irritated. He had only recently been called back from his studies at Columbia University in order to look after Papa's business in Salt Lake City.

'Not that there's anything to do after I've taken care of everything,' Mama Georgia would sniff. Even 'Aunt' Mabel, so often at odds with her sister's sentiments, would make a clucking sound of approval at this statement. There was always an uncomfortable feeling when Uncle Quentin, Mama Georgia and 'Aunt' Mabel were together.

Uncle Quentin talked all the time about New York City, of books by Tolstoy, the words of Cheng-tzu and about modern economics. He freely disapproved of Salt Lake City's 'narrow-minded, small-town ways'. He also especially seemed to dislike Barbara. She had never been much out of Salt Lake City and knew nothing else. Perhaps that was why. Or perhaps it was because once when she had jumped up quickly to save a bottle of glue from going on to the floor, she had overturned his books and he had been very angry and shouted at her.

She studied each of the candies and laid them down on her little space behind the business counter. This was just in order to draw out the anticipation of the happiness ahead. Then, finally, she opened her pink box. Everything else was forgotten. Inside were eight beautiful little dishes – a tea set, tea pot, creamer, sugar bowl, two cups and two saucers, a plate for serving cakes – tiny, perfect, dishes for fairies. She felt each one carefully. They were so wonderful she ached with their beauty.

'Mama! Look!' she cried joyfully, despite the warning that she should never interrupt the conversation of adults. She showed the treasures to Mama Georgia, Auntie May and Uncle Quentin. Mama Georgia and Auntie May made nice adult noises about the gift, but Uncle Quentin said nothing. He glared at her gift for a moment and then picked up the little serving dish. He turned over the tiny delicate plate. Suddenly he turned red and made an obvious curse in Chinese. Wrenching the other things away from Barbara's hand he flung them on the floor and smashed them under his foot.

'Japanese made!' he shouted in anger. 'They're Japanese made.'

Barbara shrieked and clutched at his leg to stop him. Then

she stood up, weeping in rage. 'I hate you,' she cried, hitting her fists against his arm. 'I'll tell Papa.'

Holding her easily away from him he looked at her with disgust.

'Do you know what the Japanese are doing in China? What do you think will happen to Uncle Willie when he's there if they get a hold of him? Go tell him. He'll feel the same way as I do.'

She stopped, still, and was silent. Her anger and her fear teetered inside her. It was true! Papa was going away back to China. No! It was a lie! Uncle was a bad man. No one but a bad man would break her beautiful dishes. She hadn't done anything wrong.

Christmas morning under the tree there were toys and toys and toys. There were four *Oz* books instead of two, and the *Yellow Fairy* book. The basket-making kit took pride of place in the middle, and there were the Lincoln logs, cowboys, Indians and bluecoated soldiers. She had a new dress and a new pair of shoes. (There was a note of apology from Santa about having run fresh out of turtles.) The purse she had made for Mama Georgia was hanging from the front of the tree, with 'Aunt' Mabel's embroidered handkerchief just slightly to the right. Papa always got another pipe (her choice from the window of the tobacco store) and a can of tobacco (his choice . . .). Both Mama Georgia and 'Aunt' Mabel seemed always to be giving him ties. And every Christmas he bought himself a handsome new suit.

But the gifts for Papa were different this year. There were two leather suitcases with WAC engraved in brass on the locks, an elaborate travel case with hair brushes and places for his shaving gear, and a built-in razor strop. Another solid-looking case was lying there that Mama Georgia called a briefcase.

'She must be sick,' 'Aunt' Mabel said.

'I told you so!' Georgia triumphed immediately. 'She always sits up all night at Christmas and looks at the tree lights until she falls asleep. It's not even eight o'clock and she's already gone to bed. She wouldn't even eat her drum-stick at Christmas dinner.'

Mabel did one of her sudden reversals of position. 'She was just overtired from playing. Her nerves are so sensitive and she takes everything so hard. She'll be happy enough in the morning when she finds the lights still on.'

Barbara lay in bed looking at the dark on the ceiling. For the first time in her life she found being alone in the dark soothing. She didn't cry, nor did she fall asleep. Before Mama Georgia went to bed she opened the door and looked in. Barbara shut her eyes and breathed in and out deeply until she went away, leaving the door slightly ajar. She kept her eyes closed for a long while. Finally the house was quiet except for the sound of the Christmas tree lights blinking, string on, string off, string on, string off, string on, string off.

She opened her eyes then and saw their reflection in her dresser mirror. String on, string off, string on, string off, string on, string off. Then all at once all dark and light. She watched them for a long time. Then she found they dazzled and hurt her eyes. So very slowly she got out of bed, quietly went into the sunroom and turned them off. She sat down then in the dark, staring at the barely visible tree, and finally fell asleep.

The Christmas Tree

Anna Paczuska

'The children are coming.' That was all the old woman heard. It was all she was interested in.

'You'll have to clean your room. Clear some of the rubbish out. The place is packed full of things you don't need . . .' Marysia continued.

The old woman was deaf to such complaints. All her being was concentrated on the one phrase 'the children are coming'. She repeated it slowly to herself over and over as she walked to her room. She was so excited she would have run but her legs were too old.

She made straight for the wardrobe, took out a black coat with a fur collar and put it on. She searched around on the shelf until she found a black felt hat which she arranged carefully on the back of her head. She opened the top drawer of her bedside chest and pulled out a shiny red plastic handbag. Holding the bag at her side she stood and looked at her reflection in the long mirror that hung on the wall. She turned sideways, then back again, and leaned forward peering at herself.

'Make-up. Make-up. I must have make-up.' As she muttered she began rummaging through the contents of the drawer. She extracted a gilt lipstick case, then an eyebrow pencil. She leaned towards the mirror and applied a layer of bright red colour to her lips. She pencilled a dark line along the outline of her eyebrows. She put the lipstick and the eye pencil in her bag, gazed at herself in the mirror and looked content, even though the lip colour had gone crookedly over the line of her lips and the eye pencil was many shades darker than the delicate grey of her hair. She glanced towards the door and shouted.

'Marysia. Marysia. Come here.'

Silence.

'Marysia. Marysia. I want you.' Her tone was peevish.

Footsteps sounded along the corridor.

'What do you want now?' Marysia was also irritated. Her face wore an expression of mild martyrdom as she peered round the door into the old woman's room. The look quickly turned to horror when she saw the old woman standing in the centre of the room with her hat and coat on.

'Mama, have you gone mad? What have you painted your face for? You look like a clown escaped from the circus.'

The old woman was not provoked. She replied calmly, 'We must buy a tree. There must be a tree for the children when they come.'

'The children won't be here until next week. There's plenty of time. We can get a tree tomorrow if you want. Or the day after. It doesn't matter anyway. They'll have a tree of their own at home. They don't need another one.'

The old woman persisted. 'We must have a tree when the children come. It won't be Christmas without a tree. I'm dressed now, we can go and buy the tree together.'

'Mama, I have things to do today. I can't just go out and buy trees. We can't go today.'

The old woman turned away from her daughter. 'I want to go today.'

'We can't go today. I've told you.'

The old woman said nothing, just stood staring out of the window in front of her. Her daughter watched. After a minute the old woman's shoulders began to shake. She sniffed loudly several times but did not look round. Marysia sighed heavily.

'All right. Stop being stupid. We'll go today.'

The old woman turned her face back towards her daughter. Tears were streaming down her cheeks but she smiled. 'Thank you my little kitten. Thank you.'

Marysia said nothing.

At the shops the old woman chose a small tree. Marysia carried it to her car and put it in the boot. Meanwhile the old woman bought tinsel, shiny coloured sweets, two pink candles, glistening glass baubles, and a long string of gold-coloured beads. She also bought flour, sugar and eggs.

Marysia spoke crossly to her mother as the food was unloaded on to the kitchen table. 'I have all those things. We don't need any more. The cupboards are full. It's ridiculous to buy more. A waste. We're not going to feed an army you know. Only children. Every week you buy flour, butter, eggs and sugar. It's a sin to have so much food.'

'You should always have plenty of food in the cupboard for emergencies, and for visitors.'

'Oh. And who were you expecting?'

Marysia picked up the tree, carried it into her sitting room and leaned it upright in the corner opposite the fireplace. The old woman followed her.

'I've put it as far away from the fire as possible. That way the needles won't drop.'

The old woman folded her arms across her stomach and stood by the tree, a scornful expression on her face. 'I don't want it in here. I want it in my room.'

'Don't be silly. There's no room in there for a tree. It will look nice in here when it's decorated. We haven't had a tree in here for years.' Marysia spoke to the old woman in the same tone you would use with a petulant child. She did not look at her as she spoke, but stared at the tree instead.

The old woman sniffed. 'I want it in my sewing room. It can stand on my table in there. It's my tree, I want it in my room.'

Marysia tutted. 'Your tree. All right, your tree. You should have told me before I brought it in here and got needles all over the carpet. There'll be needles everywhere now. I hope you realise I'm not going to clear up the needles in your room. You'll have to do it yourself.'

Marysia picked up the tree and carried it into the back

room of the house which was already crowded with a treadle sewing machine, a table, a bed for guests and a chest of drawers. She looked round briefly, tree in hand, then laid the tree on the table, which was covered with a starched white cloth. She brought in a plastic bucket, stood the tree in it and wedged it upright.

'There you are, Mama. Your Christmas tree. You can do the rest yourself.'

The old woman did not dress the tree that day, but that night Marysia heard her moving about for hours. When she got up in the morning the door of the sewing room was closed.

During the day the old woman busied herself in the kitchen in spite of Marysia's protests. She made dough, and while it was rising she strained the poppy seed she had left to soak in a large brown enamel saucepan. She put the poppy seed through a mincer. Later she put it through the mincer again. She added sultanas. Then she rolled out the dough with a rolling pin, flattened it and rolled it up again with a layer of poppy seeds inside. She divided the roll into six pieces. She baked six long cakes and when they were done she put them away in the larder wrapped in aluminium foil. She soaked the dried mushrooms she had gathered in the woods the previous summer, and from them made fillings for pirogi, small pasta rolls. She cooked beetroot and from it made clear beetroot soup such as is made on great occasions. She cooked sauerkraut and cabbage and sausage and left it standing in a big pot. Gradually the kitchen filled up with pots overflowing with the results of her cooking.

They arrived on Christmas Eve, in the afternoon. The old woman stood in the doorway as they came into the house.

'Jan, Halina, Rosa, Michael.' Their mother introduced each one to their great-grandmother in turn. The old woman greeted each child effusively in Polish, kissed their cheeks and hugged them. The boys giggled at the lipstick marks she left on their faces from the kissing. The girls licked their fingers and rubbed away the marks for each other. Meanwhile their mother blurted apologies to Marysia.

'Mark is really sorry he can't come. He was going to come only something came up at work and he couldn't get away till midnight. It's this new job. It's good money but he can never get away.' She shrugged, embraced her mother and her grandmother and followed her children into the kitchen, talking as she went.

'I said you wouldn't understand,' she said to the children. 'She's Polish. You know she can only speak Polish. You've never seen her before because she used to live a long way away. It was too far to take you all. She lives here now. Yes, I can talk to her for you. Tell me what you want to say . . .'

The table was laid with the food the old woman had prepared. As she presented each dish in turn she offered the only word of English she knew: 'Nice.'

'Nice. Very nice,' the children responded. The old woman nodded vigorously and smiled.

After they had eaten Marysia led the children to the sitting room. Their mother made as if to follow them, but the old woman grabbed her arm.

'Jasia, Jasia, come and help me with the tree. I want to finish it before the children see it.'

The old woman led Jasia into her sewing room, holding on to her arm.

'Babciu. It's beautiful.'

The tree was hung with tinsel, coloured glass balls, and sweets with shiny wrappers. Red candles in metal holders perched on the ends of branches.

'It's just like the ones you used to do for me when I was little.'

The old woman smiled, rested her hands on her stomach and admired the tree too for a few moments. Then she turned to Jasia. 'It's not finished. See, these gold beads need to go round the top branches. Then it will be finished. Will you climb up on the table and put up the beads? I'm too old.' She held up the string of gold-coloured beads.

Jasia smiled. 'Of course.' She hitched up her long straight skirt so she could climb up on to the chair beside the tree. She looked down at the table on which the tree stood, and hesitated.

'No, go on. You don't have to worry. My table is strong. It's a good table.' The old woman gave the table a thump with her fist to show how strong it was. 'It is good and strong. All my furniture was good and strong, but your mother wouldn't let me bring it here. Such a beautiful sideboard I had. And armchair. All left behind. Ay, yay, yay.'

Jasia waited until the old woman had finished speaking. She stepped on to the table and the old woman handed her the string of beads. Jasia wound the string round the topmost branches as the old woman watched. Neither spoke. When she had finished, Jasia climbed down and stood beside her grandmother. They looked up at the tree together.

'All right?'

'Oh yes. Oh yes. It's a real Christmas tree now. It looks like a tree should. It's beautiful like the trees we had in Poland when I was a girl. Such beautiful trees we had.'

The two women admired the tree again in silence.

'Babciu. Do you remember when I was little how we used to paint walnuts with gold and silver paint then hang them on the tree? I loved those gold and silver walnuts.'

'Remember. Of course I remember. And I even remember better walnuts. When I was young there was a man lived near us who worked in the Russian Orthodox Church. Their churches are full of decorations and painting. His job was to keep up the gold and the silver on all the paintings and statues. He didn't work in just one church. He gilded and silvered in nineteen different churches. One Christmas, as a present, because I was a beautiful girl then, he gilded and silvered some walnuts for me. Real gold and silver. Such beautiful walnuts they were. I kept them for years, then I lost them. I don't know where. Maybe when I left Poland. Maybe in Russia. So many things were lost.'

Jasia nodded.

The old woman smiled and grabbed her sleeve.

'But come on. There are still things to do. Help me move this sewing machine.'

The treadle machine stood between the bed and the chest of drawers, on the other side of the room. The two women dragged and pushed it towards the table holding the tree, until the machine top was level with the table top. Satisfied at last, the old woman let out a long sigh.

'We have space to put things on at last.'

She squeezed past the sewing machine and went into the room next door. She made several trips to and fro, fetching articles from her bedroom and placing them on the white starched tablecloth beneath the tree.

Two pink candles were the first. She put them in a candle holder made of antler and placed it on the sewing machine work surface. In front of the candles she stood a large plaster-of-paris vase with red roses painted on it. She took down the crucifix from above her bed and stood it in the vase. The crucified Jesus sank into the vase almost up to his armpits. If not for the tortured expression on his face, he might have been taking a bath in the vase. The old woman did not consider his privacy however. She placed a sprig of yellow plastic flowers in the vase along with the crucifix, and stood back.

'Look. You see. God is with us.'

She fetched photographs of each of the children and propped them up neatly round the base of the vase and the candle holder. She kissed Jasia and pointed at the photographs. 'See, they will be near God today.'

She fetched long pieces of orange and yellow taffeta and wound them around the sewing machine to hide it. She placed a small hand-made lace cloth on top as a finishing touch. She then brought gifts wrapped in coloured paper and decorated with red ribbon. These were placed under the tree. Last came a plain blue envelope and a hymn book. She put these down by the sewing machine and called 'Marysiu. Marysiu. Bring the matches.'

Marysia arrived, complete with martyred look, carrying matches. Jasia called the children. Once they were all in the room, the old woman lit the candles on the tree, switched out the electric light and looked at the six people squashed tightly between the items of furniture in her tiny work room. Everyone was still and quiet. The old woman luxuriated in the sense of expectancy she had created. It was her moment, her ceremony to conduct as she wished. She smiled generously at them all, like a queen facing her adoring subjects. The children stared politely. Marysia scowled.

Majestically the old woman picked up the blue envelope and held it aloft.

'The holy wafer,' she said in Polish. Her pronouncement deepened the hush.

Like a magician, she opened the envelope and drew out a clear sheet of what looked like rice paper. She held the wafer in front of her and broke it in two.

'Show the children, Jasia,' she urged, handing Jasia one half of the sheet. 'Tell them to break it carefully.'

The old woman broke a piece of wafer from her half, and holding it carefully between thumb and forefinger leaned towards the nearest child. She gestured to him to grasp the wafer, break off a piece and put it in his mouth. When he had done so she kissed him on both cheeks. The old woman moved on to the next child, and so she progressed from person to person, nibbling the wafer, kissing cheeks, and magnanimously wishing the children good health in a language they could not understand.

The children were mesmerised by the old woman's manner. They stared politely in the candlelight and broke the wafer with each other as they were told. Only Marysia stood apart, silent, not participating. The old woman glanced at her briefly but remained serene. She picked up the hymn book and thrust it into Jasia's hand.

'Here. It's open at the right place. Sing it. Sing the song of the shepherds.'

Jasia began singing. She nudged Marysia to make her sing

too. The old woman joined in. The children watched as the three woman sang. Between verses Jasia smiled at Marysia.

'Silly old fool. Silly old fool,' Marysia muttered in response, but continued singing.

When the carol was finished the old woman took the hymn book from Jasia, closed it and replaced it under the tree. Then she reached for the first present. With great deliberation she read out the name on the parcel and handed it over. Each parcel was issued with the same ritual. The children held their parcels carefully, overawed.

'Open them,' Jasia whispered loudly. 'Go on.'

The bewildered expressions vanished from the children's faces as they tore open their presents. This at least was a custom they understood. They hugged their great-grand-mother and thanked her for their presents. 'Nice. Nice,' sounded across the room on all sides.

The old woman chattered on in Polish, pointing to the children's photographs propped up against the vase with the crucifix in. The candlelight reflected in everyone's eyes. The old woman glowed with satisfaction. She looked proud and strong as she surveyed her domain. Then silence fell. Everyone waited to see what the old woman would do next.

Marysia fidgeted, moved towards the light-switch and switched on the electric light. The children blinked. The ceremony was over.

The old woman did not look as her guests filed out of the room. Instead she busied herself tidying the display beneath the tree.

As she worked she talked to herself. 'As it should be. As it should be. The wafer, the carols, the tree. All is as it should be.'

In the sitting room the children settled down in front of the television. Marysia lit a cigarette.

Jasia leaned over to her. 'That went off all right. It was fine. But you could have been a bit more helpful. Once a year doesn't hurt.'

'It's not once a year for me. She'd have me doing things

like that every day if I let her. There would be priests in the house and name days and holy days. Holy pictures and holy water everywhere and mountains of food and burned saucepans. You don't realise what she's like.'

Marysia smiled at her daughter. 'I know you think I'm cruel to her. You think she should be allowed to get on with her cooking and her celebrating. But you don't know what it's like. You only see her good side, the side she puts on for special occasions. You don't have to put up with her every day.'

Marysia took a deep puff of her cigarette, blew the smoke out slowly and leaned back in her chair. 'She's obsessive. Her stories, her memories, her customs. I'm bored to death with it all, with the old times and the old ways. I've heard all her stories over and over again. I know them off by heart. They're no good to anybody. All that overeating and drinking and carousing. It's for times and people that have gone. I don't want it here.'

'Ah but she put on a good show for the children. I'll be able to tell them what it's about. It's good for them to know where they came from. She gave the children something to remember.'

Marysia snorted. 'The children? She doesn't care about the children. She didn't do that for the children. She did it for herself. Why do you think she put the tree in her room?'

In the work room the old woman slowly got down on her knees in front of the tree, holding on to a chair to steady herself. She clasped her hands in front of her chest and stared at the half-visible Jesus in the vase surrounded by artificial yellow flowers. She reached out and touched each of the children's photographs in turn. She made the sign of the cross and fixed her eyes on Jesus-among-the-flowers.

The White Sauce

Jenny Palmer

It is twelve o'clock. Everything is ready. The turkey has been stuffed, the pudding made, the presents wrapped, the house decorated with holly, the balloons hung up. The dinner is cooking. May's sister has got up at seven o'clock and put the turkey in the oven just like their mother always did. The turkey needs five hours to cook. No more, no less. If it is in too long it will be dropping off the bone and nobody likes that. Somebody will have to take responsibility for making the gravy and there is the white sauce which goes over the Christmas pudding.

May has chosen to make the white sauce. She isn't exactly sure how to go about it, but she can find out. Auntie Irene has worked as a cook in domestic service for most of her life. She can get the instructions from her.

On the way home from dropping off the presents at Auntie Irene's, May tries to remember the ingredients for the sauce. Milk and flour and sugar. That is it. She is feeling rather cheerful now, having accepted the glass of sherry that Auntie Irene offered. Well, it is Christmas Day. If you can't drink at Christmas, when can you?

When she gets home the dinner preparations are in full swing. The turkey has just been lifted out of the oven. Her father is taking charge of it and sharpening up the carving knife, and her brother is making the gravy. Her sister is busy testing the potatoes.

They sit down and eat the dinner together. It's lovely. Everybody has done a good job. May takes herself off to the porch on the end of the house to make the sauce on the hot ring. It's what their mother always did, to save congestion around the Aga. There are always so many pans at Christmas. Besides, May welcomes the distance. She needs to think clearly about this.

Mix the flour and a bit of the milk together first – that's what Auntie Irene said. Otherwise if you put the flour in later, it will go lumpy. That is to be avoided at all costs. Nobody likes lumpy sauce. Her mother never made lumpy sauce.

It's a long time since May has spent Christmas at home. She has almost forgotten what happens. Since she moved away from home to live in London, life has changed dramatically. She's travelled a lot. Now she has a job and a flat in London. She has her own circle of friends. She goes out clubbing from time to time and if she doesn't feel like getting out of bed, she stays there all day. She's always kept in touch with family though, but she's tended to avoid family Christmases, preferring to travel to far-flung places. She's spent Christmases in Germany and Ireland and Libya. Twice she's been in Mexico where she sunned herself under tropical palms, sleeping in her hammock at night, hardly noticing Christmas Day. Perhaps the best Christmas was in Sudan. There they didn't bother with it at all.

Now what did Auntie Irene say? she thinks to herself. May is worried that she might have forgotten something. The sherry has gone to her head a bit. She will have to concentrate harder than usual.

Mix the flour and milk together and then heat the milk on the hot ring and put the sugar in while it's heating up. Not too much mind. It doesn't do to be too sweet – the pudding is sweet enough. She really must make an effort to get this right. This is to be a perfect sauce. It is to be the sauce of a lifetime. A sauce to end all sauces.

This year May has planned her Christmas holiday well in advance. She'll spend a week at home before going down to Cornwall for the New Year with friends. She'll make a 'round trip' and has bought her ticket in advance so that there can be no hitches. She's chosen her presents carefully, books mainly. It's to be a book Christmas this year. She has one present left to get but she can get it on the way up.

As the train draws out of Euston Station, May feels a pang in her stomach. It seems like excitement, but she's not quite sure. It's a feeling she often has when going on journeys, but not usually in connection with going home. Nothing really happens at home. It's always the same.

The weather has been unusually mild this year. It's a good omen. She looks forward to walks on the moor. There's nothing worse than being cooped up indoors for days on end watching television. She's bought a copy of the *Guardian* to pass the journey. There's an article in it entitled 'Going crackers for Christmas' which she reads with interest. It's funny. It doesn't apply to her though. She had already thought of everything. She has a book to read when television gets boring. She'll go for walks and she will avoid confrontation at all costs.

'Be careful not to let the milk boil over,' Auntie Irene had said; 'otherwise it leaves a nasty smell that hangs around for days.'

May stirs the pot of hot milk. It's close to simmering but it isn't quite boiling yet.

If only she could undo last night. It was last night that the crack appeared. More than a crack really. A chasm more like. She wishes she could unsay some of the words, unthink some of the thoughts. But it is too late now.

The evening had got off to a good start. She had brought out her bottle of coffee liqueur. The family had sat and toasted each other in true Christmas spirit. It was later that the feeling had come over her; later when they were all sitting together in the one room, her brother half-asleep in a chair, her father with his head in a book, her sister and niece absorbed in the television, and May wondering to herself where she fitted in it all. She had tried reading a book, but the words had hung around on the page and she couldn't make any sense of them. She had tried watching the television, but it was some awful comedy and the last thing she wanted to do was laugh. She had finally suggested a change of programme.

'There's an opera on the other channel,' she had said pointedly, knowing full well nobody would be interested. She wasn't even that interested herself. She had said it again, anyway. Finally she had said it so loudly that she had almost shouted it. Somebody had changed over the channel but she hadn't been able to enjoy the opera.

She had contemplated leaving. What was the point of sitting around like this? But then she had remembered it was Christmas Eve and there wouldn't be any trains the next day.

'Why don't you talk to me at least?' she had blurted out then. 'I'm beginning to wonder why I come up here anyway.'

'Maybe we've got nothing in common any more,' her father had said matter-of-factly.

'That's ridiculous,' she had said in retaliation. She wasn't going to stand for that. Of course they had something in common. She'd lived there for the first twenty years of her life, hadn't she? She'd visited for the next twenty. How could they not have anything in common?

'I won't be treated like this,' she had shouted at her father. 'I'm a grown woman now.' It was the first time she had ever dared to shout at him.

He raised his eyes momentarily from his book, uncomprehending, distant.

She had looked at the empty rocking chair where her mother had always sat. She would have known what to do. She would have known what to say.

For the rest of the evening they had sat in stony silence.

But today it is Christmas Day. Today everything will be all right. May will make it right, or the sauce will. The milk is starting to bubble now in the pan. May must be quick. She must lift it off the boil. It won't do to let it boil over. She'd never live that down. She can hear her brother shouting from the other room.

'How long you going to be?' he's saying. 'The pudding's ready.'

'Not long,' she shouts back. She's almost ready now. She pictures the second course. The pudding will come out of the pot, hot and steamy. May's brother will lift it out carefully by the cloth it's tied up in. He'll then carefully untie the knot. The smell will come out rich and sweet, the smell of raisins and candied peel and suet. It will smell just like it has always done, just like when their mother made it. It is the same recipe. The one she left behind the clock, a legacy for posterity.

Her brother will turn the pudding dish upside down and out it will come. Nothing will stick behind, since he will have greased the dish well. He'll set the pudding down on the table. Then will come her moment. In she will walk with the white sauce in the jug and set it down triumphantly on the table. Synchronisation will be the order of the day. Their mother had everything ready at the same time.

Everyone will sit down and take an equal share of the pudding. They'll pour the sauce over and eat. It will taste sumptuous, exquisite, just the way it always tasted. Not too sweet. It will counteract the richness of the pudding. The place where their mother sat will be empty, but they won't feel the emptiness now. They will sit and eat together. The sauce will undo all of last night's events. The silence between them will be broken. They will sit and chat about past times together. She will feel a part of it all again.

To her alarm, May suddenly notices the milk coming up to the top of the pan. She catches it just in time. Quickly she pours the milk into the jug and stirs it into the mixture. Thankfully there are no lumps. She's succeeded in spite of the sherry; perhaps because of the sherry. She stirs for a while with the wooden spoon to be sure of her achievement, and then carefully stacks all the washing-up in the sink. She wants to savour the moment. Timing is all important.

Slowly she picks up the jug of bubbling sauce, and smells its goodness as she walks through the passageway which separates the porch from the main room. She keeps her eyes fixed on the jug. It won't do to make a mistake at this point. She feels everyone's eyes on her as she sets the jug down carefully on the table.

She hears a voice coming from the television.

'My husband and I . . .'

She looks at the clock. It is three o'clock. It can't be. The Queen is already beginning her speech.

Red Rooms, White Thighs

Marijke Woolsey

In the ladies toilet with the fresh blood-coloured walls and the sour smell of damp, the woman sat and stared at the white, goose-pimpled expanse of her thighs. These grotesque mounds curved smoothly before her. She knew there was no way to conceal them. She would have to leave the safety of this red room, to go out into the noise of the club. There in the heat she would take off her heavy black coat and everyone would see her lack of discipline. The woman shivered and wrapped her flesh away in dark silk that hung long and loose.

As so often before, she stood in front of a mirror, cinnamon lipstick in hand. Her throat clogged. Her jaw clenched, to stop the sobs coming out, the food getting in. The gold loops in her ears swung as she leaned towards her reflection.

'Sloppy,' she hissed. 'Where is your self-control?'

She thought of him out there in the club. He'd peer into the gloom and tut. The same tongue-behind-teeth noise he used to make when she reached for a second custard cream. The sound that went with his little comments, digs at her when she ate, words that gnawed at her nerves.

'That's a big plateful.'

'You'll never get through that lot.'

And the reminder like a clock ticking, 'You'll get fat.'

The voice in her head shouted back – shut up, shut up. It's my body, my choice.

He'd stopped commenting now; she didn't know when or why. The woman didn't think about him or his voice these days. She thought about herself, so much to do, and food.

Back in early autumn the woman walked with long strides. The air smelt of bonfires, piles of crispy leaves turned to grey-blue smoke. The tower blocks and terraced houses were tinged with hazy sun. The walk along the edge of the park was a slightly longer route to the bus stop. In the morning it was worth the extra minutes. Air from across the flat area of common seemed fresher. A corridor of London planes bent their branches protectively above her. It was nine forty-five; she was on her way to an aerobics class.

It's difficult to pinpoint when she began to change. The woman remembered it as a revelation. A chain of thoughts one day as she marched to the bus-stop. She would get fit. Aerobics once a week, swimming twice a week. And she would only eat exactly what she wanted. If she felt like a packet of cheese-flavoured Hula Hoops then she would have them and nothing else. She would fill her days so there was no time to feel down and be cheered up by a Twix. No time to reward an achievement with a jam sandwich. The ounces passing on the scales, the shedding of her buffer fat would be her reward. She would take control of her body.

In the top hall where the junior children used to sing and dance, the musty smell of school remained. The polished boards were scarred where for years metal furniture had been dragged across and shoes had been used as skates, leaving black rubber smears. She stretched palms towards the window. Outside a fine sleet whipped through the bare branches. People down in the street huddled under woolly hats and scarves and thought about the chances of snow this Christmas, a month before the day. In the top hall the temperature was high. The radiators and twenty working bodies pulsed with heat.

'Stretch. A bit more. Really reach.'

Blood burned her face, sweat oozed from her body as she pushed herself through the pain barrier. The voice in her head said, 'The more it hurts the more good it's doing me.'

Fat cells decreased; muscles grew; her body firmed into a new shape.

'Think of those rock-hard thighs by the weekend.'

She panted, catching gulps of air. She ran on the spot to the beats of 'Sisters are Doing it for Themselves'. It was the third class she'd done that week.

She strove for perfection, chanted encouragement under her breath. Better than the round mousy woman. Better than the tomboy woman whose belly bulged like a drunk's.

The teacher yelled above the music. 'Come on, just ten more and you've done it.'

In her head. Eight. Nine. Deep breath. Ten. Eleven. Twelve. Body trembling. Got to keep going. Best. Better than the rest in mind and body. Push to the edge. Needles exploded in her stomach. She lay flat on her back in the damp black nylon leotard, and grinned.

Sharp prongs of pain poked the woman's guts. She gripped the rim of the stainless steel sink. Her nails were unpainted, weak and ripped. She didn't draw attention to them as she used to. She tilted her head back and drew a deep breath.

In the corners around the room, where the ceiling met the walls, grey mould pushed through the bright paintwork. This was the source of the foul smell. What was the point of putting fresh paint on top of the rot? You can't cover up things like that. She smiled at their shoddy work. If you're going to do a job it should be done well or not at all. The pains eased. Her grin broadened. She must leave the toilet.

The woman sat at her shabby desk. It rocked gently on its wonky legs as she wrote her list. She'd borrowed some tinsel; they would have to buy a set of fairy lights. It was mid-afternoon. The drizzly winter's day gave little light. The sharp bleep of the telephone made her start. She was expecting the phone call, feared the announcement, but she hadn't foreseen such bad news.

'Hello . . . Christmas lunch, yes . . . five-course meal?'

Her mouth went dry; armpits grew damp. Her stomach muscles contracted. I'm going to be sick, she thought. They couldn't force her, fill her up against her will. She didn't need it any more, the padding, the holding down and filling up. She laughed, a little hollow sound.

'The courses must be very small to have so many?' The plea hung in the wires.

Eight stones exactly. The morning of Christmas Eve. Chunky smoked cheese, brown bread sandwiches for him, a glass of orange juice for her. She ironed the new red dress. Its soft satin tucked around her curves. They would all notice the change. His father behind the *Daily Telegraph*, his mother with her good home cooking and disapproving glances. And his sisters: the thin horsey student, the well-groomed round one that earned so much running a hairdresser's.

The man said she looked wonderful, gorgeous, he was very proud but now she must stop. As if he had any say in the matter, as if he were in control. She laughed and teased, 'You want me fat and docile. Roly-poly just for you.'

How could she listen to him when he didn't know himself what he wanted? Like when the turkey, roast potatoes, sprouts and trimmings, wetted with thick brown gravy piled before her and he said, 'You'll put it all back on if you eat that lot,' as he helped himself to another potato.

No, I won't, she thought, as she ate on. In the cosy flock-walled restaurant with its plummy velvet drapes they sat at rich oak tables, surrounded by families in primary-coloured cracker hats, their laughing, gorging faces filled by shovelling heaped forkfuls, gulps of thick red wine. She knew she was not the same. He could keep his warning, his concern. The woman smiled as she cleared the plate. The Christmas pudding with cream and brandy-butter; the courses slipped down. She smiled triumphantly. Today she could eat anything she fancied, stuff herself fit to burst, safe in the knowledge that the couple of laxatives she took that morning would clean her out, negate the badness, the damage done by the food. He could say what he liked – eat, don't eat, eat some more. It was her body, she had the power.

The woman turned from her reflection to the heavy door. Although it would be dark out there in the club, she hesitated.

There would be smoke burning her eyes and throat, and boring conversations. That dumpy friend of a friend in a ridiculous leopardskin hat would ask. 'So, how's things?' And as she replied, the round eyes like brown bellies in that dumpy head would rove the club to see who else was there. Her interest, like the hat, imitation.

She'd been in this room a long time, how many minutes she didn't know. He would know, he would be waiting, and when he saw her he would frown and that look he had so often these days would come to his face. A shiver rippled the black silk, shook the padded wool shoulders of her coat. It was the end of April. She cursed and longed for summer. The constant cold was unbearable.

She'd always been fat. One of those round children that needed endless cuddles, endless affection and ate endlessly. In her teens she did the rounds of diets, speed and smoking. But always in the end her emotions got stirred up, feelings churned inside her, and she ate. She stuffed it all down – ice-cream that dripped with red sauce, chips soggy with vinegar, hot bread with butter slowly melting. Fat cushioned the pressure to succeed. Everything would be perfect if only she were thin, and she never was.

The man saw her approach. Several heads turned, women as well as men. She was striking, like a bare winter's tree on a ridge in the moonlight. He took her fragile hand and wrapped his arms about her waist. Under the thick coat he felt her bones poke through the taut skin. He stroked her hollow cheek and remembered the soft roundness it had replaced. He felt her shudder and saw the goose-pimples on her scraggy neck. He leaned to the right and wiped sweat from his brow.

He watched an Amazonian blonde gyrate. Her eyes were closed, her full lips mouthed the words. She moved in a trance to the rhythm, unconscious of the other people in the club. He wondered if she ever dieted. If she ever lost weight, and what people said to her. He wondered what had happened to the woman he'd met last spring, if he had said or done something wrong, and he wondered where it would end.

The muscles in her large intestine spasmed. She clenched her buttocks and gripped the man's arm. The thin cotton of his shirt creased like old flesh beneath her fingers. The thought of the thirty chocolate-flavoured laxatives made her gag. It was fair punishment for her gluttony. She didn't want to take them, but had to. It had been all right when she started. The fat had begun to go. She felt great. The scales said she had the power but the mirrors disagreed. Her eyes must be telling the truth – she was still fat. He kept on at her, 'Eat, you've got to eat,' but he couldn't make her. No one could make her and everything would be fine if it wasn't for the pain.

Her thighs quivered as waves of agony rolled downwards. She had to get back to the red room. With a weak smile and no apology, the woman turned from the man and walked away.

Unto Us

Zhana

This life is mine. I want this life for me! For me.

My first Christmas alone, away from my family, in this horrible, cold land where it's dark all the time and you can never get warm and they even sing Christmas carols to the wrong tune. The words are right, but – there's nothing to remind me of home. Nothing to remind me of 'Jingle Bells' and chestnuts roasting on an open fire. I hate 'Jingle Bells'. I hate presents under the tree, trying to find something that will please my dad and never succeeding. Never asking for what I want and never getting what I ask for. Smiling for family photos – I feel sick. Again.

Sitting in the church, crying and crying because nobody cares. Sitting in the church, my heart is breaking and people file past and everybody's singing Noël and nobody stops to see why I am crying – because the Christ child didn't come for me. It is not a silent night, and in the middle of the church I am crying alone.

This year there's none of that. A friend is coming round, she's a Muslim, and a vegetarian. She doesn't even eat turkey. There'll be no eggnog and no tree this year. Only a foetus demanding to be fed.

My friend and I laugh together. Her toddler has gone off to a grandparent's for the day. My friend's mother has never seen the toddler – refused to acknowledge that she exists. We talk and eat, and she tells me for the first time of the abortion she had, because she couldn't afford a second child. And I'm glad she's told me because, when I learned I was pregnant, she's the first person I told.

This is not a virgin birth.

The crossing-your-fingers method of birth control has been proven conclusively to be ineffective.

For about six weeks during the Christmas season, doctors in the NHS won't see anybody who wants an abortion. So I have to wait until yule-tide is finished and the New Year has begun. Of course, they must insist on having a long Christmas break – no child conceived during this season could really be unwanted.

Coming to England was the first thing I ever did for myself. Really for myself. Playing out my fantasy. A good little girl, I always did what I was told. Lived out Mommy's life for her. Kept my legs crossed, because I was a good girl. I went to college because she told me to. A good girl. I hated it, but I did it. I hate my job, but I work hard because that's what good girls do.

The one thing I ever wanted in my life – the one man I ever wanted in my life – I can't have. He doesn't want me. He threw me out – ripped my life apart. I forget. I can't remember. My mind cannot keep hold of the thought of what he did to me. He didn't want me. This cannot happen. My heart, open, trusting, giving. Everything. He could have everything I have, everything I am. But he doesn't want it. And so he threw me into the street, wide open, with my guts spilling everywhere like so much garbage.

So here I am. In this cold, cold country, all alone. And I picked up my guts strewn like so much garbage and I carefully placed them back inside myself and I came to this house, where I don't belong. To this room, where white women give me refuge, though they don't want me here. To this tiny room where I keep my guts and all my worldly goods, and now a baby. Wants to come into my life. Wants to come into my tiny space where there's not even room for me and my belongings. No!

One of the white women says to me, 'You must stand up for your rights. You're entitled to an abortion. You can't have a baby now, it would ruin your life.' That night I dream that she is trying to rip my baby from my arms.

I never wanted to have a baby. I don't see myself as the motherly type. I'm still a child myself, after all. When I first found out I was pregnant, I wanted to die. I wanted to kill myself. Visions of slitting my wrists. Then I thought, this is silly. Only one of us has to die. And I want to live. I've only begun to live my life. There's only room for one in here, in this life. And there's not even enough for me – not enough food, not enough love.

I have no family, now. My father will throw me out. I remember when my cousin fell, how she was not spoken of again. How she was not allowed to enter the house, to pollute our home with her sin. A disgrace to the family. And now me. Daughter. Whore. Slut. How dare I? Sleep with a man? Show him my secret, private place? Dirty. Forbidden. Show to no one. How dare I? My father will never want to know me, now. This child will grow up alone. No family. No daddy to love her, play with her. No home. No roots. I can never go home again.

My child deserves a home. My child deserves a daddy. I want my child to have a home. I want my child to have love, and family Christmases, and trees, and presents, and the taste of my mom's sweet potato pie. I want – my child.

My family continues in an unbroken line, through my dad, proud of his Indianness, to me. And now my child. This is your granddaddy, his great-grandmother was an Indian. You are of the land, your people are of the land. Your roots are in North American soil. And this is your grandmother, her great-grandmother was a slave. Our people built that country; we have a right to live there. We have a home, a place where we belong, our own traditions, songs our ancestors sang, foods they grew and cooked and shared and celebrated with. Even the slaves got a day off for Christmas.

I remember what it was like to know when I had to eat, to have a rough idea of when mealtimes would arrive. Now, hunger strikes at any hour. Dragging me out of bed, ravenous, at 2 a.m. The tiny creature inside me rules my life. I used to know when my bedtime was. I could stay up till 11 p.m. and still wake up in time to go to work. Now I arrive home at 6 p.m., exhausted, in the dark, and force myself to stay awake long enough to eat something. Anything. Just hoping I can eat enough so I'll be able to sleep through the night. So I won't wake up again, too hungry to sleep, too tired to eat.

I drag myself out of bed in the morning, in the dark, and struggle to stay awake through another day's work. Eat a little something to fill the hole in my stomach that the creature inside me has gnawed. It drains me, saps my energy, drinks my blood, steals my life. How can something so tiny eat so much?

I used to be toilet trained. Now, I never know when I'll have to run off to the loo. The thing inside me rules my life.

A good girl turned bad doesn't take too many precautions. She's not entitled to that much thought. In Paris, the land of licence, of too much freedom, where she goes to forget that she is not loved, a good girl is apt to forget other things as well. And when she goes bad, she deserves to suffer, for the evidence of her sin is upon her.

I want to talk to my sister. Someone has to know that the next generation is upon us – upon me.

'You know I'll support you, whatever you decide,' she tells me, and I feel better.

But my parents find out, by accident, long distance. They still love me. I am shocked. In the spirit of Christmas they welcome my unborn child. And – if it's a boy – my father will teach him to play baseball.

They want me to come home. But England is my home now. Coming to England is all that I have. Going to work and coming back to my cluttered room every night, to be sick again. This is all I have. I deserve more than this, and so does my child. I deserve a life. I will not give up my life for anyone. Not even my child. Especially not my child.

December turns to January and the days are getting longer now. There is some sunshine in the mornings. I rise early to travel to the hospital, to lie face-up on the operating table with my feet hanging in English stirrups. They do not provide support. It takes the doctor half an hour to kill my child, to remove the thing that invaded my life.

'Thank you! Thank you!' I smile up at the doctor's white face. I have my body back. Gratitude pours forth from my heart.

The Waters, Mabel, the Waters

Caroline Hallett

The room was still. Light crossed the sill, bearing news of December. It would be a mild grey day. The vine on the marble dresser stirred discreetly and a sock fell from a chair to the floor with no explanation. Above the bed motes of dust swam through the sleep-thickened air to land on the form of a sleeping woman.

Coral was dreaming. Her dream was of the sea-shore although her bed was inland and nowhere near water. She lay by the water's edge beside a wooden breakwater. The shore was sandy and freckled with stones and shells. Further inland a light wind lifted the hems of tufted dunes into flurries of fine blow-away sand. Further down, the same sand slipped in on itself and gave way beneath slow waves.

Coral lay somewhere in between, where the ground was smooth and firm, levelled by water that welled up at the lightest touch. In the distance she could see horses standing or running along the line of the waves. They looked small, like Shetlands, but perfectly proportioned. She would have liked to approach them or even to ride on them but she knew that they would run away, and besides her body felt heavy and difficult to move.

Sunlight was flying off the surface of the sea. It looked inviting. She would go for a swim instead. She dragged her heavy body into the water where it slid under easily without making a splash. She sank slowly on to the sea-bed and lay rocking backwards and forwards with the waves. Her head rested on the sand and she could hear the magnified sound of a million grains shifting under the weight of water. It was pleasant but soon she felt she must lift herself to the surface to draw breath. Her head was too heavy and her body had turned to stone. Her limbs seemed insubstantial, unable to heave her torso from the sand. She began to struggle with the weight of her body and her heavy lolling head that she could not drag from the floor of the sea. She wanted to sleep but she knew that she must climb out of the water. By now she was disorientated as well. She no longer knew which way to turn her head to find air. She could feel sand against her cheek and lips. She tried to turn the other way. A strong light broke through the water above her head. Of course, she thought, I have only to open my eyes and move towards the light. And so with enormous effort and racing heart, Coral dragged herself from her sleep.

She woke to find her head piled up with pillows and the bed lined with stones. She felt the stones when she finally rolled over and fought her way out of the pillows. There were five or six in a line on each side of her body. They were nestled on the sheet beneath the duvet. At her feet was a plastic doll, rather grubby, with wiry hair. It was almost as cold as the stones. She kicked it out of the end of the bed, threw off the pillows and began to gather up the stones.

She knew at once that the stones and the doll were a gift from her daughter. They were stones that she and her brother had gathered on their summer holiday, her first visit to the sea. They were kept in a wooden box called Treasure. They were pleasant ordinary stones, some as big as a child's fist and some the size of a toe. They were smooth and grey and very hard.

This is my present, thought Coral, my first Christmas present. Her daughter was generous by nature and at the age of two had learnt to transform bits of the world into gifts. Coral often woke to find offerings slipped under the cover: a half-eaten apple or some jigsaw pieces. Sometimes when she got to work she would find a surprise in her work bag. Her diary or her purse had been removed and in its place would be a tiny doll, a scrap of linen or a broken whistle. She would laugh at the nuisance of it all.

She sat on the bed with her hands full of stones. She felt sudden nausea rise up inside her. She dropped the stones on the ground and lay down again. Not over it yet, she thought.

After the dropping of the stones it was still again in the room. Coral hugged her knees and thought about Christmas. She hadn't intended to be pregnant at this time. It made life difficult. But Christmas couldn't be cancelled. She felt tired. She wanted to sleep all the time, but there was so much to do. And now she had slept in on Christmas Day without meaning to. She'd missed the stocking opening and breakfast in dressing-gowns. She was disappointed. She felt suddenly alone. The house was quiet. Where was everyone? She pulled the cover over her bare shoulder.

There was a clatter at the front door. Feet were pounding down the hall and up the stairs. She pulled the cover over her head.

'Wake up. Wake up.'

'Ow. Get off my head. I'm awake.'

'Where were you?' said her son. 'I looked for you. I looked under all the pillows.'

'I was here all the time. Where did you look?'

'Here, of course.'

'I was on this side.'

'But that's not your side. That's where I threw the pillows.'

'I know. I could hardly breathe.'

'You were there all the time?'

'Yes.'

'I never saw you.'

'This is your present,' said her daughter, passing Coral a grey stone, medium-sized.

'Thank you. That's lovely. So, did he come?'

'Who? Did who come?'

'Father Christmas.'

'Yes, he came. Ages ago.'

'And what did he bring?'

'I can't remember . . . a toothbrush.'

'And toothpaste.'

'Yes, toothpaste. Mandy's eaten half hers.'

'Is that all?'

'No. Chocolate. And a funny glittery thing. I don't know what it's for. And a nose with elastic and witch's fingers. I can't remember what else. We've been to the park. Move over.'

Ken brought up a tray of tea and they all sat under the cover.

'Happy Christmas, sleepy head. How are you?'

'Okay, I didn't mean to sleep in. What time is it?'

'It's only nine but we'll have to get moving soon.'

They packed the car with presents and mince pies, and locked the house. They headed up the north circular and into open country.

'It's good to leave the city behind,' said Ken.

'What's the city?' said Jack.

'It's where we live,' said Coral.

The children chattered in the back, and Ken and Coral tried to relocate their thoughts. They talked about the pregnancy and the test that Coral had been advised to have. In view of her age. In case there was chromosomal abnormality.

Coral sifted her memory for important details. The hospital didn't stop for Christmas, which was reassuring. She had ridden there on the 41 and Mandy had jumped up and down on the seat above the engine, shouting 'Going to the hisspital, the hisspital.'

The consultant had looked at her belly and felt it. He'd looked surprised.

'Are you sure of your dates?' he'd asked.

'Where's the baby?' Mandy had asked.

'In here.'

'Where? I can't see it. Is it coming out?'

'No, it's only little,' Coral had told her, 'smaller than your hand.'

'Has it got legs?'

'Not yet.'

'Poor baby,' Mandy had said, 'poor little baby.'

'In view of your age,' the consultant had said, 'I would strongly advise you . . .'

'Look,' Mandy had put her hand close to his face, 'I got a baby in my hand. It's only little. Got no legs. You can stroke it if you want, see?'

'. . . to have this test. After all, you will feel guilty if you could have prevented it.'

'The test? Could you tell me more about it?'

The consultant had looked tired. 'There's nothing to it. You don't feel a thing . . .'

'And the risk?' she'd asked him.

'Negligible.'

Coral had thought he was lying because he didn't have time to explain. His white coat was open and his stomach was bulging around his belt. Just like hers.

'Time to go,' Mandy had said. 'Nearly Kissmas.'

Coral had left the clinic feeling uneasy.

The car hurried northwards. Something about the landscape reminded her of her dream, although they were still inland. Maybe it was the horses on a hillside, but they were gone in a flash. The sky was grey and the green land looked waterlogged.

Coral considered what it would be like to be a creature with hooves, forever standing in the mire under a grey sky.

They were not the first carload or the last to arrive at the old farmhouse. Her brother's house was no longer used as a farm. It stood like a lighthouse in a sea of ploughed mud. Fields came right up to the kitchen window. Coral's brother was a sales rep for a big fertiliser company. He had always wanted to farm but he lacked capital. Coral supposed that he must get the flavour of farming when he looked out of his window at the brown plough-rippled fields that were not his. She wiped the wet off the car window and looked out. She shivered slightly. The wintering oaks on the horizon and the endless trenches of mud, and then the slightly run-down look of the house, gave an air of dereliction to the place. Hooded crows strutted across waves of earth. They reminded her of desolate places, seen in dreams.

The family Christmas would be cheerful though. They fell out of the car and began hugging the crowd of people gathering at the front door. The cousins were busy trying to remember each other's names. They ranged in age from eighteen months to twenty-five years. Coral wondered whether they would have anything in common. Apart from her family they all lived in the country. Her nieces and nephews seemed gentle to her, even the adolescents, and different from city children. They played with their young cousins and showed them card tricks that bewildered and delighted them.

The women of the older generation were sitting in a row on the long sofa. Coral's mother Iris, and her Aunt Mabel, her brother's mother-in-law Betty, and Betty's sister Moira. Three were widows and one had never married. They would stay there until they were slightly drunk. Ken was already ferrying drinks to them. Coral went to help in the kitchen, but the smell of turkey grease made her heave so she offered to lay the table. The tablecloths were heavy and white, and silver-plated candelabra had been specially polished. An old garden table had been added to the end to make room for everyone.

When Coral returned to the living room Ken was talking to Iris, who was hard of hearing, and Aunt Mabel who was a bit on the slow side and had a tendency to repeat things.

'We have to decide by the New Year whether Coral should have this test done,' he was saying.

'What test is that?' said Iris.

'What test?' said Mabel.

'It's a test where they put a needle into the womb. The consultant has advised her to have it.'

'They do what?' said Iris.

'What's that?' said Mabel.

'What on earth's it for?' said Iris.

'It's a test for congenital abnormality.'

'What?' said Iris.

'What?' said Mabel.

'For *congenital abnormality*.'

'Oh I see,' said Iris.

'What's that?' said Mabel.

'You know, Mabel, it's someone who's a bit on the slow side,' said Iris.

'Oh I see,' said Mabel.

'It sounds dreadful. How on earth does it work?' said Iris.

'Oh it's not that risky. I've got a pamphlet here. You can read it if you like.'

Coral made a sign to Ken but he didn't see it. It was a sign that said don't show, not now.

He had already fished it out of his pocket and Iris was putting on her reading glasses.

' "A needle is gently inserted through the abdomen into the amniotic sac." Oh my God,' said Iris.

'What sort of sack?' said Mabel.

'The waters, Mabel, the waters,' said Iris.

'Oh I see,' said Mabel.

' "About 20 mls of yellowish, slightly cloudy liquor is drawn off." Ugh.'

'That's about what you've got in your glass, Iris. Ha ha,' said Betty.

'What a thought,' said Moira. 'How about a top-up, Ken?'

' "A single stab should suffice," ' said Iris.

'A single stab, I see,' said Mabel.

'They might stab the baby,' said Moira.

'Oh it's not likely. They can see it all on a TV screen.'

'A TV screen?' said Iris.

'Yes, ultrasound. But there is a risk.'

Coral wished they would stop.

' "Complications" it says here, ". . . the serious complications of amnio. . . ." whatever it's called, ". . . all have the same result – loss of the pregnancy." That means you lose the baby.'

'Yes, but the risk is low.'

'She can't do it, Ken, it's horrific. I never heard anything like it. We never had anything like that.'

'No,' said Betty. 'We just got on and had the babies, didn't we? Moira was having them when she was forty-four, weren't you, Moira?'

'You see? Coral's not even forty, is she? Are you, Coral?'

'True,' said Ken. 'But there is the question still.'

'What question?' said Iris.

'About congenital abnormality.'

'Oh that. It's hardly likely. It's not in the family. And if it happens, well, bad luck. God's fault not yours. Put it in a home, that's what I say. Don't torment yourselves.'

'It's not that easy, Iris.'

'Not easy,' said Mabel.

Mabel was not congenital. She had been dropped on her head by her grandfather when she was a baby. She took fits afterwards and didn't progress. That was the story. Coral wished they had never brought up the subject.

She was glad when the older children began to organise a carol singing. And after that it would be opening of presents and then dinner. Maybe after dinner they would wade through the mud and watch the pink stain spread across the grey sky out on the horizon where the oaks were wintering.

Everyone clapped the singers, and the presents were opened. Lots of people gave each other soap in novel forms. The children were confused by their presents. Jack and Mandy didn't understand them. Some of them needed batteries and didn't work.

'Say thank you,' said Ken. They said thank you quietly to no one in particular.

Dinner was well cooked but Coral picked around the plate, looking for something not too oily.

Someone brought out the port. The party hats began to look tattered. Betty's was over one eye.

After the port the women from the older generation rose groaning from the table, and giggling and clutching their stomachs staggered back to the sofa for a little liqueur and chocolate.

Ken and Coral led a band of children through the mud towards a pond. The mud was sticky and built up on the soles of their boots until they were teetering along like Chinese women on high platforms. One by one they toppled over into the furrows. The big ones laughed and the little ones cried. Then they teetered back along the ridges. The house looked warm and inviting in the twilight. The flaky guttering and the cracked window frames hardly showed beside the glowing living-room windows. The curtains were still open and Coral could see the women laughing on the sofa, Mabel a bit behind the rest. Everything looked bright and normal.

Then there was tea. And cake. The women were talking politics and the men property.

'As far as I'm concerned she's a cow, first rate,' said Moira.

'But she got to the top,' said Betty.

'Yes, on the backs of other people,' said Moira.

'The backs of other people,' said Mabel.

'I think she's in love with Ronald Reagan. That's what makes me nervous,' said Iris. 'They might get excited and press the button.'

'We thought of moving back to the city,' said Derek, 'but it's out of the question now. We'd have to live in a shoe box.'

'It's gone crazy,' said Ken.

'You don't know where it's going to end,' said Derek.

Coral began packing the presents into a box. She noticed that bits of toys were missing already. Still Christmas was nearly over and no tantrums. Coral felt relieved. They had done well. In a while Betty or Moira might get cantankerous if they had another gin.

Now seemed a good time to leave. It's a good family, she

thought as she hugged her sister and her mother and everyone chorused goodbye.

They drove down the motorway, travelling fast like a 125, the clouds speeding grey on grey in one direction, the car in the other. Ken drove and Coral dozed with her head against the seatbelt. The children slept in the back.

They were passing through a landscape where earth had given way to water and lay scattered in strange humps in the shallow marshes. Coral knew now that she didn't want to have a needle gently inserted through the abdomen into the waters. The thought filled her with sadness for no reason that she could understand. But she didn't know either what decision she must make. There were so many people to consider besides herself. She felt that the heaviness of her abdomen and the weakness of her limbs had slowed her when she might have slipped away unnoticed. Now she was caught, awash with hormones and weighed on by a subtle pressure that muffled her thoughts.

They were near the end of the motorway. The watery flatlands were already giving way to industrial wasteland, with tall chimneys ranged on either side of the road, trailing sulphur into the wind. Coral realised it was only a short time of waiting till the New Year came in.

She was glad to get back to the room with the vine on the dresser. It always had an air of quiet about it, maybe because it faced into the evening sky. She sat there after the children were settled in their beds.

That night she dreamt of water again. It was the floodwater of the marshes, tideless, flat and still. It seeped through the land and swamped the strange-looking grassy humps. Coral lay on a ridge of damp grass. The water seemed on the verge of penetrating her skin. On one side she could see the reservoir with square beds of rusty-looking water raked through mechanically by long metal fingers. On the other side were the waters of the marsh that seemed to be increasing although she couldn't understand how. The light was already fading over the horizon and marsh birds were calling harshly to each other, circling the ridge where she lay. They scored the water's frail skin with their tail feathers as they landed. Beyond the marsh lay the motorway. Coral noticed that the waters now reached half-way up the small escarpment that carried the ribbon of concrete across the flatlands. Cars with blazing headlights and thundering lorries sped past oblivious. And still the waters grew and Coral couldn't see how this could be happening. She wondered vaguely how they would ever manage to drain them. It seemed to her as if nothing anyone could do would diminish them.

The Special Present

Malorie Blackman

Rosemary Channing knelt down slowly, feeling every weary second of her forty-seven years of age. She tugged at the bottom drawer of her dressing-table. It refused to budge. Rosemary rocked the drawer open, a slow, frustrating process. Her knees were beginning to hurt, even though the carpet beneath them was a good-quality shag pile. Shifting her weight slightly, she sat down, carefully stretching out her legs in front of her. She looked around the bedroom. How many years had she spent in this house, in this bed? More than twenty years. Almost thirty.

Rosemary smiled at the Christmas decorations her grandchildren had insisted they should put up for her. Paper chains and tinsel boas and glittering baubles covered the walls and draped from the overhead lampshade. Rosemary hadn't wanted her bedroom decorated, but as usual her beloved grandchildren had won her over.

'Oh come on, Nan. It is Christmas,' Julian had pleaded.

'Please, Nan,' Judy joined in; 'it will make your room look so pretty. *Please.*'

And of course she'd given in. When had she ever refused her grandchildren anything? Quickly, Rosemary ran her fingers across her tear-filled eyes. This wasn't helping.

'Keep searching,' Rosemary whispered. She had to find it. There had to be some clue as to why this had happened.

Rosemary turned back to the open drawer. Diaries. Diaries of different sizes, colours, shapes. All of her private diaries, holding each secret thought and fear. The yearly diaries she'd faithfully kept since her sixteenth birthday when she'd received her very first one. She'd never shown them to anyone. She'd never wanted to, never *dared* to. And she'd never reread them. Once a page was written she never returned to it. There was no point. Writing the truth but never reading it was her way of burying the past. She could leave it alone saying 'I've done with you'. Starting a new page each day had somehow been symbolic, not to mention therapeutic.

But now she *needed* to see them, to read them.

Rosemary looked down at the diary on the carpet beside her. This year's diary. Only a few more pages left before the end of the year. Just one last entry to make for today – Christmas Day. She would attend to that last.

Rosemary took her diaries out of the drawer, one at a time. Opening each one, she carefully laid them out in a line on the carpet next to her. There were so many of them that it took some time to arrange them into chronological order. Rosemary shifted again so that her back was against the dressing-table, her thirty-one diaries to either side of her.

Now that she was ready to begin, she felt a frisson of fear. This was it. The gateway to the past was now open. All she had to do was walk through.

But she was scared . . . no, terrified. This wouldn't be like arguing with her memories. They were old and frail, as she was, and could easily make mistakes. But her written words – she couldn't argue with them.

Taking a deep breath, Rosemary ran her fingers over the oldest diary. The blood-red velvet was skin-smooth and almost warm to touch. Her fingers moved to the next diary, then the next and the next – a small diary, palm-sized, with a raspberry-pink cover, decorated with yellow flowers. Rosemary smiled as she grasped it to her. She held it up to her nose. It still smelt of new playing cards and old spices. Rosemary opened it.

14 February

I'm happy, happy, happy. Alex met me outside the Mexican

restaurant. He was holding a dozen long-stemmed *red* roses in his hands. He ordered champagne with the meal. It was wonderful. Then guess what? He handed me a small box and *asked me to marry him*. I tried to stay calm, I really did. I thought to myself, 'Rosemary, act like you get marriage proposals every month at least!'

But I couldn't. I leapt up and hugged him right there in the restaurant. I didn't care.

I'm so happy I want to scream and scream and never stop. So what if Alex is thirty-five? I like older men. They're so much more mature.

And Alex is wonderful. He says that we can get married exactly a year from today. How romantic!

Yaahoo! He loves me.

And the only itsy-bitsy fly in the ointment is that he wants us to start a family as soon as we're married. When he said that, I got a peculiar stirring in my stomach . . .

I'd rather wait a while before starting a family. But never mind. We'll cross that bridge when we get to it.

He loves me. No one's ever loved me before.

I think . . .

There was a dull thud as Rosemary slammed the diary shut. She could hardly hold it, her hands were trembling so much. Putting the diary back in its place she picked up the one for the following year.

16 October
I hate this. I hate this so much. And Alex doesn't care. He has no idea how I feel. All he keeps talking about is how wonderful it will be when the baby arrives.

I've made a colossal mistake. The biggest mistake of my life.

Alex wants children. I don't. I love him desperately, but the thought of this thing inside me terrifies me. I should never have got pregnant but Alex wanted it so much. I knew the instant I conceived. It was a hollow, nauseated feeling deep down inside me. The feeling hasn't got any better. In fact it's worse. Something repulsive and alien has been planted in my body and slowly but surely it's taking me over. I'm no longer in control, it is. It dictates when I should eat, when I should sleep, even when I should have a pee.

I'm going crazy.

I fight against it but it's too strong. It's got to the stage now where I can't bear to look at any part of my body, except my face. At least my black hair and my brown-black eyes are the same. My cheeks are a little thinner but they're still mine. Nothing else is.

I lie in bed at night, clawing at my hideously swollen stomach whilst Alex lies gently snoring beside me. I feel like a balloon that's going to explode and there's nothing I can do about it.

I envy Alex and with that envy comes burning resentment.

I'm trying to suffer in silence, but then I find myself resenting Alex even more. Why should I be the only one to suffer?

I hate this.

I swear that this pregnancy will be my last. Never again, not even for Alex will I go through this. Another pregnancy and I can kiss my sanity goodbye. If it hasn't gone already.

26 December

It's over. At last. The thing was born quite easily on the day before Christmas Eve. It was born within two hours of my contractions starting. The pain wasn't too bad and it slipped out of my body like a greased eel. That made it worse. The whole process disgusted me. I didn't want to take the baby when one of the nurses handed it to me. It was bloody and slippery and it smelt foul. I only took it in my arms because Alex was standing there, tears of joy in his eyes.

He never cried for me.

'We'll call her Nicole shall we?' he whispered.

I looked down at Nicole in my arms. I was so revolted I could feel my stomach churning.

'Isn't she perfect?' Alex beamed. 'Look, she's got your eyes. She's got my nose though. Isn't she lovely?'

Everyone around me was telling me what a lovely baby I had. Wasn't she an angel? Adorable?

I looked down at her scrunched-up, screaming face and I couldn't see it. I really couldn't see it.

And I think . . . I think Alex knew I couldn't.

She doesn't even look like Alex. She looks like me. The same almond-shaped eyes tilting up slightly at the outer corners and extra-long fingers and toes. Alex has short, pudgy digits. Nicole couldn't even get that right.

Rosemary shut the book slowly, put it carefully back in its place and picked up the next one in line. An A4-sized diary with a blue vinyl cover.

12 May

I feed her when I have to, clothe her when I have to, change her nappy when I have to – but that's it. Alex of course is the complete opposite. He worships the ground Nicole crawls on. If she starts crying at night, he's up and at her side in an instant, her first sob somehow penetrating even his deepest sleep. But his snores deafen me if I cry at his side.

Every day, *every day*, he tells Nicole how lovely she is and how much he loves her. Humiliated, I said to him tonight, 'Why don't you say that to me any more?'

'But Rosemary, you already know all that,' he replied.

I'll never ask him to say it again.

It's all her fault. I'll never forgive Nicole for spoiling what Alex and I had. Never, never. She's turned me into the invisible woman.

Rosemary shut the diary and let it drop from her hand. For several moments she sat still, staring at one diary in particular. The diary which marked her twenty-eighth year and Nicole's seventh.

'I can't . . .' she muttered. Yet even as she spoke, she

reached out for the grey leather-bound, paperback-sized diary which she'd sworn she would never touch again.

1 December
What am I going to do? I'm losing it.

Today I lost my temper with Nicole. 'Mum, is Dad going to die?' she asked me.

It was as if each muscle in my body was immediately pulled taut. God forgive me, but I slapped her. She looked up at me, as if she'd never seen me before. But she didn't cry.

I don't know which one of us was more shocked.

I didn't mean to do it. It's just that . . . she put into words something that I wouldn't even let myself think.

But I didn't mean to slap her.

'Nicole, I'm sorry . . .' I started to say.

She turned her back on me and walked out of the living room.

Alex, don't you dare die. What will I do without you? You're only forty-four for God's sake. No one has a heart attack at forty-four.

What am I going to do?

23 December
Nicole's seventh birthday.

I wish I was dead.

Rosemary stared down at the blue ink on the yellowing page, smudged by her tears all those years ago. Fresh tears splashed on to the page. Her life hadn't been so bad. There had been good times, happy times. So why were all the clues tied up in the moments of despair and misery? It didn't make sense.

Rosemary closed the book and put it back in its place. She allowed her fingers to skim over the cover of the next few diaries. It was all coming back now. The years of carrying on even though she never knew why. The years spent buried in grief, living her life on auto-pilot. The years of shutting out Nicole, until at sixteen, Nicole had run away from home. Then the slowly building guilt and shame and loneliness.

Rosemary looked at the diaries at the end of the line. The ones that covered the previous three years of her life.

The last three years of her life.

These diaries contained the final clues. The pointers that had been there, ready to be acted upon had Rosemary but noticed them.

She picked up the diary of three years ago.

25 December

I've always dreaded Christmas, but I must admit, I was really looking forward to this one. And I wasn't disappointed.

It was wonderful.

My first Christmas with my grandchildren. Nicole still hasn't told me what happened between her and her ex-husband Robert, and of course I can't ask. It's not my place to ask Nicole her business. I'm just grateful that she turned to me three months ago. I realise that I was her last resort but I don't mind about that. I feel I have so much to make up to her, but I haven't a clue where to begin. I don't think we'll ever have the mother and daughter relationship that most of my friends seem to have, but if we could at least be friends then I'd happily settle for that.

But as for my grandchildren, they're perfect. I'm totally besotted by them. Why? Maybe it's because I didn't carry them. Writing that makes me feel uneasy but if I can't be truthful in my own diary then where can I?

I remember the very first time I saw them. A jolt, like an electric flash, shook my body. Julian is a miniature Alex. Even Judith looks like Alex; a small, sweet, feminine version. They both have his cat-like eyes, his lazy, uncertain smile. They're seven-year-old angels. The resemblance to their grandfather really is uncanny. He would have adored them. That thought makes me a bit sad, but I really feel I can't be too unhappy today, even though I still miss Alex terribly.

This morning was the best. I was in the kitchen when I

heard the twins crashing down the stairs. Thinking that Nicole was still in bed, I went into the living room to be with them. They were so enthusiastic and eager they made me laugh. They kneeled down in front of the Christmas tree.

'What is it, Nan? What is it?' Judith asked. She sniffed at the large box-shaped present I had bought them.

'Open it and you'll find out,' I said.

Nicole came into the room and sat down on the sofa, watching them. I knelt down next to Judith and Julian as they tore open the wrapping paper.

They do everything together.

When the wrapping paper was in pieces, strewn all over the floor, Julian sat back on his heels.

'It's a cage,' he said, surprised.

'It's a hutch,' I said. 'And you'll find what goes in it in a cardboard box in the cupboard under the sink.'

The twins almost knocked me over in their haste to get to the kitchen. 'Be careful with it,' I called after them.

The living room was eerily silent after Julian and Judy had left. The hair on my nape began to prickle. With a frown I turned. Nicole's eyes were narrowed slits as she regarded me.

'Why Mum?' she said.

'Why what?' I asked.

'Why can . . .' Nicole's voice trailed off.

'Go on,' I prompted.

'It doesn't matter.'

I don't know which one of us felt more frustrated. Nicole turned away from me.

'You've got a lot of photographs on your mantelpiece,' Nicole said. The subject change was too abrupt to be even remotely subtle, but it was Christmas Day. I didn't want to quarrel with Nicole. Not today. Not when the twins were so happy. I looked at the mantelpiece as well. There was the wedding photo of Alex and me, two of Alex by himself and two of Julian and Judith. Terribly sentimental I know but I love looking at my photographs – especially when I'm alone.

'Look, Mum, oh look.' Julian ran into the room. He was closely followed by Judy who walked with measured, careful steps, a grey rabbit cradled in her arms.

'Nan, it's a rabbit,' Judy said, her eyes sparkling.

'I know, dear. I bought it for you – remember?' I teased.

'What's his name?' Julian asked.

'*Her* name is up to you and your sister,' I told him. 'You choose.'

'Let's call her . . .'

Julian and Judy looked at each other.

'Cloudy,' they said in unison.

'She's just the colour . . .' began Julian.

'Of a cloudy day,' finished Judy.

They're always doing things like that. Sometimes I'd swear they can read each other's minds.

Nicole had bought each of them a burgundy, turtle-neck jumper and some puzzle books and one of those pocket computer games, but they spent all day playing with the rabbit. I was a bit uncomfortable at that. I caught Nicole looking at me once or twice but she didn't say anything. She looked disapprovingly at the rabbit as the children played with it. I tried to get the twins to play with the things Nicole had bought them but Nicole stopped me, saying, 'Let them play with Cloudy if they want to. They can play with my stuff any time.'

Well that's Christmas Day over. All in all it hasn't been too bad.

30 December

Chaos reigned in the house this morning. For some reason, Cloudy bit Julian. I think Julian was more scared than seriously hurt but he was crying and Judy was crying and their mother was panicking like a good 'un. Nicole kept insisting that she should take Julian to the local hospital for a tetanus injection. Have you ever heard the like? For a little rabbit bite!

'That rabbit is dangerous,' she shouted. 'It ought to be put down.' I didn't mean to but I laughed in her face. Anyone would think we were talking about a ten-ton Rottweiler rather than a two-pound rabbit. In the end I lent her my car and she drove Julian to the hospital. Judy insisted on being with her brother of course. I was alone in the house for the first time since Christmas Eve. For the first ten minutes I cherished the peace and quiet but after that I just wanted them all back. I missed them terribly. Nicole and the twins have only been in my life for a few months but already it feels like they've always been here. I just wish that Nicole and I had been closer when she was younger. Then Judy and Julian would have been a part of my life from the time they were born. When I think of what I missed, I do feel a kind of ache inside of me. But then I think of all the future years we'll have together. And you know my motto. Look forward, not back.

31st December

When I went down for breakfast this morning, Nicole and the twins were already in the kitchen ahead of me. They weren't exactly whispering but their voices were very low. They were silent the moment they realised I was in the room.

'Mum . . . I've got some bad news,' Nicole said slowly.

'What is it?' My heart started to beat faster. Please God, don't let them leave, not now I've just found them, was the first thing I thought.

'It's . . . it's just that . . . Cloudy's dead,' Nicole replied. 'I came downstairs this morning and she was lying on her side in the cage. I don't know what she died of . . .'

I felt guilty at the relief I felt. Cloudy's death didn't begin to compare with losing my family. I looked at Julian and Judy.

'Are you two all right?' I asked.

They nodded.

'But our rabbit's dead,' Judy sniffed.

'Never mind. I'll get you another one. We'll pick it out next week, as soon as the pet shop is open,' I said.

'Promise, Nan?' Julian said.

'Promise.' With a smile, I crossed my heart and hoped to die.

Luckily it seemed that the twins hadn't grown *too* attached to Cloudy in the few days they had had her.

I looked at Nicole. To my surprise, Nicole lowered her gaze and turned away from me. I hadn't seen that look in a long, long time but I still recognised it. She was hiding something.

'Where's Cloudy now?' I asked.

'I put the hutch out into the garden,' Nicole said. 'I thought we should bury her.'

'Yes, please.'

'Oh let's.'

The twins hopped up and down with excitement.

'You two have got over your grief quickly.' I frowned.

'Well, Cloudy's dead now . . .' Judy said very seriously.

'And we can't bring her back.' Julian shook his head.

'She was dead when we came downstairs for our breakfast. Wasn't she, Julian?' Judy asked her brother.

Julian nodded.

I looked at Nicole. She was glaring down at her children, her face set. Sometimes Nicole is too hard on the twins. I must admit, I did think it was a bit gruesome of them to be eager to see Cloudy buried, but children bounce back so quickly don't they? And besides, they've probably never seen anything buried before. Poor Cloudy. I wonder what happened to her.

Nicole took me to one side later on today and asked me *not* to buy another rabbit. God forgive me, but sometimes I can't help thinking that she can't stand to see her children happy. She's always watching them. She doesn't even trust me enough to let me watch them alone for more than a couple of hours at a time.

Rosemary placed the diary, pages down, on to her lap. She reached for the next one. A big, black leather-bound diary that had been a present from her work colleagues when she'd left her job. This diary would be the most damning of them all. All of last year's secrets were contained within its pages, secrets she had written out but which paradoxically she'd been unaware of – until now. Last year's diary.

23 December

I just had to give it to them today. Besides, a puppy isn't like a rabbit. I couldn't hide it in a box under the sink until Christmas Day. So as soon as Julian and Judy had come downstairs for their breakfast, I told them what I'd bought them.

'Okay, you two,' I began. 'You remember what happened to Cloudy last year?'

'Cloudy?' Julian frowned.

'The rabbit I bought you,' I said impatiently.

Their memories sure were short!

Judy and Julian looked at each other before turning back to me and nodding slowly.

'Well because of what happened last year, I decided to get you another pet. So I bought you a certain something that's out in the garden shed,' I said.

'Can we get it now?' Judy asked, excitedly.

'After your breakfast,' I told her. 'And that's not an excuse for gobbling down your food.'

Ignoring me completely, the twins were half-way through wolfing down their food when Nicole ambled into the kitchen, rubbing her eyes.

'Good morning, Nicole. And many happy returns,' I said.

'Mum, Mum, guess what? Nan's bought us a pet for Christmas,' said Julian.

'Only we can have it now,' Judy added.

Nicole stared at me.

'Is something wrong?' I frowned.

'You didn't. Tell me you didn't get them another pet,' Nicole hissed.

Shocked at her tone, I stared at her.

'What's the matter?' I asked. 'It's only a puppy.'

'A puppy. Hooray!' the twins shouted. They stood up, their breakfast forgotten, and headed for the back door.

'You two aren't to go out there until you're dressed warmly and wearing your wellies,' I said. 'It's freezing outside.'

Judy and Julian barely answered me. They went rushing up the stairs.

'I wish you hadn't, Mum,' Nicole said quietly.

'Why ever not?'

'I don't want this puppy to end up the way the rabbit did,' Nicole replied.

I stared at her. 'Why on earth should it?'

Nicole opened her mouth, only to close it again without saying a word. She pursed her lips as she looked at me.

'Nicole?' I said, uncertainly. 'Is there something wrong?'

Nicole shook her head slowly.

'Oh before I forget,' I said, 'I didn't have a chance to buy you a birthday present. What would you like?'

'You don't have to get me anything,' Nicole said.

'I know I don't have to. I want to.' I smiled.

Silence.

'Do you know what I'd like? What I'd really like?' Nicole said at last.

I shrugged. 'Tell me.'

'I'd like my photograph on the mantelpiece. Just one photograph with me in it.' The words were choked with bitterness.

I stared at her, I started to protest . . . then I realised she was right. Of all the photos on my sacred mantelpiece, she wasn't in one.

'You'd love it if I was really out of the picture, wouldn't you? You want me out of this house, out of your life. Julian and Judith can stay of course, but me? I could go to hell for all you care. All my life I've been waiting for you to love me. And then I realised I was aiming too high. So I thought I could settle for you just liking me. But I'm nothing to you, am I? Just the anonymous woman who gave you your precious grandchildren.'

Shocked, I struggled to get the words out. What words? Any words. Any words that would let her know just how wrong she was. I might have felt like that a long time ago but not now.

But I couldn't say anything. My words kept tripping over themselves.

'Mum, are you and Nan not friends any more?' Judy asked from the door.

I hadn't even heard them come down the stairs.

'Of course we are.' I forced a smile on to my lips. 'Your mum and me just have a few things to sort out, that's all. Now off you go and play with your puppy.'

Julian and Judy slowly left the room, casting backward glances at us as they left.

'Nicole, you're wrong . . .' I began.

'Mum, I don't want to talk about it,' Nicole sighed, heading for the door herself. 'I just wish you hadn't got them another pet without consulting me first.'

And I thought Nicole and I were doing so well recently. I'll have to do something to put us on a better footing. She was wrong though. I do care for her – in my own way. I'm learning too.

Well, Nicole and the twins will have the house to themselves on Boxing Day. I'm spending the day with my friend Andi, who lives in Bolton. It's quite a drive so I'll have to set off early.

I think maybe I've been cramping Nicole by always being underfoot. It struck me a while ago that if Nicole wants to be alone with the twins then she has to leave the house with them, now that I no longer work. I'll have to watch that next year. It will be one of my New Year's resolutions. I will give Nicole more time alone with her children. I have to remember that they're *her* children not mine. Maybe I'm trying to make it up to Nicole, through her children. I think about that sort of thing a lot these days. The whys and wherefores of the past. Nicole and I still aren't close. I guess we'll never be. That saddens me. I do care about her, really I do. And what I feel has nothing to do with Julian and Judy. I just find that sort of thing very hard to say. I never had any trouble saying those things to Alex, so why do I find it so difficult to let Nicole know how much I care about her? If Alex was still alive, maybe Nicole and I would be closer. He would have stopped me making so many mistakes.

God! I'm going to worry myself into an early grave if I carry on like this.

27 December
The puppy is dead.

I can't believe it. First Cloudy, then Joey. When I tucked Julian up in bed tonight, he was still crying. I got back from Andi's house this morning and even before she said hello, Nicole told me that Joey was dead and that she'd already buried him.

'What did he die of?' I asked.

'He just died,' Nicole told me, storming out of the room.

He just died. What does that mean? I couldn't get much out of Julian and Judy either. They were too upset at Joey's death.

Judy did say something that made me think though. She said, 'Mum was really angry with Joey.'

'Why?' I asked.

'Cause you bought him for us,' she replied.

'That's why she was mad at our rabbit,' Julian said.

And Julian and Judy then nodded up at me several times.

I can't believe . . . Does Nicole really hate me so much that she would kill a rabbit and a puppy? Just to get back at me?

I *won't* believe it. The twins do have very active imaginations. I'm sure that there's a perfectly reasonable explanation for Joey's death. I just wish I knew what it was.

So the clues *were* there. All the time. They were glaringly obvious. Rosemary turned the diary over and placed it on the floor. She should have noticed them; she should have realised. Then maybe she could have prevented what had happened.

It was all her fault. She should have prevented it.

Rosemary picked up her latest diary. This year's diary.

22 December

This evening I did the one thing I swore I'd never do. I quarrelled with Nicole about the twins. And what's more, Judy and Julian were there, listening to every word. It all started over something so stupid. We sat down to a late dinner because Nicole was back late from her office. She said she'd gone round the pub for a quick drink. From the smell of her breath, I thought a quick half-dozen was closer to the mark. Then Julian asked me what I was getting them for Christmas.

'Can we have another pet, Nan?'

'A cat this time,' Judy piped up.

'You two aren't having any more pets. Not whilst I have anything to do with it,' Nicole leapt in before I had a chance to open my mouth.

'But you don't have to buy it for us, Mum. Nan could buy it for us,' Julian said.

'Oh no she couldn't. You're not having a pet and that's final,' Nicole said.

'Nicole, I don't mind . . .'

'I said no,' Nicole shouted.

'Don't take that tone with me. I'm not one of your children.' I frowned.

'Thank God! What would I do with three of you? Two children are two too many.'

'Nicole!'

'Don't "Nicole" me, Mum. You don't know the half of what I've been through. You think the twins are so sweet and innocent? Well I could tell you a thing or two . . .'

'Nicole, you don't know what you're saying,' I said icily.

'Mum, Mum please . . .' Judy began.

'Please what? Please don't tell your nan what you two are really like . . . ?' Nicole's words were getting faster and more slurred now.

'Nicole, I think you should go and lie down.' I tried – and failed – to keep the censure out of my voice.

'Lie down. I don't need to lie down. I should have guessed you'd take their side against me. Nothing changes. They're always right and I'm always wrong.'

'That's not true. You're being ridiculous,' I said.

'Of course it's true. D'you think I'm stupid. Well, I've got a little secret for you, Mum . . .'

'Mum, don't . . .' Julian was crying.

'No, Mum . . .' Judy ran to Nicole and tried to take her hand. Nicole pushed her away – hard.

'And the little secret is . . .' Nicole's laugh turned into a hic, 'Prepare yourself, Mum . . . The sun does *not* shine out of your grandchildren's backsides.'

'I'm not listening to any more of this.' I stood up, absolutely disgusted.

Nicole leapt to her feet so quickly her chair toppled over behind her. 'Mum, you must listen to me. Julian and Judith . . .' Even from where I stood, I could see that Nicole was shaking. 'Those two . . . they're the devil's children . . .'

I'd had enough.

I marched around the table and slapped Nicole hard. It was only the second time I'd ever laid a hand on her. The first time I didn't mean to. This time I did.

'You deserve to burn in hell for saying such wicked, wicked things,' I told her. 'Julian, Judy, go to your room – now. And as for you, Nicole, I suggest you stay down here and sober up.'

I pushed my grandchildren out of the room.

I don't know what got into Nicole tonight. Judith and Julian were almost hysterical. It took me ages to calm them down.

I can't help feeling that in some way I'm responsible for Nicole's behaviour. She still sees me the way I used to be – not the way I am. She holds on to the past so tightly that I despair of ever getting her to see I've changed. I know my grandchildren aren't perfect, they have their moods just like everyone else. And I know I spoil them. But to call them the devil's children . . .

I've just heard her slam out of the house.

I hope she realises just what she said and makes amends to the twins. How could their own mother say something like that? I *never* thought of Nicole as the devil's child – not even when she was born – much less said it to her face. I can't understand why she would say something like that. I'm trying not to condemn her, after all who am I to judge? I was never exactly given any cups for being the world's best mother.

In a way I'm glad I'm driving to see Andi on Christmas Eve. I think both Nicole and I could use a break from each other. When I get back on Christmas Day, the dust should have settled. Things are always better on Christmas Day.

Rosemary laughed bitterly at the last sentence she'd written. She glanced down at her watch. Christmas Day was nearly over. There was a knock at the bedroom door.

'Nan, aren't you going to make us our hot chocolate?'

Julian and Judith stood just inside the bedroom. Rosemary smiled. They really did look like two angels. So calm, so serene.

'Of course I am, darlings. Back to bed and I'll bring it up for you,' Rosemary said as she got to her feet.

'We're glad you're our nan,' Julian said. 'Aren't we, Judy?'

Judith nodded enthusiastically.

'And I'm glad you're my grandchildren. Now back to bed, you rascals.' Rosemary forced a laugh.

God, she loved them so much. She would do anything for them.

The twins ran back to their own room. Rosemary followed them and watched as they scampered into their bunk beds.

'Count to two hundred and I'll be here,' Rosemary told them, before closing their bedroom door behind her. She heard their muffled counting through the door. After stopping off in the bathroom first, Rosemary made her way downstairs. She had this year's diary in one hand, the bottle she'd retrieved from the bathroom in the other. Rosemary looked at her diary. She had to hold on to it. She'd never let it go again. She couldn't. The diary would have to be her strength, her courage.

In the kitchen, she worked quickly until the hot chocolate was ready. Placing three steaming mugs on a tray, she carefully carried it upstairs.

'Here we are. Hot chocolates all round.' Rosemary smiled as she walked into the bedroom, tray in hand.

She handed one cup to Julian on the lower bunk, and one cup to Judith before taking the third cup for herself.

'Nan, this tastes a bit funny,' Judith complained at first taste.

'That's because I wasn't watching the milk and it boiled. Milk should be warmed, not boiled if you're making hot chocolate, otherwise it tastes a bit bitter. That's why I put extra sugars in each cup.'

Rosemary smiled, sipping at her hot chocolate. 'Come on, you two. Drink it down. It'll help you sleep.'

Without another word, the twins drank to the bottom of their cups. Then Rosemary did the same.

'I'll tell you what. Would you two like to sleep in my bed tonight? I could hold each of you and we could all fall asleep together.'

'That would be great.'

'Yeepee!'

'Come on then.' Rosemary smiled.

The twins were out of bed and ahead of her within moments. Rosemary fingered the now empty tablet bottle that was in her pocket.

'Forgive me,' she said to the empty room.

She followed the twins into her bedroom. They were already sitting up in the bed.

'What are all these books on the floor, Nan?' Judy asked.

'My diaries.'

'Can we read them?' said Julian.

'Maybe some time.'

Rosemary pulled off her dressing-gown and got into the middle of the bed, where she sat, her back against the head-board.

'Are you going to read us a story, Nan?' Judy yawned.

'Not tonight, precious. I've got something to finish. Snuggle down, you two, and go to sleep.' Rosemary smiled.

The twins did as she asked.

'What are we . . . going to . . . do . . . tomorrow?' Julian's voice was getting softer and softer.

'Anything we want to do, dear,' Rosemary replied.

And the twins were asleep. Rosemary smiled down at them, then stroked their hair. She opened her diary and began to write.

25 December

I got back from Bolton at about four o'clock in the morning and fell straight into bed. It seemed like I'd only just shut my eyes when the twins came bounding into the room, waking me up. Without warning Julian pulled back the curtains, nearly frying my eyeballs it was so bright outside.

'Get up, Nan, it's Christmas,' they yelled, and pulled me out of the bed.

Where do they get their energy from?

I had a shower and got dressed before popping into Nicole's room. She wasn't there. I went downstairs. I called Nicole several times but there was no answer. I went into the kitchen to make a cup of tea.

'Do you know where your mother is?' I asked the twins, who were lying on the floor poring over a junior puzzle

book. They got to their feet immediately. Judy giggled. And
that giggle sent an icy chill racing down my spine.

'Where is she?' I asked, my voice sharper than I'd intended.

'Nan, Nan, come on. We've got a surprise for you. We
want to show you what we got you for Christmas. It's a
special present,' Julian said.

'Yeah, very special. You will like it, won't you?' Judy
asked anxiously.

At that moment I was more interested in where their
mother was, and my cup of tea, but it was the twins' day
and I didn't want to be a spoilsport. Besides, I wasn't going
to get a thing out of them until the presents were opened.
They took me by the hands and pulled me into the living
room. Nicole was sitting on the sofa with her back to me.
She was facing the Christmas tree.

'Nicole, your children are kidnapping me!' I laughed.

Nicole didn't reply. She didn't even turn her head. She sat
absolutely still. I sighed inwardly, guessing that she was still
mad at me. Julian and Judy pulled me around the sofa. I
looked at the tree; green tinsel branches decorated with silver
and gold and scarlet tinsel boas and fairy lights. It looked so
beautiful. And underneath it were the presents, most of
which had already been opened. I smiled at the sight, not at
all surprised that the twins couldn't wait.

'Nan, Nan, look at your present,' Julian said proudly.

He and Judy spun me around. I smiled ruefully at Nicole.
My smile froze and died on my lips. Bile stung the back of
my throat. Both hands flew to my mouth. I had to clench
my teeth and lips together to stifle the scream inside me.

Nicole's unseeing eyes were open and staring straight
ahead. She didn't blink. She *couldn't* blink. A thin stream of
dark blood ran from the corner of her mouth down her chin
and on to her neck. I fell to my knees. My stomach was
churning and turning.

'Nan, Nan, don't you like it?' Judy asked, her lips quivering with disappointment.

I tightly closed my eyes at the sight. My whole body was

quivering now. My face was so set I felt I'd never be able to open my mouth or my eyes again.

'You don't like it,' Julian said sadly.

'What have you done? *What have you done?*' I swallowed convulsively. I was going to be sick. *I couldn't be sick.*

I opened my eyes to stare at my grandchildren. Out of the corner of my eye, I was aware of Nicole. Nicole . . . sitting and staring . . .

'But Nan, you said she should burn in hell. You said she deserved to,' Judy pouted.

'Only we couldn't burn her because you always told us not to play with matches and fire . . .' Julian said.

'So we did the next best thing,' Judy continued. 'We waited until she was sitting down, opening her presents. That's when we got her. We only did it for you. We thought you'd be pleased.'

'Besides she deserved it. She said all those nasty things about us,' Julian sniffed. '*And* she didn't like what we did to the rabbit and the puppy.'

I stared at them. Such beautiful eyes. Such angelic, serene faces.

'Cloudy bit Julian's finger,' Judy said, frowning at the memory. 'We couldn't let her get away with that, could we?'

Julian started laughing. 'So I stood on her neck. It was so funny. Do you remember, Judy?'

I covered my mouth with a trembling hand. Several seconds passed and I still couldn't trust myself to speak. Nicole . . .

Judy nodded and laughed with her brother. It was the laughter that did it. I was no longer shaking. I was very still.

'Then you got us Joey,' Julian said, his smile fading into anger.

'He widdled on me when I was holding him,' Judy said indignantly. 'It was disgusting.'

'So we . . .'

'Don't . . . oh don't . . .' I raised my hand. My voice shocked me. It was so weak. I'd never felt so alone or afraid

– not even when Alex died. This was much, much worse. Because I wasn't afraid for myself.

'Anyway that was ages ago,' Julian said dismissively.

'Nan, don't you like your special present?' Judy asked.

I looked at her. My granddaughter. My precious Judith. I turned my head to look at Nicole. Nicole . . . sitting and staring . . .

I stood up slowly, feeling old. Very old.

'We're going to play with our presents now.' Judy smiled, first at me, then at her brother.

They skipped away from me into the kitchen. I closed my eyes and turned away from them. I sank down on to the floor as if I'd been struck. I tried to get up but I couldn't move. A long, long time passed and still I couldn't move. At last I felt I had to stand up or I'd never stand again. My legs numb, I stood slowly and stumbled over to the mantelpiece. A photo of my daughter Nicole with the twins now took pride of place in the centre. Nicole was laughing, Julian and Judy proudly cradled to her.

Nicole.

I couldn't help it. I buried my head in my hands. If I clamped my teeth any harder together, they would crumble. If I separated them just a fraction I knew I would howl and scream and never, ever stop.

I don't really know what Julian and Judith did for the rest of the day. They played quietly and whispered between themselves. I sat in the kitchen, drinking cup after cup of tea, trying my best to decide what I should do next.

This evening it came to me. The answer was quite simple really.

They won't separate Judith and Julian and me. I can't allow that. We only have each other now.

So we'll go to sleep.

And where we're going, no one will split us up.

Merry Christmas and a ha . . .

A Dangerous Christmas

Eleanor Dare

Laura thought the house lights looked beautiful from the car. House bulbs and Christmas tree colours all merging into each other.

Kate sat beside her. Her upper lip was shiny with snot; it irritated her but she felt too dizzy to airlift a handkerchief all the way from her coat pocket to her nose. The taxi cab driver held lightly to his steering wheel with one hand, enforcing a holiday ease which Kate could not rise to.

It was a very dark Christmas morning. When they reached the wide parade at Crystal Palace the driver flicked on his fog lights and swept past a Ford camper van loaded up with children and Christmas presents. The roads were clear for London. No rush-hour traffic filled them, just relations driving to visit each other on Christmas morning.

As they swerved round a 'temporary' roundabout which had been there for as long as Kate could remember, she felt Laura's hand brush the back of her neck where the hair was just starting to outgrow a haircut from two weeks before.

'Do you still feel really sick?' Laura said, feeling the softness of Kate's hair.

'About the same,' she replied, speaking weakly as if it was an effort.

Laura smiled. 'Don't you ever think it's strange how you always get ill at Christmas?'

Kate sank down into the car seat, wrapping her coat protectively around herself.

'No, I think it's very natural to fall ill at this time of year.'

She sniffed self-pityingly. 'I feel delirious and car sick. It isn't too late to turn around.'

The driver looked back for a second and gave his expensive car seat material a worried glance.

'Don't worry,' said Laura, addressing him. 'She isn't really sick, she just doesn't like family Christmases very much.'

'I'm not that keen on them myself,' he answered, driving and looking back at the same time. 'I'm a very health-conscious person. Most people don't realise what a dangerous time Christmas can be.'

'I'm very aware of the dangers,' said Kate, rousing herself enough to make meaningful contact between her nose and a handkerchief.

Laura hugged a heavy bag of presents she was supporting on her lap. 'Well I really like the way your mother does Christmas,' she said. 'I'm looking forward to it.'

As the front door swung open Kate felt her temperature rise. The spacious Edwardian rooms of her mother's house looked like they had been cleaned twice over, which was probably the case as Kate's mother, Anne, frequently got up early to tidy the house before her cleaning lady arrived. There was little concession to Christmas in the way of traditional decoration, though a small tree had been placed in one corner of the sitting room and carefully embellished with silver tinsel.

'I've been given a cold for Christmas,' said Kate, giving her mother a small dry kiss on the cheek.

Anne put her hand affectionately on Laura's shoulder. 'How do you put up with this sickly creature?' she said. 'She always seems to be coming down with a touch of death when she visits me.'

Kate was slumped on a stool, her head supported in her arms on the kitchen table. The kitchen was already steamy from potatoes put on to par-boil before roasting. I could be trainspotting right now, she thought, or cleaning round the back of the oven, anything but spending Christmas Day knocking back sickly chocolates and playing Trivial Pursuit.

Kate's stepfather, Alex, put his warm hand on her forehead and held it there for a few seconds. 'It feels like a bad case of Kate's Christmas temperature,' he said, adding, 'Do you think a lie down and one of my special cures would help?'

Kate nodded. Her throat was raw now. She reached up to feel her throat glands which had swollen perceptibly within the last half-hour.

Once in her old room, now transformed into a tastefully decorated spare bedroom, Kate began to drift into a half-sleep. Alex's 'cure' – a good-sized tumbler of whisky mixed with honey and lemon – had immediately relaxed her. She felt warm underneath the bed covers. Her thoughts began to roam with an independent momentum. They washed over and through her, and were laced with house sounds and cooking smells. She thought she could hear Laura talking to her mother and Alex, their voices alternating, occasionally breaking into laughter. Laura's laugh was low and comfortable; her mother's was a generous booming sound which reminded her of the lifeboat flares they had sometimes heard during childhood holidays in Cornwall. She couldn't hear Alex laugh; he usually laughed silently, just beneath his breath.

Outside on the street a car changed gear, groaning under the strain. The sound broke up Kate's thoughts. She wondered what presents her mother and Alex had chosen for her this year. She wasn't eager to 'have' whatever it was they had bought her. There was always something about their gifts which missed the essence of her personality. A sense that their assessment of her needs and interests was not quite right. They really don't know me any better than they know their neighbours, Kate thought. This was also true of her father over in Canada. He sent me an appliquéd clutch bag last year *and* he still thinks I'm craving for my own pony.

She wasn't surprised by these thoughts; they always cropped up at Christmas. It was part of the reason for not liking it, that and her annual Christmas delirium. She pulled the bed covers right up to her chin. Just as the goose was going into the oven and more members of the family arrived she fell into a deep sleep.

Laura was leaning over her in the bed, stroking her breasts very softly. Kate knew it was a dream. She nearly always did know the difference between a dream and reality, though she wasn't what they call a 'lucid dreamer', she couldn't control the direction her dreams would take. She felt the smoothness of Laura's skin moving against her own as Laura pulled herself a little further up the bed to kiss her. As their lips touched Kate felt a sudden wave of panic. 'We can't,' she said, 'not here – this is my mother's house,' then she looked up and realised that her entire family were leaning over the bed as if they were visiting a new-born baby in hospital.

'You'll have to be stripped of your skin for Christmas,' said Kate's father in a surprisingly matter-of-fact way as if he was suggesting they mash potatoes instead of roasting them. Kate's heart felt as if it was stopping.

Laura said, 'I'm sure we could sort this matter out over a glass of sherry. I really don't think it will be necessary to strip anyone's skin off.' She sounded so reasonable and intelligent that the family appeared to agree that some sort of discussion would be acceptable.

Kate whispered to Laura, 'For God's sake let's just run.'

'It's all right,' she answered, 'I think everything will be fine if we just talk things through.'

Kate felt a reservoir of tears building up. She turned violently in her sleep several times. When she woke, the duvet was corkscrewed around her body like a straight jacket. Laura was sitting beside the bed holding a cup of tea.

The dinner table was contorted out of its usual shape by the pulling out of flaps and the addition of an extra table from another room. In her delirium the table looked enormous to Kate, a strip of the M1 laid out with cutlery and napkins stretching across the whole of south-east London and lined on either side by scores of blood sisters and brothers, aunts and half-brothers, uncles and stepsisters, all accompanied by their spouses and children dressed in new jumpers and scarves, for every one of them had received at least one item of clothing that morning.

Kate squeezed into an empty chair between her oldest brother, Robert, and a young woman called Emma, whose exact relationship to her Kate had never worked out. As she sat down several remarks were made about how pale she looked, followed by jokes relating to the rareness of her appearance at family gatherings.

'Oh, it's a lesser-spotted Kate,' Robert said.

'Don't tell me your name, I'm sure it will come to me in a minute,' remarked one of the stepbrothers.

'Have you made anyone laugh since I saw you last?' Kate answered, looking round to see where Laura had been placed.

'Over here!' a familiar voice called, followed by a blurred hand waving from a few miles up the table on the opposite side. Kate waved back across the vast expanse of the table-cloth as her mother came into the room carrying a large silver dish with an unusual green mound on top of it.

'It's spinach and coriander terrine. I haven't made it before, so you'll have to be my guinea pigs.'

Her mother's food was never boring. The family made all the right noises of appreciation and surprise – the same noises they made every year. Alex came in a few minutes later holding a china gravy boat.

'I've made a very delicate sauce from our home-grown tomatoes. We grew them last year and preserved half of them in kilner jars.'

Kate thought how proud they were of their achievements. They were both from lower-middle-class backgrounds with parents who had hardly read anything but gas bills and reactionary newspapers. Kate's mother had always emphasised how dull her childhood had been in the stultifying suburbs around Croydon – grey meals eaten in a grey house, grey school uniforms and long dull weekends spent avoiding a bad-tempered and rigid father. That Anne had worked her way into Oxford was of course astonishing and wonderful, but Kate felt it was her duty to be perpetually impressed by these facts.

When Kate was eighteen and just about to come out as a lesbian, she had envisaged Anne and Alex reeling with shock and disgusted outrage. In fact her mother had said, 'Oh, you shouldn't work yourself into a frenzy about that – we've known you're a lesbian for years.' When she had told them she wasn't going to university they had hardly spoken to her for weeks.

While they were waiting for the goose to be carved Robert and Emma started a discussion about German workers in the Weimar republic. The sound of Alex dragging the carving knife against the old-fashioned spike of the knife sharpener set Kate's teeth on edge. The knife flashed backwards and forwards. She followed its movements and became mesmerised. By the time the huge goose had been half-carved the conversation had escalated into a raucous argument, with Kate sitting between their raised voices.

A good slanging match was a family tradition at Christmas; it entailed loud-mouthed denunciations of other people's most cherished ideas, all undertaken with an underlying jokiness which ensured things didn't get embarrassingly aggressive. Kate was silent. She thought how much she loathed these arguments which often lasted the whole day and usually revolved around subjects she knew nothing about.

Laura joined in from across the table. Her voice sounded muffled as if she was speaking under water.

'In that case, why did Stresemann fall short of extending the mutual guarantee to cover the eastern frontiers?' The words meant nothing to Kate who was still beguiled by the flashing silver of the carving knife. Robert rested his elbows on the tablecloth, now dotted with flecks of spinach.

'You're both missing the point. For years most people had become habituated to thuggery in their own backyards . . .' His voice pounded on.

Kate thought of her latest painting, waiting for her at home. If she could just get back to it, her temperature would drop. It was a large canvas, long and narrow like a child's alphabet frieze. She had been working on it for three weeks, painting all day then going into work in the early evening. She didn't mind working in a restaurant; in fact it had given her the idea for this painting – a visual document of her experiences there, the faces of women who came in for tea every day loaded down with shopping and laundry, the weight of their bags increasing as Christmas approached. The work was easy – automatic really after two years. Her real work was painting. Laura was the only person in the room who seemed to understand this. Anne and Alex had asked Kate several hundred times with a fairly narrow variation of the same sentence: 'When are you going to get a proper job?'

Kate's answer was equally repetitive: 'If you mean a posh pen-pushing job, never.'

The Weimar argument died down when Kate found to her surprise that she had opened her mouth and casually said, 'A Weimaraner is a silver dog, isn't it?'

Emma, Robert and Laura had all looked at each other and burst out laughing.

The goose meat was rich and fatty, a posher and more carbohydrate-filled version of traditional Christmas turkey. More dangerous, the taxi driver would probably say.

Kate thought her family looked quite normal when they just ate instead of talking. There were no vulgar paper hats or sentimental religious overtones. At least I wasn't born into a fundamentalist family, she thought. At least they don't expect me to go to Bible college or breed babies.

When the main course was finished the goose carcass dominated the table. It was still immense. Anne and Alex would make superb salads and sandwiches from it, slowly decommissioning the bird like a ship sold off for scrap, stripping it down until it would finally revert to its essence – rich and jellified blocks of bouillon resting at the bottom of a freezer.

Just the pudding to get through, thought Kate. Just the

pudding then the giving out of presents. Conversations whirled around her. A flood of wine seemed to pass across the table, back and forth a hundred different hands reached out for it.

At one point the dining-room curtains were drawn and the lights suddenly switched out. She felt calm for a second. Now I can shut my eyes and sleep, she thought, but instead her mother came into the room carrying an old-fashioned terrorist bomb licked in flames, sizzling and spitting.

'What a magnificent pudding,' someone said as the blue flames changed colour and died down.

Kate had survived the giving and receiving of presents, embarrassing and not quite right as she had predicted. They had moved into the front sitting room where Kate had chosen a seat beside a large picture window looking out on to her mother's front garden and the road which ran along at the end of it.

The family were discussing New Year resolutions. Kate was paying very little attention, for the same ones turned up every year – smoking, losing weight and spending less money on expensive food at Marks and Spencer's. A little way up the street she could see a small group of children trying out new bicycles, watched over by their parents who looked bloated and bad-tempered.

'And how about you, Kate – will this be the year your intellect finally emerges before all the universities are shut down?'

Kate turned slowly. It was her mother who had spoken. She was surprised to be the focus of attention. Everyone was gazing at her. They suddenly looked angry. The room was silent until Laura sighed. She had been hoping the subject of Kate's 'academic career' wouldn't crop up, but there it was, as predictable as Christmas itself. She recognised the look on her lover's face – a look of exhaustion which always emerged when this subject was broached – Kate's I-wish-I-had-been-orphaned-at-birth look.

'I know you think I'm just being a bossy and irritating mother, but mothers *do* worry about their daughters, especially their youngest and sickliest.'

'Sickliest?' said Kate. 'Most of the time I'm a very healthy person, apart from when I come here.'

Anne and Alex laughed.

They're going to skin me, Kate thought. I should have known what this was all leading up to – sharpening the carving knife, flashing it back and forth at the end of my nose then bringing up the subject of dull New Year resolutions as a decoy so I wouldn't see sense and run away.

Anne was suddenly standing beside her. 'I didn't mean to upset you on Christmas Day,' she said, gently putting an arm around her.

Kate flinched instinctively, then thought, I never confuse my dreams with reality. I'm a very stable person – I scored forty-two in the *Observer* personality profile. I'm virtually incapable of displaying paranoid tendencies.

Her mother smelt to Kate of vanilla and cognac. They usually felt too embarrassed to touch each other for more than a few seconds but Anne was moderately drunk and Kate felt too weak to pull away from her. At least I am safe now, she thought. The quietest part of Christmas is always after a scene.

She watched two poplar trees swaying slowly above the houses on the other side of the street. As a child she had watched them many times from her bedroom window. In high winds they had terrified her, for she had been certain that one day the massive forms would snap, crashing through both rows of houses. She felt the texture of her mother's blouse against the skin of her neck – it was cool and smooth, like a pebble under water. The cool silk soothed her headache. I should introduce more cool colours into the painting, she thought, picturing the canvas waiting for her at home. Across the room Laura was talking quietly with one of Robert's children. They were looking through a book which contained aerial photographs of London in winter. Laura looked up from the book and smiled at her. It was a serious, loving smile. Just a few more minutes to go, the smile said. Just the subtle easing away from the family. Polite and reconciled goodbyes, then Kate and Laura would be home and their Christmas celebrations would begin.

The Man Who Loved Presents

Eileen Fairweather

Buying presents for Harry was such fun that Shona thought she must still be in love with him. She felt privileged, superior to the other women scurrying around the Christmas shops, anxiously searching for something suitably unfeminine. How they frowned over the safe if uninspiring filofaxes, ties, seasonally packaged underpants and anti-freeze. How desperately they hoped the manufacturers were right, and that holly-strewn blister packs really did make Superglue That Special Gift, For That Special Man. She was lucky, her man was different, a man unashamed to be playful, soppy, funny. Ten years since they first met, Shona still loved indulging him.

She found her first present, a badge, in a joke shop. 'Sticks and stones may hurt my bones But whips and chains excite me'. Harry, with his unabashed fondness for black stockings, and the odd bit of rough handling by Shona, would chuckle hugely over that. It was the stress, he said, of being always in control, of having 300 lives in his hands every time he flew, that made occasional escape into *being* controlled so blissful.

Shona knew him so well. That is how gifts succeed or fail, by what they reveal about our knowledge of, intimacy with, the person to whom we give.

Shona's family's presents never failed to disappoint her, the childish excitement she still felt at Christmas going flat as she unwrapped the inevitable Avon lipstick from her sister, the plastic figurines from her parents.

They could not help not having much money. But they

could help not noticing that she had changed, had hardly worn make-up since her teens (and then only Beauty Without Cruelty), and had put Bambi ornaments behind her when she hit medical school.

Their presents always made her feel lonely.

It was Harry who gave her magic. If he was wonderful to buy presents for, he was also a master present giver. He had courted her with presents, brought from his travels around the globe: silky kimonos from Japan, lingerie from LA, a delightfully kitsch little music-box from Amsterdam which played 'You Are My Sunshine', and made her cry as Harry looked deep into her eyes and sang tunelessly along. He was her big baby, such a gift after the exhausting penny-pinching years of study and being endlessly on call. He was glamour, frivolity, final escape from the greying Aertex vests of her childhood, and the pebbledash council home. He was her very own Father Christmas.

Shona wasn't unrealistic. Marriage had taught her that Harry wasn't all glamour. She often thought that if people knew how much air crews drink, they would never fly again. She knew Harry's sprees with the duty-frees, and his morning-after remorse. She knew his caffeine-high twitchiness, his bleary irritability when he hadn't slept, his explosions of rage over incompetence. She laughed, then, when she found the sloganised T-shirt, 'Leave me alone. I'm having a nervous breakdown'. Harry wouldn't be above wearing that beneath his uniform and flashing it, mid-Atlantic, at anyone foolish enough to disturb him.

For his serious present, the one that shows you care enough to spend real money, Shona found a beautiful hand-carved puppet. That first night, she'd thought it just a play on the old line when he twinkled, 'Come home and see my collection.' She'd gone anyway, and let him roam all over her body with an explorer's ease and daring, and delight in new discoveries that left her with shaking limbs, little muscle spasms of relaxation, and coming out with a hoary old line of her own, but meaning it, 'Yes, I know, it's never been like this for me before, either . . .'

Control yourself, Shona, she'd thought; this man is a wonder between the sheets, a goat with a magnificent dong, but that's all there is to it – hormones. Despite the soft words, he's dangerous, a charmer in gold braid with probably a girl in every airport. She was all set to rearrange her limbs and go home to her flatmate (for Shona was not the sort to shock with all-night stop-outs), when he jumped out of bed himself, protesting that she still hadn't seen his collection.

He opened his wardrobe, and there, dangling between an untidy jumble of shirts and ties, hung some sweet, faded puppets, relics, he said, from his childhood.

'I keep meaning to display them properly, but I never seem to get the time. I need a woman,' he said, with a mischievous dart of his tongue into her mouth, 'to look after me.'

That was it. She was lost, she was gone. This man had it all. He was strong but tender, sexy but sentimental, sufficiently sure of his masculinity not to hide the child within. He was a stallion with soul, the man her Women in Medicine group collectively fantasised over in the pub after meetings, neither a wimp forever apologising for his sex, nor a deadhead unaware there was anything to apologise for.

Just like that, Shona, who had meticulously fought off men during medical school, sure her mother was right, that men only led to one thing, babies and smelling of cabbage, fell head over heels in love.

Now, ten years later, amongst the mothers in the crowded toy shop, Shona considered which puppet to buy for her big baby. There was a bagpipe player, a bomber pilot, a green-jerkined Pinocchio, and a pouting, scarlet-lipped ballerina.

She did not realise, until she got it home, quite why she made the choice she did.

Once there, safe from the dazed, frantic shoppers, Shona brewed herself some peppermint tea – she should not have drunk so much last night – and wrapped the presents. She signed them all 'To Daddy. Love Jack'. She deliberated for a moment, then smiled – why not? She wrapped one final present, and signed her own name. This one cost her nothing. But it was something she had made, only she could give, and only Harry would appreciate. She knew her Harry. It would touch him deeply; it would make him cry. It would ruin his new girlfriend's Christmas.

Laughter had always been the big bond between her and Harry. Well, that and mind-boggling sex. Beneath Shona's reserve was an irreverent streak, which with her po-faced colleagues often went down like a cup of cold sick. But Harry too was fond of cutting through the crap with a quick perceptive shaft of irony, and Shona loved this when she felt her profession demanded that she take it, and herself, too seriously. She was never again quite so scared of her morose consultant after Harry met him, and his wife, at a hospital function. The pair held hands the entire time, he in a wrinkled corduroy suit, she in a bizarrely inappropriate English garden-party hat.

'Oh, they're not so bad,' she protested, when Harry characterised them as 'drabbies'. 'And they've got their problems. They're desperate for a baby, but think they're infertile.'

'No wonder,' Harry had said. 'That hat and hand-holding say it all. They never fuck.'

Then he shook hands with the man, while with his other hand he goosed Shona's bum.

They were an unlikely pair, the psychiatrist and the pilot, the small, serious woman of medicine, and the bulky joker in the pack. But from when they first met, they took to each other like their lost halves.

Harry spirited her away from that party, with a confidence she was unused to in the earnest medics she usually dated, to a luxurious restaurant. Then with glamorous humility he explained that his wasn't really a glamorous life, that flying a plane was no more exciting or difficult really than driving a bus.

'But to you, Doctor,' he smiled, 'I can confess it's stressful. Whatever goes wrong, you have to act cool, in command.'

He was so openly vulnerable, she longed to comfort him.

He told her of the poverty he saw in Africa, the orphans he sponsored, how money wasn't everything, though you'd never know that from the gold-digging stewardesses who were all he mostly met. If his pill-popping ex-wife had taught him anything, it was that he was tired of women with long nails and *Daily Mail* minds, just waiting for a man to shoulder their every burden.

She couldn't believe it. A man who actually *liked* independent women! Heady on the wine, she confided her own dreams in turn. She no longer had the stomach for macho hospital medicine; she wanted to train in psychiatry, rescue those pill-poppers like his ex and her mother. She would be wonderful, he said; she was such a good listener, and so gentle.

She flushed. Her parents had never overcome their disappointment that she wasn't a nurse.

Chewing their Châteaubriand, admiring each other's compassion, good sense and liberal views, mentally they undressed each other and made illiberal love before they even left the table.

Five years later, the independent wife number two was a psychiatry registrar, and in love again. But this time round, love left her shattered, plummeting between exhilaration and exhaustion, as the mother of the baby Harry had longed to make.

'You need to grieve,' she said, of his ex-wife's miscarriages, when four weeks after Jack's birth Harry still seemed loath to help with him.

'What I love about you,' mumbled Harry, 'is you never nag.' That was one of his favourite endearments. 'Now can I get back to sleep?'

'You need to explore your relationship with your own father,' she suggested, some weeks later, when Harry cried,

'I've done two long hauls in a week, I'm wrecked – of course I can't "relate" to a three-month-old that does nothing but fill his nappy and cry for your tits. You've got the breasts. What can I do?'

'Maybe you need.to think about your images of women,' she said, trying not to sound hurt, angry, when Harry accused her of letting herself go. Jack was six months old, she had only been back at work three weeks, and somehow the stylish, feathery haircut in which she had given birth had become a jagged, grown-out mane. She did need to visit a hairdresser, but from where in her relentlessly packed day could she pluck the time?

'I'm sick of hearing what *I* need,' said Harry, '*you* need to give up work, all this hopeless ambition, and be a real woman and look after me and our son.'

She felt as though Harry had hit her. It was he who had worn down her resistance when she had told him, sorrowfully, that combining medicine and motherhood was still made heartbreakingly hard. Couldn't they at least wait till she made senior registrar? But Harry had been impatient; she would look so beautiful, pregnant.

'Don't be afraid, little one,' he said, 'you're not doing this alone.'

So much for her feminist-approved diaphragm. Unlike the pill, its protection could be discarded in a moment. Just one hormone-high moment of weakness, one middle-of-the-month broody response to Harry's encouragement; that was all it took for her to melt then swell.

And now they had Jack, and although Harry had cried buckets at his birth, and took endless snaps to show his crews, he was scarcely ever around. Suddenly the airline had him permanently on long-haul schedules.

But still the presents flowed in. By Jack's first birthday, his room resembled a toy shop. He had everything a child could want save a father he saw more than for the odd ten minutes.

As for Shona, she had perfume for every conceivable

occasion, save her most usual date – lying awake, insomniac with loneliness and frustration, watching her jet-lagged husband snore.

'I ended it because we didn't laugh any more,' Shona told her therapist. God, she was sick of being in therapy, even if it was a requirement of her training. Have done unto yourself what you would do unto others. How dare her previous therapist retire and leave her, hurt and in pain, and next week facing her second Christmas alone, forced to pull off all her old scabs for this ungiving pillar of salt?

'Although,' she admitted, 'what finally ruined things was the wandering willy syndrome.'

Her therapist did not laugh.

She picked at the bubbling varnish on her chair arm.

'I used to love Harry going away. It was like a permanent honeymoon. Until Jack was born.

'Then I didn't want to jump about the bed any more. I felt sucked dry – by my patients, by the baby. I wanted to *be* loved, gently; have someone mother *me* . . .'

She fell silent, wondering how the small boy they both loved so much had come between them.

But really, it was Kelly who did that. Such a prissy, air hostessy kind of name; Harry's reversion to type, the one whose shoulder he cried on when Shona packed his bags.

What comfort did he find there? What hard-hearted sister first sleeps with a man just weeks after his wife tears, bearing his baby?

'Kelly wasn't the only one. She was just the one who made sure I knew that when he flew he wasn't exactly wearing a chastity truss.'

A joke to dispel the pain, the injured pride, the memory of all those lies she'd chosen to believe. Harry's powerlessness over his schedules, his surprise at the condoms in his toilet bag – a gift he'd 'forgotten' for friends in AIDS-plagued Zambia. All the times she'd rung his hotel, to share a joke of Jack's or remind him about the pills to stop his ears popping, and a receptionist, whose smirk she could almost see, yawned, 'The Captain's room does not answer.'

Oh it hurt, it hurt. She had not understood her own history, even while she was living it.

'Kelly was forever ringing the house, asking for Harry. He pretended it was work, her checking roster changes. Then one day she came straight out with it, asked, why didn't I "let him go"? I'd "never meant much to him anyway".'

She burst into tears.

'I hate her,' she mumbled, shocked, because she rarely admitted even to disliking anyone. Her job was to understand.

Her therapist looked pleased. She was at last admitting to negative emotions. What a breakthrough!

Rushing home on the tube to relieve the nanny, Shona worried was she being unfair to Kelly, unsisterly? She knew Harry's power to charm, and to appear misunderstood.

The tube was jam-packed, rush hour, and from her precious seat Shona found herself looking protectively at a girl standing, flushed, sandwiched between three men. At her age, Shona had been rubbed up against numerous times.

Why, she wondered, were men so vulnerable to that dangly bit of flesh? 'Because they want power,' said her colleagues in her women's group, but Shona shrank from so depressing, unforgiving an answer. Maybe the wandering willy syndrome really was a physiologically inevitable part of their make-up, the biological command to go out and procreate before the dinosaurs eat you. If so, it was men, not women, who were really the victims of biological destiny.

For how many men, nowadays, got away with it? Harry expected her to understand – 'None of them meant a thing. Only you and Jack do' – when actually she was appalled that he considered her most secret parts interchangeable, and the truth dispensable.

By the time Shona got off the tube she had quite worked

herself up into forgiving Kelly, as a mere receptacle of convenience, and Harry too, as a tragic slave of his poor body.

She did not like to hate anyone.

Buying a comic for Jack, Shona laughed over a joke card, and bought it for Harry. Tomorrow she would buy his presents. She felt glad, proud, that their almost-divorce was a civilised one, in which access, presents and family jokes were still shared, and even the odd nostalgic, lingering kiss.

Once Shona was home, Jack punctured her hard-won calm. He was watching some sentimental children's programme, all nuclear family bliss, Daddy manly with a carving knife, Mummy wreathed in admiring smiles.

'Is my daddy coming home for Christmas?' he demanded, although Shona had already patiently explained that Harry and Kelly would be skiing in Austria.

'Well, they need the fresh air, after being cooped up in those stuffy planes.'

Sometimes Shona wished she could be like the mothers she counselled, the kind who'd guiltlessly retort, 'No, because the rotten lying bastard is going to be up a mountain having it off with his bit of skirt.'

But she had seen enough children poisoned by their parents to want to avoid inflicting that on Jack. He adored his father, the man in the splendid uniform who showered him with presents, tickled him and pulled funny faces, and she was glad. Even if their visits sometimes ended tearfully, on Harry's side too, this was how separated parenthood should be.

But still it hurt her when, clambering into bed, Jack again became weepy as he punched out a space for himself between the giant pandas and bears.

'Why did you make my daddy leave?' he asked. 'You're horrid, you're stupid, you let that stupid Kelly have him. Why didn't you think about me?'

She waited until Jack's tense, angry body became floppy, and he reached for her, her cuddles, the reassurance that she would always love him, and Daddy would too – yes, really.

How could she explain to this tiny child that she didn't jump, she was pushed? That there came a time when the absences, the lies, drained her of confidence, made her the kind of mistrustful nag Harry despised, and she had never wanted to become?

Now that they no longer lived together, the laughter was back.

As if reading her thoughts, Jack mumbled, as he fiddled absent-mindedly with a loose tooth, his first, 'Daddy doesn't laugh with Kelly like he does with you. She's boring.'

'Oh – why?' asked Shona, trying to sound casual. After Jack's visits to Harry and Kelly, she always conscientiously avoided pumping him, even though she would have relished hearing anything about her rival that was comfortingly critical.

'Oh, you know,' said Jack, adopting a silly falsetto, 'she's always saying things like, "Come on, gang! Lunch is ready!" He gratifyingly added, 'Yuck,' yawned and turned away.

Once Jack was settled, Shona hunted for a drink. She rarely drank, but needed one now, to unwind. Neither of her boys knew how much it took out of her, keeping their love for each other intact.

Searching for the last of Harry's whisky, Shona found the post that Jack's affectionate but untidy nanny had stuffed behind some storage jars. Only the slim Jiffy bag, addressed in a hand she didn't recognise, looked interesting.

Shona opened it to find a Christmas present. The attached card read, 'To my favourite little fella. I'm sure gonna miss you when we're away. This is to remind you of me and Crimble till we get back. Loadsa luv, Kelly.'

What *had* this illiterate, egotistical floozie sent her son? He wasn't going to miss *her* over Christmas, but the father she stole.

Shona carefully undid the wrapping paper, to find a book. A Christmas book. She didn't read the story, just flicked through the no-expense-spared, gold leaf illustrations. They showed an olde worlde mummy, daddy, and their little son.

In the final drawing they were all holding hands and dancing, happily united, around a candle-bedecked Christmas tree.

It was unbelievable. How could the woman be so insensitive? Was she trying to rub Jack's nose in it – or Shona's, who would have to read this thing to him?

Trembling, Shona crushed the wrapping paper and dropped it and the book into the bin. Then she reached for the whisky, determined to empty it, finally desperate to free her grief and rage.

Very early in the morning Shona was jolted awake by Jack bouncing on top of her. She was hungover, and in an erotic dream whose ending she was desperate to feel. Dutifully she let go of it, and tried to look excited as Jack presented her triumphantly with his first lost tooth.

'I wriggled it out all myself, Mummy!' he shouted. Shona had to admit he looked very sweet, so ludicrously proud of the blood around his mouth, his new gummy grin.

This was exactly the kind of moment parents should share. But there was no other parent, not even another man, Shona thought regretfully as she settled Jack's small body against hers, lulling him with her warmth back to sleep. The men who were interested in her rarely awoke her own interest. They were nice enough, but after Harry seemed flat, two-dimensional. Inside she was frozen, still hypnotised by Harry's charm.

'Are all men bastards,' she asked her friend Helen that lunchtime, 'or is it our fault for picking unsuitable men?'

'Show me a suitable man,' said Helen cheerfully, 'and I'll show you a corpse.'

Almost all the thirty-something women in psychiatry were single. Yet their male equivalents in this unit, liberal *Spare Rib* readers all, almost all had ex-nurses or part-time physios at home, to care for them and their offspring.

'There must be *some* men who'd like women like us, equals, thrusting pioneers of science?' Desperately Shona racked her brains for role models. 'Marie Curie?'

'Dead,' said Helen.

'Miriam Stoppard?'

'She wears false eyelashes,' said Helen.

'Well – how about Hannah?'

They both laughed. Hannah, their supervisor, was married to an adoring husband at whom she permanently barked.

'Poor Simon,' said Helen. 'That's not the solution.'

'But he *accepts* being downtrodden,' mused Shona. 'Maybe that's our problem, too. Maybe we don't even *see* the nice men. Maybe our hearts and bodies are still so conditioned by Brown Sugar we only turn on to cave men.'

'Yeah. And my name's dicky bird and I live up a tree,' said Helen, the only other vulgar shrink Shona knew. 'Face it, kid. We're not exactly spoiled for choice. Let's stop blaming the victims.'

Shona didn't dare confess to Helen why she was back on the subject of men. They had banned it last week as beneath them. Harry had rung from LA just as she was leaving her office. He had sounded tired, harassed. As she had expected, he'd only have time in London to pick up his skiing gear; seeing Jack, and his new gappy grin, would have to wait till the 27th.

'I should have been there,' he said sadly.

'I know. It's not my fault you weren't.'

'Oh, Shona . . . *love*. It's you who threw me out.'

Her heart skipped. Go on, say it, 'Harry, I'd take you back gladly – but only if you change.'

She didn't. Harry's main complaint against her, in the last years, had been, 'You're always trying to change me. I wanted to marry a woman, not a live-in trick cyclist.'

'Oh well,' she said, resuming her flippant *divorcée du monde* tone, 'I suppose you'll do it some time with Kelly. Have another sprog so you can watch its teeth fall out.'

That was a subject they had never broached.

'No way,' said Harry, with a vehemence that surprised her. 'Kelly's keen but . . . you may think I'm a shit, Shona, but I've learned my lesson. I'm a good uncle – and a lousy father. I don't want another kid to go through what Jack has.'

This was the nearest he had ever come to admitting he'd done it wrong. 'You've no idea,' he said, 'how much I missed him last Christmas.'

'Then why are you gadding off to Gstaad again?'

'Oh, you know,' he said bitterly, 'it's what all Kelly's chums are doing.'

It was also, she reflected, Kelly's way of keeping him away from them over Christmas.

'So,' she quipped, 'you've got to keep up with the Traceys?'

He laughed. 'Something like that. God, you're perceptive when you try.'

'I thought that was why you fell in love with me.'

'It is. And why I miss you.'

It was so comfortingly familiar, this flirtatiousness, yet unbearable. She didn't mean to, but suddenly she was yelling at Harry about the book Kelly had sent.

She believed him when he said he knew nothing about it.

'I don't know why she picked it,' he said wearily. 'She doesn't buy books much. She probably just thought the pictures looked pretty.'

Why, she wondered, had she not realised that? She had wasted all that rage and whisky, when the truth was that Kelly inflicted pain less through malice than mere stupidity. Yet she would rather have been deserted for an equal.

'Kelly, Hell-y, why should I care?' she lied glibly. 'I expect living with Hellish will one day prove its own penance.'

Harry chuckled at her renaming, disloyal to the last. 'At least with me off in sackcloth and ashes, your own admirers can flock round.'

Did he care? She wanted him to feel jealous.

'Well, there's Andy,' she improvised. 'He's very keen.'

That was true. Andy, the unit's art therapist, was forever bagging her for coffee, lunch. He was good-looking, warm, a natural healer, someone who elicited wonders from even the most withdrawn patients. She acted as though their talks were just the 'team work' their unit encouraged. Yet she knew, from the way he kept enquiring about her free time – oh yes, he loved country walking too, and it was ages since he'd been to a concert, either – that he wanted, but never quite dared, to ask her out.

For she was still the senior registrar, just two years off consultancy, a woman with double his status, and nearly double his salary.

Why was she so sexist, so passive, why didn't she help him out? The best she could manage was, 'Pop in some time if you're passing.'

He was the kind of new man whom Harry always dismissed as 'a green-cardiganed wimp'.

Have this one on me, Harry, thought Shona the next morning, as she left his presents with his flats' porter.

She wanted to re-enchant Harry, so she could break his spell.

Harry rang at nine on Christmas Eve, while she was struggling, full of self-pity, to erect Jack's train set. She considered asking Harry's advice, but he was slurring, extremely drunk.

'We all did like the Krauts,' he bellowed, 'opened our presents today. Liddle one, I wanna thank you.'

'What did you get?' she asked, meanly perking up.

'You mean from Hellish?' Harry's voice became distant. She heard him call out, 'Wha' d'you give me, eh, Hellish?' He came back to the phone and mumbled, 'A jumper, NSU, an ashtray.'

NSU? Harry must already have strayed.

'It's an Yves St Laurent jumper!' she heard Kelly, poor Hell-y, yell.

There was a loud crash.

'Tha' was the ashtray,' laughed Harry.

There was another crash.

'She's gone back downstairs,' said Harry, and burped. 'She wan's me t'boogie, I wanna ring you.'

'Shona. Baby. Why don' I gerron with women? She di'n't even 'preciate what I gave her. Tell me. You're the only one unnerstans me.'

This was the moment Shona had longed for. But now that it had arrived, she could only giggle.

'I can't tell you, love,' she said. 'I haven't got a spare six months.'

'Bitch,' said Harry, affectionately. 'You an' yer whips an' chains. You're wunnerful. An' yer presents. Specially the liddle one. Hellish thinks you're really weird, wrappin' that in a satin bow. But tha's why I love you, Shona. An' Jack. I love you,' he repeated, half sobbing. 'I'm sorry. I *need* you. I want to – '

There was another crash, then silence. Shona knew, from experience, that Harry must have passed out. Their call was still connected. Harry was probably still clutching the receiver as he snored.

Oh well. It was his phone bill.

Shona replaced her own receiver, and hugged herself. Poor, darling Harry. So her gifts had struck home. But so what if she really was the only woman who had ever understood him? Harry didn't understand himself, and never would. In the morning he wouldn't even remember this call until he saw Kelly's face.

She would always love Harry if only as the father of her child. But no, he would never change.

Half an hour later Shona's eyes were still shining when she answered the door. There stood Andy, bravely lying through his teeth, saying he was just on his way to a party nearby, thought he'd say hello, check she was surviving Christmas.

'Never felt better,' she cried, as high, yet calm, as if stoned. 'I've just realised I don't want my husband back. That's taken me nearly two years!'

She led him in, gratefully let him fiddle with Jack's train

set, uncorked the wine, then thought, why not? Why waste that treat tomorrow on a child?

Unexpectedly bold, she made him close his eyes, then popped the caviar into his mouth. Inside her own, she felt the burst of the salty capsules, the creamy smetana, the crisp bread, the blend of sharp and soft upon her tongue. When their eyes opened, they lingered upon each other just a moment more than socially correct. Not a Me Tarzan You Jane calculated heavy come-on, just affectionate, faintly surprised lust.

Later, when she showed him out, they kissed, a comradely first kiss that only on second thoughts became a tasting of the salt in each other's mouth. He tasted like innocence.

She shut the door after agreeing to a walk on Boxing Day. They would swim towards each other in their own time, nothing rushed, nothing hurried; neither rash nor boring . . .

He would not sweep her off her feet, so that she ended up on the floor, being walked over. He would not display his neediness, then hate her for seeing it. He might be a short-term lover, or a forever lover, she did not know. But he would be precious to her, for he would be the first, the man who lent his warmth as she thawed.

Best of all, he was no po-faced, green-cardiganed wimp.

'What did you give your ex?' he asked, seeing Harry's many presents for her around the tree.

'A puppet,' she said, 'Pinocchio – whose nose grew and grew, because he lied. And – '

She hesitated. Would he think her cheap, tacky, a bitch?

But he laughed, she laughed, as she imitated Harry gratefully slurring, 'Only you, darlin', would give me a bit of a child's body.'

She had given him, wrapped in baby-blue satin, his only child's first tooth.

She felt mean, vulgar, and wonderful. She was healing.

Two's Company . . .

Alison Campbell

They waited all Christmas week for the weather to change. The newscaster in the turquoise suit and hollyberry earrings told them of storms, structural damage, severe gales in the north.

Night after night Hazel turned off the television and crept into the bed beside Donald's, listening to the wild, shrieking, winds buzzing and zinging through the loose window frames.

God it had been so good to be away from Donald for a week, last summer. Hazel had left him with his father, promising postcards and phonecalls. She had danced to the station with Alain, awash with a delicious sense of freedom.

Out of the train, they had caught the early morning ferry to the island. The sea stretched with the smoothness of newly pressed linen. The sky arched above them, a startling steel blue.

That first night they had kissed outside a pub. A group of young locals, inside playing pool, had seen them. One of them in a striped T-shirt had pulled down the window blind.

Hazel and Alain had broken out of their hug, giggling.

'We've put them off their game,' Hazel had said. 'We can't go in there now.'

'Why not? They've seen it all before.' Alain had taken her in by the hand and they'd sat in a corner seat, a Guinness and whisky each, looking out at the sea and a heron stalking the beach.

She remembered those single malts. They'd tried them one

by one that week: Bowmore, Bunnahabhain, Glenlivet, Jura, Lagavulin, Talisker . . .

They'd climbed the island's main mountain – standing on the summit, staring. Ireland to the south, Kintyre and Islay directly west. A cloud enveloped them in mist and swirled by. The ring of the silence, she'd thought.

They'd stayed as long as they dared, knowing it would take them three hours to come down.

Next morning Alain wrote a postcard ending it with the words, *Toi et Moi*. 'It's to Lisette – for old times' sake,' he said, when Hazel looked at it. She knew only that Lisette had been a past lover.

'*Toi et Moi*'s pretty exclusive isn't it?' she said, handing him a stamp. She sat on the wicker chair and stared through the window. She felt tight inside. Tight with trying to believe his words.

'Oh. *Merde*.' Alain threw the stamp back at her. It spiralled and fell gently on to the bedcover. He walked to the corner of the room and tore the postcard into four pieces before throwing it into the wastepaper basket. He picked up his rucksack and slung it across the floor.

'I didn't ask you to be here,' Hazel said. 'You suggested this trip. You said it was all finished with her. Nothing messy, you said. If she's sitting there in Paris waiting for you, go back to her.' Outside the room, the guesthouse proprietor was hoovering the landing. The drone of the vacuum cleaner diminished as it was bumped down the stairs.

Hazel gripped the bedrail to stop herself shaking. Tears, fizzing and thick, turned the inside of her throat pulpy.

'And what about you?' said Alain. 'We've been together six months and it's taken you all this time to leave your child for one week. And then you want to phone him every five minutes.' He smashed his hand down on Hazel's pile of tenpence pieces on the dressing table.

'Look, I struggled to get this week free,' she said. 'And I *am* the one Donald lives with. I can't suddenly switch off when I'm with you and pretend he doesn't exist. He is my son, for Christ's sake.'

'Well he's too close to you. You've made him totally dependent.'

'And weren't you dependent at four years old?'

Hazel stood looking at him. Alain turned away and grabbed some clothes. The shirt buttons caught on the metal frame of the rucksack and made tiny popping sounds like ice cubes crackling.

'Lisette was going to have my child. She had an abortion. Of course I'm always going to feel connected to her.'

Hazel put her hands to her face and bent so that her forehead rested on her knees as she sat in the chair. Part of her wished she was under the bedcovers so that she could cry unrestrained. She wanted Alain to hold her so that the reeling inside her belly would stop. Until she was herself again. Back into gear. Fully integrated. Like she had to be for Donald. She swallowed tears.

'Well. That's very sad . . . Potentially your first child and all that. But you can't know what it's like to have full responsibility for a kid if you say these crappy things to me about Donald all the time. If you can't acknowledge him, you can't love me.'

Alain pulled the drawstrings of the rucksack and snapped the fasteners shut.

'I'm getting the next train back,' he said.

'No. Don't.' She moved towards him. Her arms encircled his waist and her hands gripped opposite forearms. Her first finger and thumb smoothed the cold narrowness of his belt and the ridged corduroy waistband of his trousers. He stood, unmoving.

At last she propelled him to the bed.

'Don't go. What we argued over. It's not worth it . . .'

They packed nuts and apples into the small red rucksack that Donald had let her borrow, and walked to the south of the island instead. They could not see the sealine because the path wove through forestry commission land. The sun hit

them full on their backs, sweeping through the gap in the
sea of pines. The tracks were unsmoothed and their shoes
threw up sand and grit.

Then all at once, as you do on small islands, they reached
a crest and saw the tiny offshore lump of land, which they
knew to be due south. It looked like a conical haystack rising
from the water wrinkling and winking around it. There was
a solitary white lighthouse.

'The landmark,' they said to each other, flapping open the
map to check. 'Three miles to the hotel bar at Kilcreggan.'

For Hazel, the landmark had been coming through the
anger of that morning. She shook her hair back for the last
lap and linked her arm through his. She thought how bright
they must seem to observers . . . the lightness of her hair
over her shoulders. His polished bare arms, and hair fair and
straggly, curling over the collar of his open-necked shirt.
They might well look like an established couple, striding out
in perfect parallel.

No one would guess that she, Hazel, was silenced in some
raw unattainable way, by the morning, still. That she somehow sensed the tightrope quality of it all. *She* might have to
move towards *him* always, when that anger surfaced again.
She wondered if that would always be the pattern.

She saw her father sitting forward, forearms resting on the
table, a school report held lightly in his fingers.

'Geography. Why are you distracted?' Then, 'Maths,
what's "could be more forthcoming" supposed to mean?'

Hazel sat opposite. A girl. Nearly a woman, in her navy
and maroon school uniform, her skirt shiny at the back from
sliding on to so many wooden bench-type seats, the ones
with squeaking hinges. They seemed stiff at first until they
sprang down with a surprising screech-twang as you sat.

She saw her white bri-nylon blouse, her navy cardigan,
unbuttoned. If she looked down almost closing her eyes, she
could see the shadow of her bra. Her hair, parted in the
middle, hung ('dripped' her mother called it) on to her
shoulders.

It was as if a voice unknown to her had jumped into her mouth, when she said to her father, 'What *is* this? The Spanish Inquisition?'

Her father stood up. She could see the tiny patch of cotton her mother had sewn on to his shirt cuff, covering the frayed bit.

She sat silent, not looking at him but at his shadow cast on the cream ridged wallpaper, by the coal fire and the Anglepoise lamp lungeing from the bookshelf behind.

The firelight picked out the reds and whites of various holly and mistletoe cards, and she knew it was once again coming to that time of the evening when her father would look at all the signatures inside, and throw into the fire those Christmas cards from people he no longer acknowledged. She had watched year after year as he tore the cards precisely in two and flung them into the flames with a quick flicking motion of the wrist.

Hazel shivered lightly and pressed the palm of her hand against Alain's as they walked, till the pressure made her stumble. He linked hands with her and stroked his finger against hers. She liked the way their little fingers were exactly the same length, but his other fingers and his thumb were much longer than hers, and narrower.

At the hotel they drank too much, and ran down the driveway in the faint hope that they had not missed the six o'clock bus. A few cars passed by, then a couple in a land-rover stopped for them.

Their names were Grant and Jan and they wore identical green oilskins. His hair was thick and matted and pushed under a black cap with a peak. Jan sat with her hands on her legs. Grant talked, while Hazel and Alain hunched, knees up, in the back, watching the conical islet disappear in a heat haze behind.

'Turned out the very place we'd set our hearts on was up for sale,' Grant was saying. 'By that time we were ready to kiss the city life goodbye and come to the island.'

'How do you make a living?' Hazel turned slowly towards the couple wondering if they ever went out without waterproofs. It made them look fit for anything – a march through the fields to rescue lambs or a hike to the village to collect the papers off the morning ferry.

'With difficulty. Barter system usually.' Grant lifted a finger from the steering wheel to indicate a croft house clinging into a sharply rising scree hill. 'Neighbour up there needed a hand with the peat cutting. Did two days with him. Next week round he came with three ducks.'

Jan spoke for the first time. 'We're off to collect a kitten from a farm – for the mice in our place.' Hazel wondered why Jan looked as though raindrops were caught in her eyelashes, and whether she and Grant also lived on a tightrope. She thought somehow that the couple did not seem to base their lives round words. Hazel imagined them outdoors repairing stone walls, putting new slates on the roof, filling up the lean-to with sticks and chopped wood ready for winter, throwing scraps and stale bread to the ducks.

That night, in a hotel with tartan carpets and clan crests over the bar, Hazel told Alain about the incident she'd remembered with her father. 'I never showed my anger to him – except that once.' She looked carefully at the bar for her own clan crest. 'I suppose it was never allowed,' she said.

They talked round the issue as though it were a challenge, something that the two of them, not only she, Hazel, needed to face up to.

Hazel went for last orders: two doubles of Bowmore. She bent her head to catch its tangy, almost spicy aroma, as she waited for the change. A man with stubble on his sunken cheeks toppled off the tall bar stool as Hazel carried the drinks back.

'We should come here again for New Year,' said Alain. 'A Scottish Hogmanay. We could bring Donald.'

'What about babysitting?' Hazel said. But Alain was watching the barman. He had slung a towel over his shoulder and had come round to the front to help the man back on to the stool again.

On their last day they found the old hotel up a long, beech-fringed track that twisted beyond a shield of pines.

They knocked on the heavy door to ask about winter accommodation. The old woman said that not everyone liked self-catering, but . . . that was how the place was run now.

Hazel and Alain looked round. Rooms sparsely furnished. Dim. Artificial silk curtains flung with geometric shapes and leaves. Short double beds with loose headboards. Metal Will's Capstan ashtrays, squarely placed on dressers. Small bedside lights with yellow shades and dangling bobble fringes.

They booked up for New Year then and there. Hazel though that the woman looked approachable enough for at least one night's babysitting . . .

'MV Islander will berth in four minutes. All passengers please be ready to board.'

Hazel watched as the ferry lurched into the harbour, spray coursing the prow.

Two young brothers in commando hats and anoraks jumped across puddles on the quay. A woman pulled her coat collar over her neck, and picked up a cat basket. Four men in navy jackets and hats heaved the mobile gangway along the ground to the side of the ferry.

On board, the rolling motion forced Hazel to plant her feet apart and grip the metal rail with one hand. She manoeuvred Donald in front of her, curling the fingers of her other hand round his face so that he would not bump his chin.

Up and around, down again. The vessel heaved and ploughed its way to the island. They tried to walk to the front of the boat but the strong south westerly drove hail into their faces and sent them scuttling back to the shelter of the port side, directly under the suspended lifeboats, creaking on pulleys.

The sky was splintering. Deep metallic clouds fought off arctic blues.

In the calmer weather of summer she would have seen the island clearly by now and, on coming closer, seen the familiar patchwork of fields, translucent and vivid green. Today they were hidden in early afternoon dusk. The mountain, clad in its eerie whiteness, gleamed against heavy cloud.

The jetty was grey and empty of people as the ferry loomed closer. The metal ramp clanged home and Hazel walked ashore, Donald's mittened hand in hers.

She knew the route now. Along the shore road, up the mud and gravel path. It settled her to see the hotel again, granite solid, opening on to a wide drive and a small bank of snowy grass.

Upstairs she threw their coats on to the heavy candlewick bedspread, and rubbed at the window. Donald dragged off his boots and jumped on to the bed. He drew a spider in the corner of the pane, legs spilling from it like sunflower petals.

'Can we get a hamburger?'

'There aren't any hamburger shops here. But there's a big oven downstairs. We can made some soup.'

Hazel pulled a thick sweater over Donald's head and wondered how they would ever keep warm. Already her fingers were stiffening with the cold.

'Can we go mountain climbing?'

'Tomorrow, perhaps. Let's go down and get warm.'

She chopped the vegetables that she'd carried in her rucksack. Exotic things from the mainland. Aubergines, sweet potatoes, pumpkin.

Tucking in the green tartan scarf closer about her neck, she rested one thigh against the Raeburn as she worked. Above her, from the ceiling, vests and long johns dangled from a rack. She must remember to bring Donald's pyjamas down to warm before bed.

As the soup bubbled she picked out bone-handled cutlery from the dresser and laid it on a large tray with two projecting metal handles, a relic from the hotel when it was run as such, before the owners had got too old and tired. She imagined the place in its heyday, brimming with guests and student waitresses.

Donald skipped along the dim corridor to the dining room, and she followed with the soup and a chunk of bread each. The tables stood fringing the room, white cloths unused since the summer. She didn't switch on the lights.

In one corner a grandmother clock ticked irregularly. The huge mirror on the mantelpiece reflected a ridged pink vase containing purple hydrangeas and honesty, now browning and crinkled.

Donald swung his legs under the table to the clock's rhythm. Hazel sipped the soup, nibbling at the pearl barley and rice. Through the bay window the huge pine tops moved in the wind. Rubbing one clenched hand on her thigh, Hazel held it out to the calor gas fire beside the table.

'Why did we come here?' Donald submerged bits of bread in his soup and slurped up the sludge on his spoon, which he still held like a drumstick.

'I thought it would be fun to come to the island in winter.'

'We could have stayed in Glasgow.'

Hazel guessed he was remembering their stopover at her cousin's rambling flat in the student quarter of the city, and the evening excursion to see the lights in Sauchiehall Street.

She said, 'You know I told you I went to the beaches when I came here in summer?'

'When I was staying with my dad, and you phoned me every day?'

'Yes. Well, it's not just a summer place. You get to like it when it's cold and snowy too.' She groped for a reason within herself, and then for a way to translate it for her son. 'It's like a person. You don't just like someone when they're all smiling and happy. You get to like them when they're cold and wet and sad too.'

'Mmm.' He crumbled the crust into the soup. The bits floated like coarse black pepper.

'So is the island a friend?'

'A best friend,' she said.

Donald stirred the crumbs round and round. 'Is that why Alain didn't come with us?' He prounouced it 'Ah-len'.

Hazel put down her spoon and waited.

'Because he didn't like to see a best friend cold and wet and sad?'

Hazel looked at him and brushed the fringe out of his eyes. 'I don't know,' she said at last. She couldn't tell him that Alain had sent a card to say he had gone back to Paris.

They cleared away. Donald carried his bowl, then hers, to the kitchen. They washed up and Hazel showed him how to hang the teatowel straight, over the front bar of the Raeburn, so that it would not scorch.

She sat beside him upstairs as he drowsed.

'What's this night called again?'

'Hogmanay.'

The wind gave a sudden gust, clattering the window frames. The stiff pink curtains moved. Across the corridor in the bathroom, wallpapered in straight blue rows of roses, water dripped. Tap. Tap. Tap.

'January the first tomorrow,' she whispered to him, as she switched off his bedside light.

'A new year.'

Confessions and Lullabies

Rukhsana Ahmad

Then there was the laying on of hands. Amy stood absolutely still, sensing the spirits fluttering in the hushed light of the hall. People with heads bowed stood still. Suddenly, but slowly, she began to move, like a Frankenstein struck by lightning, energised, charged, invincible. She left the hall before the others, putting an abrupt end to the healing session.

Her senses were heightened. Her mouth felt dry, her hands burned, her eyes smarted and blinked at the brightness of the Christmas lights and decorations which clustered the shops outside. Memories, people and spirits swirled inside her head so that it threatened to explode. She panicked at the extraordinary clarity that detailed everything around her. Why had she never noticed before the tiny grains of poison floating in every glass of water she filled from the kitchen sink? She washed the glass, ran the tap for hours and filled it again, and there they were, clear as daylight!

When she asked Mrs Friedman next door for a couple of jugs of water from her kitchen, later that day, she looked wary and suspicious.

'Don't you believe me?' Amy asked, slightly irritated.

'You may be right,' Mrs F conceded, the frown never leaving her brow, her eyes watching Amy intently as she filled the jugs for her.

Amy looked at the jug triumphantly. 'See, yours isn't poisoned, is it?' Mrs Friedman did not debate the point.

Amy returned to her kitchen to make herself some tea, her gaunt figure stooping in the dusk, the lines on her face deep with anxiety. She screwed up her eyes at the green mould on the bread. It appeared to move. She shuddered and put the bread down. She had difficulty drinking the weak tea that stood on the table.

Her eyes were held by the layers of browned grease on the stove. Each and every section of glass had been knocked out of the glazed door that divided the kitchen from the living room. The old green and yellow chintz curtains with their heavily stained frills looked strangely out of place, a forgotten attempt at home-making buried in the sea of neglect, the only reminder among the burnt pots and pans of better days. The chequered marble floor in the hall, dusty and cold, looked bizarre against the bald door frames. Amy dodged the heaps of black plastic bags which stood in the hall. She cursed inwardly. 'They keep bringing in the rubbish I throw out,' she had moaned to the sceptical Mrs F. In the bedroom webbed icicles hung on the window panes. The grand wardrobes looked haggard as they stood sentinel over her bed, their doors pushed ajar by the chaos that surged inside. She pulled the black quilt wearily round her shoulders, her head singing with the noises They made just to keep her awake all night. She couldn't sleep. Then she started looking for it: that creamy lace doily, turning sepia with age. That always worked. It sang her songs, told her stories. She held it in her tense, nervous fingers, listening to its gentle murmur. The tips of her fingers stroked it with the featherlight tenderness of an adoring mother.

Here I am, across the black waters, with no hope. No hope of a return to Narsapur, the place of my birth. Miles and miles I've travelled, boxed, blindfolded. I shiver now, longing for the sun, in the musty stench and gloom of a battered old bedroom in this elegant suburb of London.

From an inert distance years-long I watched life, without being watched; dispassionate neuter entity, receiving comment without comment. Now memories keep me going, stimulate jaded consciousness. The past, rich with its pains and joys, shuffles before me, jolting the weary dullness of limp hours. I rejoice; I agonise.

Not many can remember what it's like pushing through the birth canal, or the time of the pre-birth when a mere thread of demented, infinitesimal energy, wriggling to attain an identity, shoots, in blind passion, into the mother's womb. I do. Even the time before, when I waited, passive, inanimate, breathless, in that colourless skein that held me, waiting, for the quickening, in those far-away, long, long summer days.

I see it clearly, a dusty little shop in Palakol where the whiff of the salt sea, when it blew, carried the tang of fish of an afternoon, reviving the villagers in the summer.

He had an enterprising gleam to his dark eyes, the tireless Mr Venkanna, who started his own lace business. He began exporting lace, then became a thread stockist, back in the thirties. He couldn't read or write so he got the village scribe to write to Messrs Coats in London, and became their agent. Now, fifty years on, it's a thriving business, a limited company run by his son. Venkanna Junior has something of a monopoly over the supply of thread in the area, which gives him lots of power and control over the lace business, even over the lives of the lace makers, all those women around Palakol and Narsapur.

Boxed and blindfolded we all arrived at his shop, fifty years ago. New country, new smells. India! Rich, strange and exciting they'd all promised it would be. Huh, books! They always lie, I remember thinking, for I never really got to see much of the place except the dusty old shop, not for a long time anyway, not until I was delivered into the convent in Narsapur.

Then it all changed, suddenly, remarkably, when she took me out of the cellophane wraps and held me in her warm, moist, square hands: Sister Josephine! Her memory still has such power over me as a mother has over the very thoughts of her babes. I can remember the living touch of her fingers, smell her breath, her body, hear her voice speaking, low when she remembered to lower it, loud when she forgot. Everyone knew she would never make it; she would have to die a 'sister', poor thing. There is not enough self-discipline in her for one thing; much too much passion in her caring for humans. The only one who is late for prayers, meals, meetings, everything. She gets so involved in teaching the girls, sitting on the whitewashed verandah, she forgets where she is. Or forgets to return to the cloisters like the others do, for the long afternoon siesta; stays out instead, enjoying the sea breeze and a little gossip about one of her old pupils in the cool shade of a tree. She has no ambition to pull herself together. Too happy, too content. Younger novices come to the convent, zoom past in their speedy spiritual progress, pursing their lips at her slipshod ways and her grimy habit, never quite as white as Mother Superior's, shaking their heads in guarded disapproval.

Adilakshmi adores her. She seeks her out with so many little excuses. Sometimes Mother Superior casts a frowning look at the pair of them. She sees the young girl, dark-skinned, bubbly, her vibrant youthfulness bursting out of every pore of her rounded body, and she worries. Then she looks at Sister Josephine's serious face, the single hair, now turning grey, that grows out of the mole on her left cheek, at her sagging breasts, her spreading middle, and decides to say nothing. If she hasn't learnt at nearly fifty, she never will she thinks. Sister Josephine learns all the time, from Adilakshmi, from Padmini, from the women who come selling the fish, and from Krishan who comes to deliver the milk. She chats with all of them, evading Mother Superior's frowns. Every week, she must offer the same confessions, the same penances. It doesn't bother her, she doesn't seem to learn.

Amy's eyes were mesmerised by the drops of blood that dripped out of Jesus' heart. His fingers were long and delicate, and his face looked like a woman's. It was young and sad. The nails staked through his fine bones must hurt. She could see where they punctured the flesh, making it bleed. She clutched her little palms together and pressed them between her thighs. Her eyes were held by the drops of blood.

'Put your hands together, and pray,' her mother's voice whispered in her ear. 'God can see you wherever you are. He's always watching.' Amy brought her hands on to her lap.

It was hard to confess. She tried to find the words but they evaded her. Not the words so much as the sentences. Where was the sense in stringing sentences when all you had was the odd gasp of insight? If He's always watching then He must know. Nothing makes sense. Nothing hangs together.

Still, something akin to instinct brings her back unfailingly to the vast shell of the house that was her home. She clings to the stale odours of the house with a blend of fear and passion, like an abandoned cat still waiting for the owners to return. She waits for Leo to return to her, even though the outline of his face is blurred in her memory.

All she remembers is giving birth to the children. That is the clearest memory of all. The pain, insistent, virulent, attacking her spine from inside. The nettles of pain clinging round her muscles, tautening and pulling her abdomen, ripping her open with an unimagined violence. She clutches the doily to her heart. Her palms feel sore as if nails had been hammered through them. In her dream she can see the drops of blood falling from Christ's heart on to her doily, muffling its voice.

Adilakshmi is desperate to learn how to make lace so she rushes after the lessons, forgetting about lunch, to find Sister. Adi loves beautiful things; she loves lace. She's seen her friend Geeta's new petticoat with a delicate lace edging. Maa's irritated with Adi when she asks her if she can make lace edging for her petticoat.

'Lace,' she says, 'is for people who live in big houses and dress in fancy clothes, not for people who live in mud houses.

There's plenty to do here to keep the roof together over our heads, to keep the younger ones fed, the animals watered and your father happy.'

Then, noticing the tears in Adi's eyes, she says, 'Ask the sisters at the convent; they taught many of the women who know. Someone there will find time to teach you. You're old enough, Geeta's mother was only a girl like you when she learnt.'

Sister Josephine agrees to teach her. Adi is overjoyed. she doesn't know yet how happy these memories will become for her in the future that waits to mangle her vibrant youth, grind down the fullness of her body. Later on, she will remember with terrible yearning these hours spent under the old gnarled banyan tree in the courtyard of the convent. Now she struggles, desperate to learn how to make a fine lace trim for her petticoat. Her fingers are clumsy, envious of the speed with which Sister Josephine can crochet. She finds it hard, very hard, to synchronise the movement of her young fingers with the eager lurch of the crochet needle as it plunges into the loops with hungry energy, using up the thread, using it up fast . . . Using it up, as Deshu used her.

The red carpet with its brave green and gold pattern camouflages the cigarette burns in its worn pile. It must be the darkest pub in Stepney. The wooden beams frown in the shadowy light sieved through the pink glass lampshades. Amy waits tensely for Leo to come, unsure of how he will react to her family.

He was fascinated by her adventurous tales of shoplifting and streetfighting as a child. Life in a flat above the pub in the East End with an unconventional mother and her gentle but unremarkable stepfather, Fred, had sounded quite unusual and exciting to him. He listens spellbound as he looks adoringly at her grey-blue eyes, her blonde hair hugging her swaying shoulders, her long slender legs, omitting to censure the nose, a trifle too sharp, and the chin, a trifle too square.

When he visits that evening, the reality, no longer muted

by its distance from the Chelsea School of Art, seems coarsely mundane. Amy tries to quash the word 'common' as it surfaces again and again in her head with reference to Mum's conversations with Leo. Her references to a prospective marriage become crudely obvious. Leo seems not to notice, thank God. Fred's grey mildness helps to alleviate the situation. Mum had always kept a sharp eye on Fred. She'd read *Peyton Place* more than once in her time. From the moment she noticed Amy's breasts developing under her blouse she kept a hawk's eye on customers and Fred alike. Amy was out in digs before the urge to leave home had even taken a clear shape in her head. Boldness rather than subtlety had been Mum's strength, and it had served her well enough.

Visits to the pub became fewer and fewer after the marriage. As time went on it was Leo who was confounded by the crudities of her family, and he went to great lengths to avoid seeing them. Christmas dinners inevitably ran aground over trivia, leaving a foul taste behind. It seemed kinder in the end not to ask Fred and Mum at all, rather than have them come and see them being ignored or, worse, snubbed over their ignorance. There were always tears at Christmas.

Amy stares sadly at the cigarette burns in the powder-blue carpet, angry with thoughtless customers for not noticing the ashtrays . . . It strikes her vaguely that the face peering at her is Benjy's.

'This is not the pub; I'm in my own home.' She tries to hold that fact in her fist as she looks up at her son's face, a little bemused by his anger. He towers above her, scowling.

'There's not a thing to eat in the kitchen. I got a take-away from the chip shop. There's a bit of saveloy and chips left if you fancy any. I wish you'd pull yourself together.'

'No thanks.' Amy tries to raise her head to show her gratitude but she feels faintly sick at the mention of saveloy and chips.

'Somehow, the paintings never turn out as wonderful as the image in my head, no matter how hard I try!' She is bitterly aware that the portfolio never added up to much.

She looks bewildered as she explains to Leo what she was trying to express. He looks untouched. She can see the images so clearly in her head, but it is so hard to put them on to canvas, even harder to describe them. The holes in the powder-blue carpet don't make sense. She hides herself from those ugly holes in the soft, lacy comfort of the whispering doily.

Years later, Adi looks at her crochet needle as it weaves the thread, using it up fast, and thinks how tired she is of Deshu and his demands. She can crochet faster than Sister Josephine, much, much faster, if only Sister could see her now.

In between feeding the baby and milking the goat, in between kneading the dough and preparing the vegetables, in between preparing the mixture for kallapi and making lunch, in between making cow-dung cakes for fuel and fetching the water, she picks it up for short snatches, fingers flying, and she can finish a couple of squares for a table-cloth, or a couple of rounds if it's only a doily she's working on. By evening her fingers ache and her nipples feel sore, her eyes hurt and her neck feels ever so tired. But doilies are easy to finish.

Doilies are small, insignificant things. They don't take that long. In the afternoon she gets a clear stretch of two or three hours if that monkey of a baby sleeps through. Small, insignificant, I watch. It's a long weary day for her. She lies down at about eleven, bones crackling, muscles desperate to thaw into sleep, and then Deshu reaches out for her. A soundless sigh whispers to the darkness as she turns, unbuttons her blouse and pulls up her cotton petticoat. There's never time to make a lace trim for it. She's always behind with the orders.

The lace trim for her petticoat, that first one, took her hours and hours to finish. Three weeks to finish a metre of lace less than three centimetres wide! Years later she could do a bundle and a half in three weeks. She wouldn't have guessed that was possible when she started.

She struggles, putting a brave face on it. Sister Josephine applauds every inch as it grows, gently pointing out where the tension sags or has become too taut. I watch the struggle with amusement. It's fun watching things grow. Then it's time to move on and Sister teaches her how to make a lace doily.

'What do they do with these?' Adi asks, looking at the doily in Sister's hands.

Sister sneaks her round to the nuns' parlour, points to the table in the middle of the room made from the best Godavri teak. It has a high polish on it. On top of it sits a little doily for the silver bowl of fresh roses that are replaced every day.

'That is a doily,' she says. 'It saves the table from being marked. You can use it for drinks, ornaments, anything that goes on a polished table.'

'But we haven't a table like this in our house for which we could use it,' Adi argues. She wants to make a lace trim for her new blouse now, instead of a doily. Her mother would rather have her help with the baby.

'Still, you should learn how to make it. It may come in handy for a gift some time. Or you could sell them as a set if you did enough of them.' Sister remembers all those girls who learnt from her. Always, they grew into women who were glad they knew how to make lace. Some time in their lives it came in handy; got them a few rupees for rice, oil, lentils, whatever.

'All right, Sister, if you want me to,' Adi says dully. She knows Sister can be stubborn. 'But can I do a lace trim if there's any thread left, please, please Sister, for my new blouse,' she begs.

'Once you've done one of these,' says Sister, who knows about incentives.

That's how I came about. A doily without a polished table to sit on. The years I spent in a battered old trunk stored under the string bed in that crumbling, dusty hut, desperate for a whiff of fresh air and sunlight. Sometimes her mother would find a moment to rummage through before popping in some new-found treasure to save for Adi's marriage, and I'd draw in long deep breaths to revive my spirits while I lay dormant, dead to the world.

Amy looks around her in horror. Benjy's asthma is frightening. Alone in India with two little children! 'Not quite alone,' Leo says, as he leaves, 'there's the ayah and the cook and the driver when you need the car. There's not a thing to worry about.'

He has to tour round all the manufacturing units, he tells her, to make sure they are keeping to the colours and the designs. Amy sighs in resignation.

'The dust doesn't help any,' explains the American doctor. 'The kids here develop immunity over the years. Our kids have a problem; they're delicate, they're not used to these conditions.'

The wheezing sounds dreadful through the night. Sophie whines for her attention, jealous of the cosseting being lavished on Benjy. Amy, exhausted and confused, worries about Leo and herself. His eyes are always evasive, his conversation vague. Where does he spend all this time away from home? Yet when he is near her she flits about nervously, fearful that he might tell her.

She looks at the architecture around her, the colours, the motifs, the landscapes, with longing. If only she had a moment to herself to subsume her experience, to see, to understand what was going on, to capture it all and put it on canvas. The pain inside her head grows and grows until it blurs the images. She walks round the beach wondering why beaches in England looks so different.

She remembers walking on the pebbly, foam-grey beach at Brighton with her father and his 'woman' on those few but special weekends when she was invited. Her father steeped in alcohol and idealism would ramble about a Utopia which was near at hand. 'Huh, ideas are cheap,' Mum would comment cynically on her admiration for him, 'when's the last time he's bought you a pair of shoes? Don't you believe him, girl. You need a bob or two to get by in life, you take my word for it.'

Leo is the same. 'Without money you can achieve nothing,' he says. 'With money comes culture, the awareness of beauty, the avoidance of that which is ugly, cheap, coarse and shoddy. You like to surround yourself with beautiful things, don't you, Amy?' Amy twirls the stem of the crystal glass in her left hand thinking of Leo's family home where labels are sacrosanct. Hallmarked. Genuine. Real. 100% Pure – silk, wool, leather! Quality is underwritten by price. They all know it, accept it.

Everything is cheap in India. 'Is it tacky?' she wonders whenever she comes across something unusually beautiful. Enamelled boxes, hand-carved ivories, polished brass, engraved copper, inlaid marble: everything is cheaper than it is in Europe. India is too vast and frightening to comprehend. She longs for peace, struggling to pray in the tiny chapel inside the convent, but her mouth feels dry and her hands twist frantically.

Get a hold on yourself, girl. Look at what you've got on! He'll leave you if ya don't pull yourself together. Mum's greeting on their return to England haunts her. Leo is busy designing tiles for an upmarket company: the ethnic look is in this year.

Fear galvanises Amy. She clings to Leo, the children, the house, their lovely home. Leo resents her clinging. He accuses her of perverse suspicion and jealousy. She tries to remain poised but panic besets her when she sees cold distance glaze his pupils. She longs for grace and dignity. Leo's mother is always elegant and calm in her world of mellow opulence, where the right balance of chintzes and lace, brocade and velvet strikes the perfect note; ritual and decorum choreograph every move she makes. Amy tries to achieve that effect in her own home, uncertain of her own taste, after years of being 'just a housewife!' Nothing blends, nothing jells. Leo moves out even before the children decide to leave for universities in the regions, eager to get away from her.

She looks round. Now only the house remains, decaying and damp, but always there. She returns from her wanderings, wheeling her shopper crammed with her most precious belongings, and the house is still there. Suddenly she starts rifling through the shopper. *The lace, this time They've taken my lace away, just like They snatched Leo from me.* She rummages in the shopper and finds it; it is still there, gentle and reassuring.

'Adi, you must find time to work harder at your books,' Sister used to say.

Books! They don't seem relevant to Adi, years later. She remembers a sliver of a poem, stirring the onions over the fire or picking the stones out of the rice. Or some small detail from her geography lesson puckers the surface of her thoughts as she crouches over the lace, eyes screwed, back aching, and wonders if that can matter to her now.

If only I'd done some extra bits of lace and put them by instead of spending all those hours in those grim classrooms, learning, she thinks with some regret. Learning, for what?

She reckons if she had a few bundles of lace-work stored in her old trunk instead of just half a dozen silly little doilies and a couple of tablecloths she could be out of debt by now, forgetting that the money for the thread was always the problem then, as it is now. But the debt keeps multiplying, adding up.

Mind you, at least because of that bit of time at school I can work out my money better than Maa was ever able to. She lost money sometimes, poor old Maa, Adi reminds herself. No one can cheat me out of my due wages, not the sharpest agent in Narsapur or Palakol. They've tried hard enough, God knows they have. It's a small triumph but it keeps her going when times are hard.

Except that there was one occasion when she did get cheated but memory also cheats her now, not letting her recall that mistake, a little mistake that cost her quite a lot.

He looked nice enough, respectable. He had been at the shandy plenty of times before. She had seen him often enough, sold him stuff before. He paid her the right amount every time. Until that day when he fell for the bedcover. It was beautiful! It had taken her three months to finish. The thread alone was worth two hundred rupees. She borrowed to buy the thread at black market prices; Venkanna stopped selling it to the women when he had large orders himself. She hoped to make fifty or sixty rupees on it. He smiled when she asked her price, said nothing, and letting it drop back into her nylon basket, walked off. She saw him turn and leave but held herself back. She was going to hold out for her asking price. I applauded silently! Even twenty rupees a month was too little for the laborious hours she'd spent over the wretched thing.

He hovered round the other stalls. Adi stole a quick side-ways glance, hoping. Not many enquirers. She needed money desperately. She decided to drop down to two hundred and fifty rupees.

He did come back, just as the crowd was thinning and the market looked about to fade. He didn't haggle.

'Look,' he said, 'I like that bedcover. You have a good hand. I like your work. It's tight and neat.' She tried to look cool and detached. 'I'll take it,' he said after a pause, quite decisively. Relief glowed through her body.

'I'm an exporter myself. I've got good links in Germany. I could probably order a few more of these if this goes down well.'

Adi's heart nearly missed a beat. She began folding the bedcover neatly, lovingly. He was pulling his wallet out.

'Oh no! What a shame! I'm not carrying enough cash!' He beat his brow in despair, and Adi's heart sank. 'Never mind, I'll take it next week.'

He seemed disappointed, 'Pity, such a pity! The German

contact was going to be visiting my shop in the city. But, well, oh, never mind.'

Adi was more disappointed than he could have been. She looked at him helplessly.

'I hardly know you. I don't know if I should even ask,' he began delicately. 'There's fifty rupees here. I am a regular at this shandy, I know you know me because I've seen you myself before. Would you consider . . . ?'

She did. Foolish, reckless thing to do. He never showed up again. After the first four Wednesdays of desperate waiting, her hopes of his return grew dim. She didn't tell most people. No one would have sympathised: foolish thing to do, they were sure to say to her. She had to sell her only gold earrings to return the loan and the interest. Now she forgets; claims she has never been cheated. Women! So given to self-deception, so adept at it!

I'd say Deshu's cheated on her. You'll never catch her admitting to any such thing though. She tells everyone this story of how he really needed to go to Calcutta six months ago, in search of a job. She never remembers to say how he's been forgetting to send her money now for almost four months. He'd said he was going to find out about how to become a lace exporter. Only the exporters seem to have money round here, he'd reasoned. It may be he has found out. No one knows where he is now.

That was five years ago. She's still hoping. She sits, fingers frantically busy, lace tablecloth clutched between her knees, peering at it through her cheap spectacles, still hoping he'll return to her. Preoccupied. Not with him though, more with the anxiety of how she can concoct a meal for tonight from next to nothing in her meagre stores. She thinks of food, rich, spicy, warming, nourishing, with an intense longing. There is going to be a good Christmas dinner this week for all of them at the convent. A fabulous meal, fragrant rice glistening with oil, spicy yoghurt, curried vegetables, steaming, satisfying, filling. Thank God for Christmas, she thinks.

Unbidden, the Lord's Prayer echoes through her head:

'Our Father Who art in Heaven, hallowed be Thy name. Thy Kingdom come, Thy will be done on earth as it is in Heaven. Give us this day our daily bread and forgive us our trespasses as we forgive those who trespass against us . . .' As always the words give her strength. A picture flashes through her mind of Deshu walking in through the door, his arms full of presents, his eyes penitent, begging her for forgiveness. Her eyes fill up with tears of compassion. She is ready to forgive him in that instant.

Occasionally she glances at the tatty curtain of sacking which acts as her door. Not much of a door to hold people in, or to keep intruders out, but then there is nothing much in here anyone would care to steal. Nothing stirs outside. There is no sign of Deshu.

Perhaps he will come home for Christmas, she thinks. Her faith in Christmas is unshakeable. She has seen the glow of absolute faith in Sister Josephine's eyes, all those years ago, as a child. It is the love of Jesus that keeps the nuns in Palakol and Narsapur. She has seen miracles sparked off by prayers. She knows it was Our Lord's hand that saved her first baby when the doctor at the Mission had told her to prepare for the worst. She decides that before Chritmas she must buy some incense and a garland of marigolds for the crucifix that hangs on the wall of her only room.

Amy looks fearfully at the image of Christ, with his hand on his heart, on the chapel wall. She is relieved to see that it is a comforting picture, no blood, no nails. She steals a glance at Mary, who looks passive, unconcerned. She is discomfited by her indifference. She looks again but Mary still gazes away from her, heavenward.

Suddenly the tears burst forth in a deluge of anguish. 'Dear Mary, don't ask more of me than I can give,' she begs.

But Mary looks blandly indifferent to her capacity for self-sacrifice, almost scornful at her outburst. Amy is unsure of what Mary wants of her, and of what makes her sob like this in anguish alone in the fragrant darkness of the chapel.

Outside in the cheerful brightness of the verandah a tiny crowd jostles round the convent's Christmas fête. The smell of home-made cake wafts around, tempting the punters. Sister Josephine asks her how Benjy's asthma has been this week. Amy stands, pretending to be her normal self, answering her carefully. Then she notices Adi, whose eyes look appealingly at her.

'Lace, madam? All hand-made, all pure cotton. Want to see, haan?' Amy picks up a bundle of six doilies without thinking, and asks her, 'How much for these?'

The doilies capture her imagination. They suggest gracious surroundings to her. Far away from dusty Narsapur, she can see them breathing more easily in the clean, pure air of elegant rooms, sitting on polished sideboards or grand pianos, on white lacquered dressing tables and mahogany consoles. She can't put them down.

'Ten rupees only, madam.'

Amy wonders if she should haggle about the price. So often people tell her she must. So often it works. 'Isn't that too much?' she asks uncertainly.

'No, madam. All hand-made, very neat. It is fifteen rupees in the shops. You can ask anywhere. It is more in Delhi, Calcutta, everywhere.'

Amy hesitates. Adi looks keen on the sale, 'Take it please, madam. Good for Christmas present. And Christmas will be here very soon!'

Amy looks for the money in her bag, her eyes a little wary of Adi's confident smile. Adi is puzzled as she hands Amy the bundle wrapped in a piece of old newspaper.

'Happy Christmas,' she says reassuringly.

Amy nods as she leaves. She clutches the lace doily, stroking it with featherlight fingertips, and whispers to herself, 'Christmas will be here soon . . .'

Adi's voice, cheery, confident, gives her new hope. She enters her front door breezily, light-footed, drunk on that renewed hope. 'Christmas will be here soon!'

There is no message from Leo. Ayah looks up with a

suggestion of reproach in her glance as she walks into Benjy's room. He is listless and wheezy. Sophie has gone to bed without eating again. Amy's heart sinks as she wonders for the thousandth time that day whether Leo will be back before Christmas or not. She looks at the doilies sweating her hand now. Adi's voice sings out a miraculous message of hope once more, 'Christmas will be here soon . . .' Amy shakes off the disbelief and listens to that voice, spellbound. Pressing the doilies to herself, she lies down on her bed, shutting out all else from her mind but the silent hum of that wild promise.

Outside her window, snowflakes silently fill the gaps between the laurel hedge and the brilliant green of the holly.

The Blackbird's Heart

Suniti Namjoshi

'Hang your heart on a tree! Hang your heart on a tree!' an irascible old woman had once told a blackbird. And the blackbird had believed her. The blackbird had reasoned that high and hidden in a tree somewhere, her heart would be sheltered. Then, when a cat leaped on her, the cat would discover that she had no heart and would let her go. Then, when a boy with a shotgun aimed at her breast, it wouldn't much matter. The pellets might lodge, or the pellets might shoot clean through her, but her heart, high and swinging on a tree somewhere, would remain unpierced. But it so happened that this unfortunate bird fell most fiercely and unsuitably in love. Her heart was now demanded of her. She flew away quickly in search of it. She had hidden it away in the early spring, it was now November. The wind helped her, and the trees divested themselves with lavish abandon, but the blackbird whirled in uncertain circles. Each time she spied a red berry she thought it was her heart, but how could she be sure? In the end she gathered all the berries that she could find and dropped them one by one in the lap of her true love.

'Choose one,' said the blackbird.

'But which one is your heart?'

'I don't know,' replied the blackbird.

Then the blackbird's true love gobbled the berries, while the blackbird watched and fell completely and cleanly out of love.

A few remained. 'Are any of these your heart?' But the blackbird had gone. The blackbird's sweetheart looked around her. Windy November was nearly over. She scooped up the berries and took them indoors for her tree at Christmas.

One Dark and Starry Night

Sara Maitland

Once upon a time, long long ago and far far away, there was a young queen in a tower.

Lest you should get the wrong idea about this story I should say at once that this was not a standard model fairy-story princess with goldy locks and a simpering smile. On the contrary, this was a dark witch queen, tall and slender and sternly beautiful, and the tight curls of her hair, which was cropped very short in the fashion of that place, broke like waves on the broad black beach of her forehead. She was very sad. And she was very pregnant.

Nor was she a prisoner in the tower; she had climbed the three hundred and thirty steps freely and now leaned against the solid parapet and looked down, trying not to think, nor to remember. The tower was in the centre of the city. I do not know if you have ever been to great Zimbabwe, the ancient ruin which is the heart and mother of that brave new country. The huge walls there are thick and solid, the entrance ways are narrow and welcoming, but despite the size they are made of millions and millions of tiny slivers of rock, dry stone, and bonded by their weight and the skill of their masons. The walls curve round, vast and embracing. I think this young queen's city was like that. And inside the walls it was part busy market, part safe haven, part great palace and part strange temple, and above it all, at the very centre, rose the tower; high above the busyness it reached up towards the heavens and at night its shapeliness was a darker black against the dark black sky. The people of the city had built the tower, with love and labour, so that anyone who wished could climb up and watch the stars, for in that city, unusually, it was judged nobler to be a magician and astronomer than to be a warrior or a king.

But now the queen did not want to look at the stars. She did not want to think about stars. She did not want to think about her husband either. For the young queen had a husband whom she loved very much, and she was right to do so, for he was merry and wise and very beautiful and his eyes sparkled not just in sunlight but in moonlight also. But now she did not want to think about him, nor about the stars.

So instead she looked down on the great courtyard, where in daylight there was constant activity; where the long caravans from the east met the traders from the western forests and exchanged goods and gossip, wares and worries, merchandise and magic; where the people of the city, serene and dignified, listened and learned, taught and told the old stories. Now under the pale lemon moon the courtyard was still and calm, but the memories caught the young queen unawares and she could not help but remember.

She remembered the evening, only a few precious months ago, when her husband had come leaping down the tower, his scarlet cloak flying, swirling around him, and his earrings gleaming gold. He had snatched her from her work, laughing, loving.

'Come,' he had said, pulling on her hand in his excitement, 'come and look. I have found a new star.' And she had run with him up the tower, nearly as light and lithe as he, for all she was five months pregnant. And there, in the navy-blue band of sky low on the eastern horizon, hung, pale and pure, a bright white star.

He said, 'That is a star for the birth of a king; a greater king than the world has ever known – a king who will be for the rise and fall of many nations.' And he looked at her with love and passion and awe. He knelt at her feet and kissed her belly, just below the navel; and the child inside her wriggled with appreciation and delight and the three of them were full of joy.

But then . . . but then . . . how to account for, how to remember a changing so gradual that it may just be the fears and tremblings of pregnancy, and at the same time is so sturdy and real that there can be no return? Over the next few weeks her husband had withdrawn from her, had gone away inside his own dreams and would not talk to her. He was busy all the time. He spent long hours in his manuscript room, poring over his maps, and star charts, and ancient documents. And he would not talk to her. He spent wide spaces of time in the incense and myrrh factory, talking to the old spice mixers – women so skilled and industrious in labours that even after bathing their fingers never lose the faint aroma of holiness. And he would not talk to her. He sent out long letters across the whole world; from her room she could see, if she chose to look up from her own star-casting and spell-weaving and daily business, the messengers going out, running or mounted, across the wide plain beyond the city walls. He sent messages to his old friend, the Arabian desert ranger, whose people's camels bestrode the great golden sand dunes beyond the hills of morning. He sent messages to the mage king of the northern mountains, whose people lived half the time in darkness and whose land mourned the vanishing of the sun by covering itself in moon dust, white and cold like a funeral robe. They sent messages back and he would not meet her eyes and he would not talk to her.

One morning she had come out from her chamber and found the great courtyard frantic with busyness. There were pack ponies already laden, and the guides had gathered to a summons she had not known of, and were there leaning on their spears with their leopardskins already tossed over their shoulders ready for a departure. His great white stallion was brought out, harnessed for the long road and eager for the travelling, and she heard the shrilling of her own black mare left behind in the stables.

Then he came out, solemn, dressed for a journey. He still

did not meet her eyes. He kissed her, formally, for a long parting, between the breasts and said, 'Well, I must be off.'

'Off!' she cried. 'Off where?'

'Off on my journey,' but he had the grace to look embarrassed.

She clutched at the baby in her belly which turned and lurched. 'Now?' she cried. And hearing the shriek in her own voice and hating it, fearing that he would think she would limit his freedom, she said in a calmer voice, 'Why now, just at the worst time of the year?'

'I'm off to find the baby king,' he said and looked proud and excited.

'Well,' she replied with a forced smile, 'if it's baby kings you want, I have one right here for you.'

But he did not smile back; he looked irritated and said, 'Don't be trivial. This is history. This is important.'

And after that she said nothing more, because there were no words that could ever put right so great a betrayal.

Then he went.

So now the young queen was in the tower, trying not to think or to remember, not knowing whether she was sad or angry. Then suddenly her body was shaken with pain. Then suddenly she found that her ankles were soaked with warm water and her face was soaked with warm tears. Then suddenly she did not think or remember him any more, because she had her own important thing to do.

She half-ran, half-groped her way down the tower and into the arms of her midwife, who was also her old nurse and her friend. And there for a while she was comforted.

But much later, in the long hours of the night, struggling and weary, she called out for him and her need for him was so great that she blamed herself for his absence.

'Men,' muttered the old woman, wiping her darling's face. 'They're like that. Always under your feet, and never there when you want them.'

But the young queen had gone on a longer journey even than her husband's, and such gentle irony cannot reach to the dark country where she sojourned now. 'No. No. No,' she cried, and the unborn child, hearing her and misunderstanding, felt rejected and sulked and made the pain worse.

'I want him, I want him,' sobbed the young queen. 'I want him. Why isn't he here?'

'Husha, husha, my lovey,' said the crone. 'Haven't you learned yet? They can think of the silliest thing – destiny, politics, history – just about anything to get out of doing the difficult and important work.'

'No,' she said, and wept. 'It is me. I am not good enough for him. I don't deserve it. I am too silly and trivial and stupid. My child is not good enough for him, I do not deserve him. He is too big for me. He and his friends, they're right to go. They know things; they are important, wonderful, wise.'

The old woman laughed; cackled from her stomach. 'In one generation? In one universe! *Three* wise men. You've got to be joking!'

And after that they settled down to the important task of birthing her baby daughter.

Rukhsana Ahmad taught English Literature at the University of Karachi before coming to live in Britain in 1973. She has been writing short stories and plays since 1986 and has worked for a year as a writer-in-residence in Cleveland, and for six months in the London Borough of Harrow. She was one of the founding members of the Asian Women Writers' Collective.

Her most recent play, *Sanctuary*, toured London and the regions in May and June 1991. She has compiled, edited and translated a collection of feminist Urdu poetry from Pakistan, entitled *We Sinful Women* (The Women's Press, 1991). Her short stories have appeared in *Right of Way* and *The Inner Courtyard* (Virago).

Linda Anderson comes from Belfast and now lives in North London. She has written two acclaimed novels: *To Stay Alive* (Bodley Head, 1984) and *Cuckoo* (Bodley Head, 1986; Brandon, 1988). Her stories and poetry have been published in various anthologies, including *Storia* (Pandora), *Wildish Things* (Attic) and *Women On War* (Simon & Schuster). She has also worked recently as a reader and producer for BBC Radio Drama.

Maeve Binchy was born in Dublin, where she worked first as a teacher and then as a journalist for the *Irish Times*. She has written four collections of short stories and five novels. The novels, which have brought her an international readership and which are translated into seven languages, are: *Light a Penny Candle, Echoes, Firefly Summer, Silver Wedding*, and *Circle of Friends*.

Maeve Binchy is married to the writer Gordon Snell and they divide their time between London and Dublin.

Malorie Blackman is an ex-computer programmer who now writes full time. *Not So Stupid!* her first collection of short stories (Livewire Books for Teenagers, The Women's Press), was a Selected Twenty title for Feminist Book Fortnight, 1991. Since then she has published a children's picture book, *The New Dress* (Simon & Schuster), and two early readers, *Girl Wonder and The Terrific Twins* (Victor Gollancz) and *Elaine, You're a Brat* (Orchard Books). She lives in London with several assorted stuffed toys and a Scottish lunatic.

Alison Campbell is from Aberdeen and now lives in London. She is co-author of a children's picture book, *Are You Asleep, Rabbit?* (Collins, 1990), and has a short story in *New Writing Scotland*, Vol. 5 (Association for Scottish Literary Studies, 1987). She is working on more short stories and a novel, and is currently completing a counselling course at Birkbeck College. She is co-editor of this anthology.

Katie Campbell, a Canadian living in London, writes journalism and plays for both radio and stage. She also has a collection of short stories, *What He Really Wants is a Dog* (Methuen, 1989), and a poetry collection, *Let Us Leave Them Believing* (Methuen, 1991).

Fiona Cooper lives on Tyneside. She is the author of four novels, *Rotary Spokes* (Black Swan), *Heartbreak on the High Sierra* (Virago), *Not the Swiss Family Robinson* (Virago), *Jay Loves Lucy* (Serpent's Tail), and several short stories. 'Not Another Clucking Christmas' was first used in a cabaret night at The Bridge Hotel, Newcastle-upon-Tyne, in December 1990.

Eleanor Dare
A friend writes: She's a snake from 1965. She's written a Bibleful of words (some dull, some divine), maybe more, even through previous careers pearldiving, some 'market research' and the current shelving bore. Now she's writing a choreopoem about a vile detective who interrogates her suspects under South London flyovers, a graphic novel about metaphysical lesbian bodybuilders, and other stories.

Zoë Fairbairns was born in 1948. She is the author of novels including *Benefits* (Virago, 1979), *Stand We At Last* (Virago, 1987), *Here Today* (Methuen, 1984), *Closing* (Methuen, 1983) and *Daddy's Girls* (Methuen, 1991). Her short stories have appeared in anthologies including *Despatches from the Frontiers of the Female Mind* (The Women's Press, 1985) and *The Seven Deadly Sins* (Serpent's Tail, 1989).

Eileen Fairweather currently works as a freelance journalist for a strange variety of publications from *The Mail on Sunday* to the *Guardian*. She is a previous winner of the Catherine Pakenham/Standard Award for young women journalists.

She is a co-author with Melanie McFadyean and Roisin McDonough of *Only the Rivers Run Free: Northern Ireland, the Women's War* (Pluto, 1984), a Selected Twenty title, Feminist Book Fortnight, 1985. She is also author of a comic novel for young people, *French Letters* (Livewire Books for Teenagers 1987, The Women's Press), which (some) critics kindly called 'the female Adrian Mole'. It has been translated into several languages, and she has just completed the sequel, *French Leave* (Livewire Books for Teenagers, 1992).

She has contributed to numerous other anthologies, including *Fathers: Reflections by Daughters* (Virago, 1983) and *Transforming Moments* (Virago Upstarts, 1989).

Caroline Hallett lives and works in North London, where she has helped to set up a counselling service for young people. Writing is a recent interest which persists alongside job, training and family of three young children. She has had a story shortlisted in the Bridport competition. She is gradually adding to a small number of completed stories which she hopes to make into a collection. She is co-editor of this collection.

Bernadette Halpin was born in late July 1954 in a hospital where Italian nuns held placards up to her mother with PUSH written large on them. This might have been an omen of her own fascination with the difficulties of language and creativity. She's been published in *Serious Pleasure* and *Woman's Own*, which indicates 'either my thematic range, or utter lack of political credential'. She has lived alone for ten years in a 'short-life' squat in Hackney, and works at a local community publishers, Centerprise.

Mary Ann Hushlak is Ukrainian-Canadian, but has lived much of her adult life in London. She studied political philosophy and did social science research before turning to writing plays, poetry and short stories. She is presently finishing her first novel.

Sara Maitland was born in 1950. For the last fifteen years she has been a full-time writer, producing both fiction and non-fiction. Most recently she has published a novel *Three Times Table* (Virago), and, with Lisa Appignanesi, edited *The Rushdie File* (Fourth Estate). She wrote a specially commissioned series for 'Morning Story' (BBC Radio 4) broadcast during Holy Week 1991. She has been a feminist since the early 1970s, and feminist concerns – especially in the arena of theology and mythology – are central to most of her writing.

Ann Chinn Maud was born in Los Angeles in 1931 but grew up and was educated in Salt Lake City, Utah. She read anthropology at the University of Utah and then travelled in Europe and the USA before settling in Minneapolis, Minnesota, with her husband and their four daughters. Since 1984 she has spent half of each year in England and Europe to research medieval dance iconography.

Suniti Namjoshi was born in India in 1941. Her first book of fiction, *Feminist Fables*, was published by Sheba Feminist Publishers in 1981. *The Conversations of Cow* was published by The Women's Press in 1985. *The Blue Donkey Fables* (The Women's Press, 1988) was a Selected Twenty title for

Feminist Book Fortnight, 1988. Her latest books are *Because of India: Selected Poems* (Onlywomen Press, 1989) and *The Mothers of Maya Diip* (The Women's Press, 1989), a satire set on an island off the west coast of India, 'where matriarchy bloomed unashamedly'. She now lives and writes in Devon.

Anna Paczuska is a second-generation Pole. She lives in London with her two children, and dreams of meeting a fat fisherman and settling down on the west coast of Ireland. She is currently working on a collection 'Love Poems for Bad Men' with graphic artist Nora Connolly.

Jenny Palmer is a feminist living in Dalston. She lectures at Goldsmiths' College in English for Academic Purposes and is currently completing a novel and collection of short stories. She has published on Third World issues in *Spare Rib*, *Everywoman*, *Tribune* and *Outwrite* and draws inspiration from Bolivia, her spiritual home. She is a co-editor of this collection.

Joanna Rosenthall was born and brought up in Leeds. Her family are second-generation Jewish immigrants from Lithuania. She studied psychology at Sussex University, in the early 1970s, where she went through an impassioned and enlightening discovery of the women's movement. It was enormously helpful and a delight at the time. Since then she has tried to reshape feminism to fit in with her life and the world. She has worked as a social worker and more recently as a psychotherapist. She has been writing for the last five years only in the sense that it fits in with having a three-year-old daughter. Some of her stories have appeared in assorted anthologies and one in *Critical Quarterly*.

Marijke Woolsey was born in North London, where she still lives with her husband, and two daughters. She writes mainly short stories, but she is presently working on her third novel ('The Eye of the Beholder'). Her first novel, *True*

Love, Dare, Kiss or Promise, was shortlisted for the Betty Trask Award and for Faber and Faber Introductions.

She works part time for the women's co-operative Letterbox Library, a children's book club that specialises in non-sexist, multi-cultural books. She is a founder member of the Purple Room Women's Writing Group, and co-editor of this anthology.

Zhana's previous work includes *Sojourn*, an anthology exploring relationships between and among Black women, which she edited and co-authored. She is a performance poet and is currently working on a novel, entitled *The Treasures of Darkness*, and a collection of poetry, entitled *Sisters and Other Goddesses*.